Date: 02/14/12

J 741.5 JUG
Jughead with Archie in A day
to remember.

D1157002

the Archie DIGEST LIBRARY

Jughead with Archie

– in –

A Day to Remember

visit us at
www.abdopublishing.com

Exclusive Spotlight library bound edition published in 2007 by Spotlight, a division of ABDO Publishing Group, Edina, Minnesota. Spotlight produces high quality reinforced library bound editions for schools and libraries. Published by agreement with Archie Comic Publications, Inc.

Library of Congress Cataloging-in-Publication Data

Jughead with Archie in A day to remember / edited by Nelson Ribeiro & Victor Gorelick.
    p. cm. -- (The Archie digest library)
    Revision of issue no. 189 (Feb. 2004) of Jughead with Archie digest magazine.
    ISBN-13: 978-1-59961-272-0
    ISBN-10: 1-59961-272-0
    1. Comic books, strips, etc. I. Ribeiro, Nelson. II. Gorelick, Victor. III. Jughead with Archie digest magazine. 189. IV. Title: Day to remember.

PN6728.A72J83 2007
741.5'973--dc22

                         2006050551

All Spotlight books are reinforced library binding
and manufactured in the United States of America.

Contents

Jughead® with Archie®

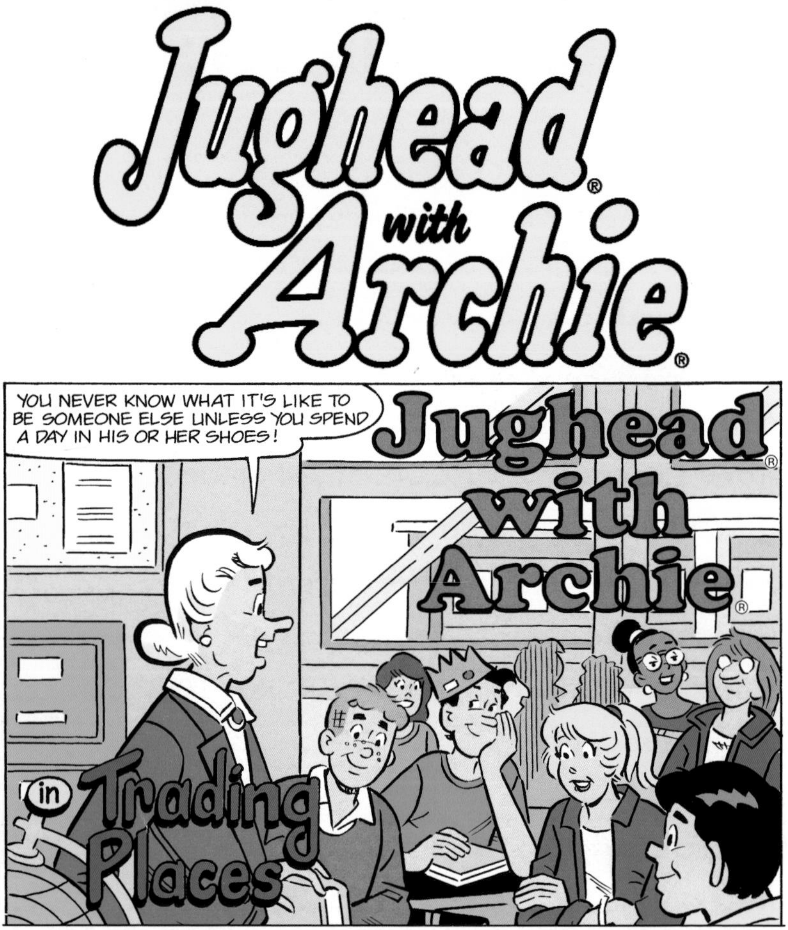

YOU NEVER KNOW WHAT IT'S LIKE TO BE SOMEONE ELSE UNLESS YOU SPEND A DAY IN HIS OR HER SHOES!
Jughead® with Archie®
in Trading Places

SCRIPT: MIKE PELLOWSKI PENCILS: TIM KENNEDY INKS: RUDY LAPICK
COLORS: BARRY GROSSMAN LETTERS: VICKIE WILLIAMS
EDITORS: NELSON RIBEIRO & VICTOR GORELICK EDITOR-IN-CHIEF: RICHARD GOLDWATER

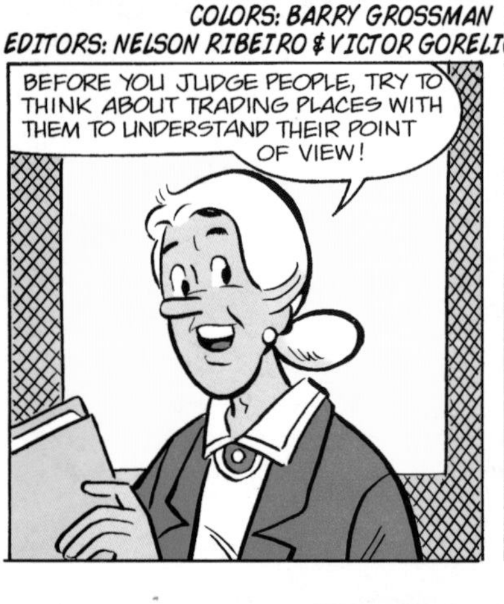

BEFORE YOU JUDGE PEOPLE, TRY TO THINK ABOUT TRADING PLACES WITH THEM TO UNDERSTAND THEIR POINT OF VIEW!

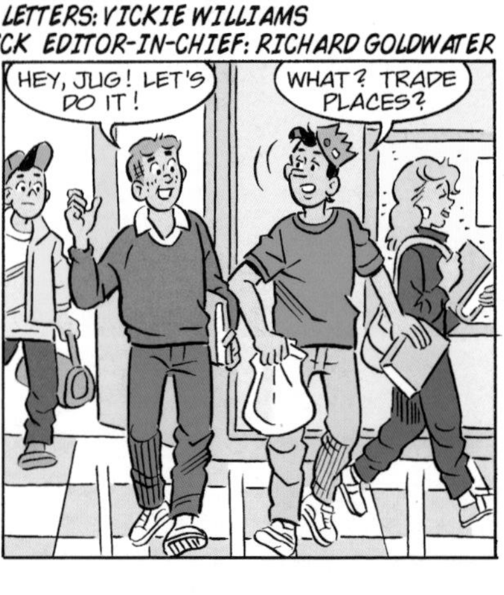

HEY, JUG! LET'S DO IT!
WHAT? TRADE PLACES?

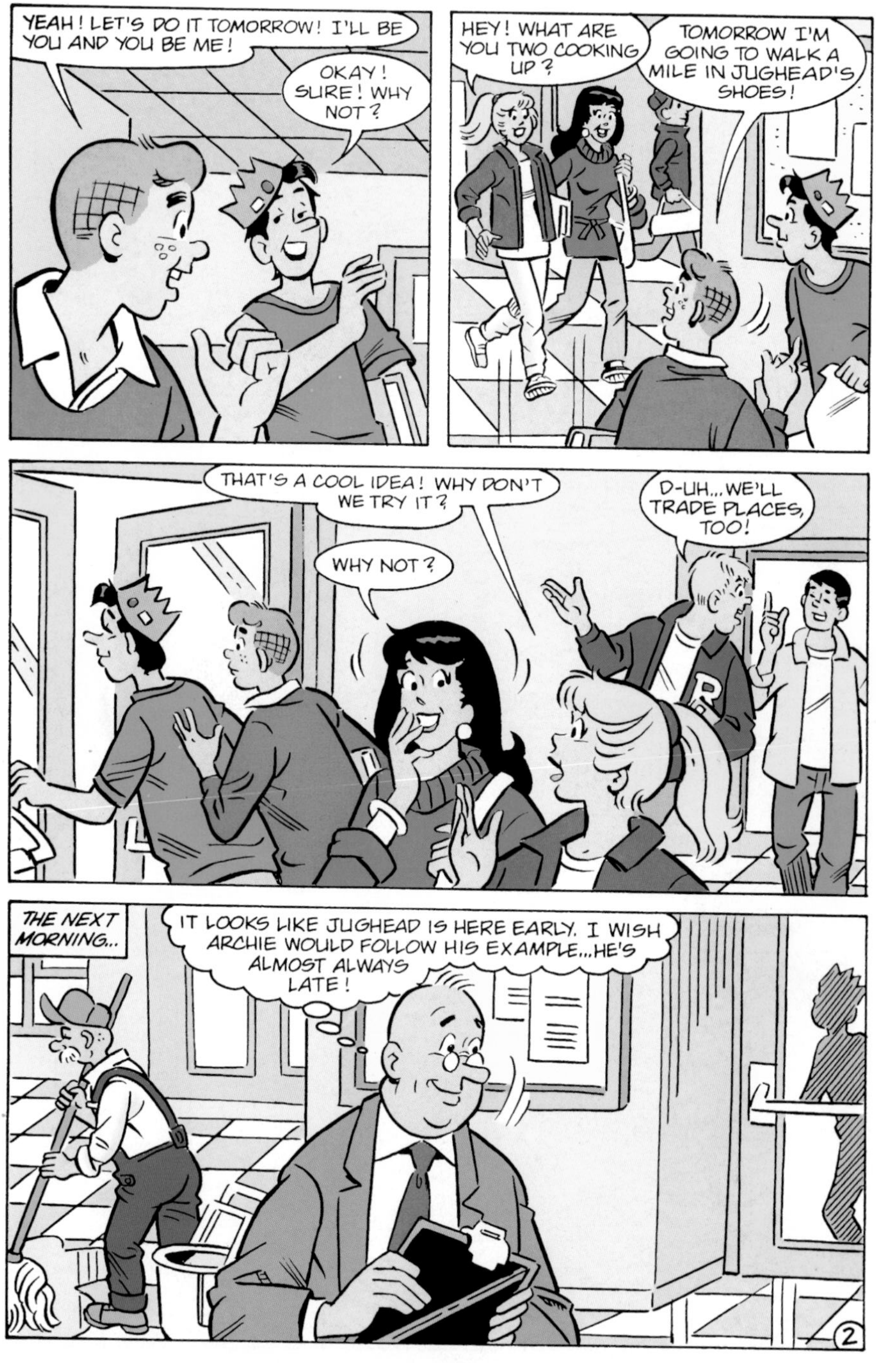
YEAH! LET'S DO IT TOMORROW! I'LL BE YOU AND YOU BE ME!
OKAY! SURE! WHY NOT?
HEY! WHAT ARE YOU TWO COOKING UP?
TOMORROW I'M GOING TO WALK A MILE IN JUGHEAD'S SHOES!
THAT'S A COOL IDEA! WHY DON'T WE TRY IT?
WHY NOT?
D-UH... WE'LL TRADE PLACES, TOO!
THE NEXT MORNING...
IT LOOKS LIKE JUGHEAD IS HERE EARLY. I WISH ARCHIE WOULD FOLLOW HIS EXAMPLE...HE'S ALMOST ALWAYS LATE!
2

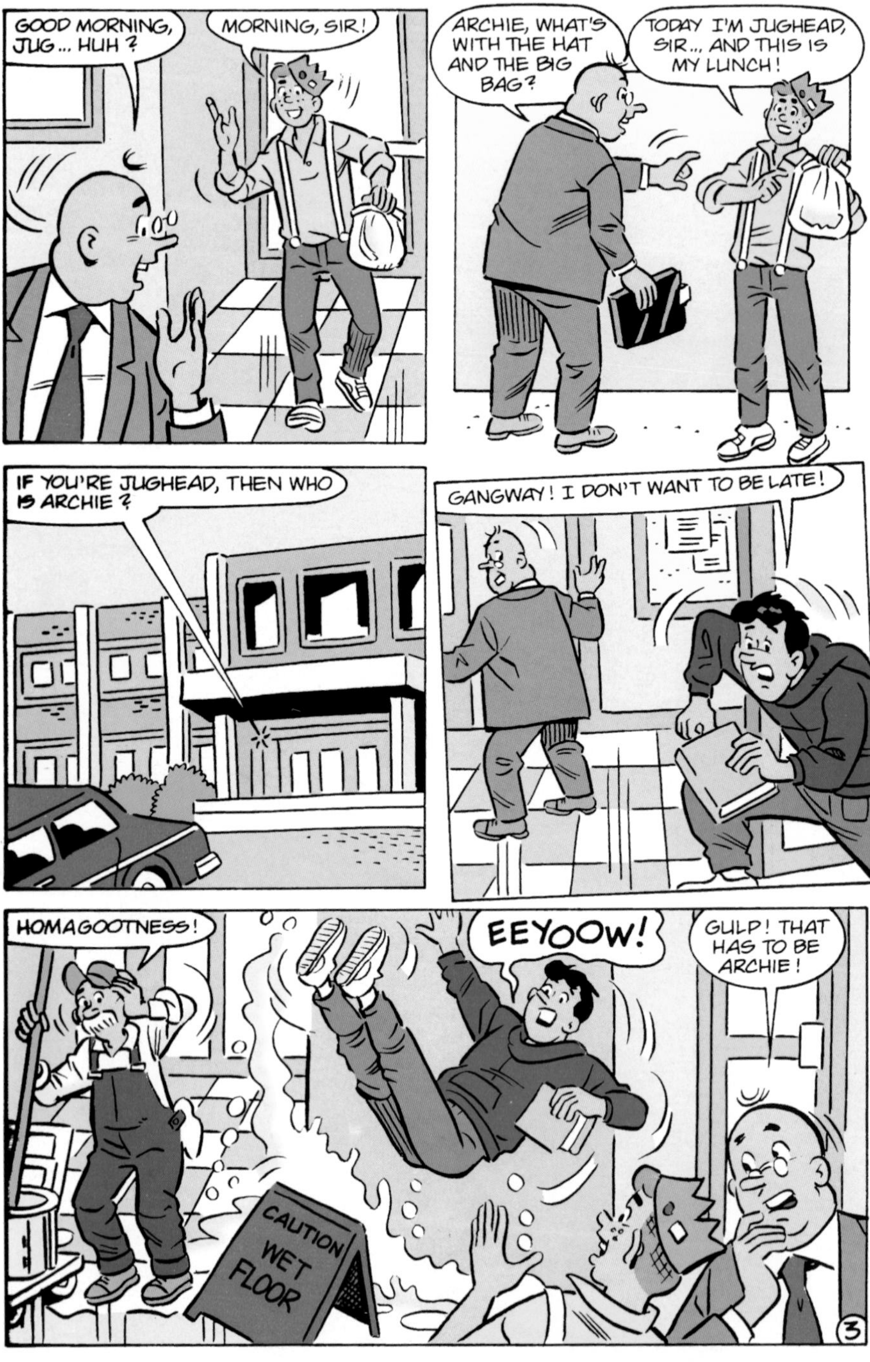
GOOD MORNING, JUG... HUH ?
MORNING, SIR!
ARCHIE, WHAT'S WITH THE HAT AND THE BIG BAG?
TODAY I'M JUGHEAD, SIR..., AND THIS IS MY LUNCH!
IF YOU'RE JUGHEAD, THEN WHO IS ARCHIE ?
GANGWAY! I DON'T WANT TO BE LATE!
HOMAGOOTNESS!
EEYOOW!
GULP! THAT HAS TO BE ARCHIE!
CAUTION WET FLOOR
3

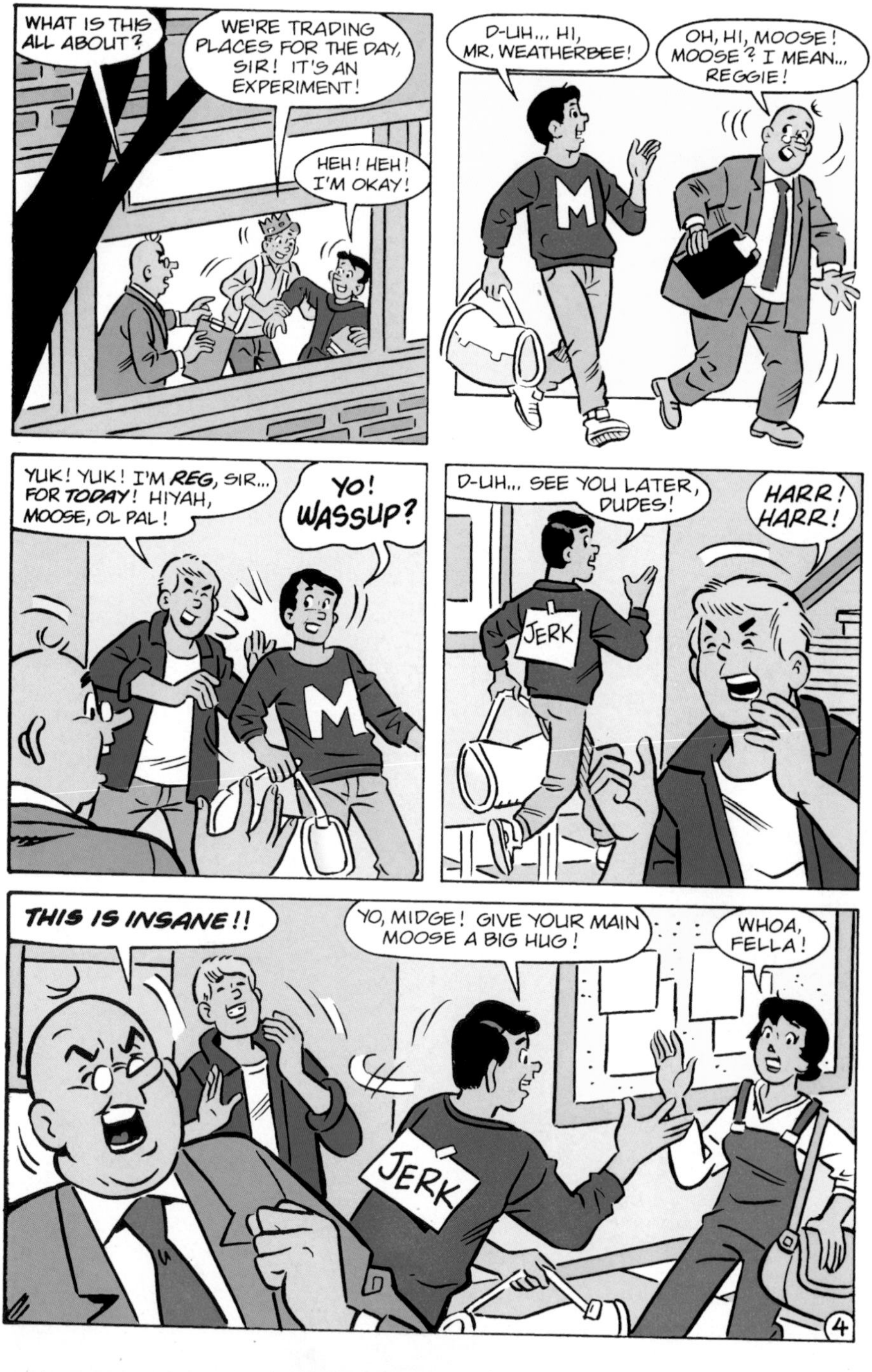
WHAT IS THIS ALL ABOUT?
WE'RE TRADING PLACES FOR THE DAY, SIR! IT'S AN EXPERIMENT!
HEH! HEH! I'M OKAY!
D-UH... HI, MR. WEATHERBEE!
OH, HI, MOOSE! MOOSE? I MEAN... REGGIE!
YUK! YUK! I'M REG, SIR... FOR TODAY! HIYAH, MOOSE, OL PAL!
YO! WASSUP?
D-UH... SEE YOU LATER, DUDES!
JERK
HARR! HARR!
THIS IS INSANE!!
YO, MIDGE! GIVE YOUR MAIN MOOSE A BIG HUG!
WHOA, FELLA!
JERK
4

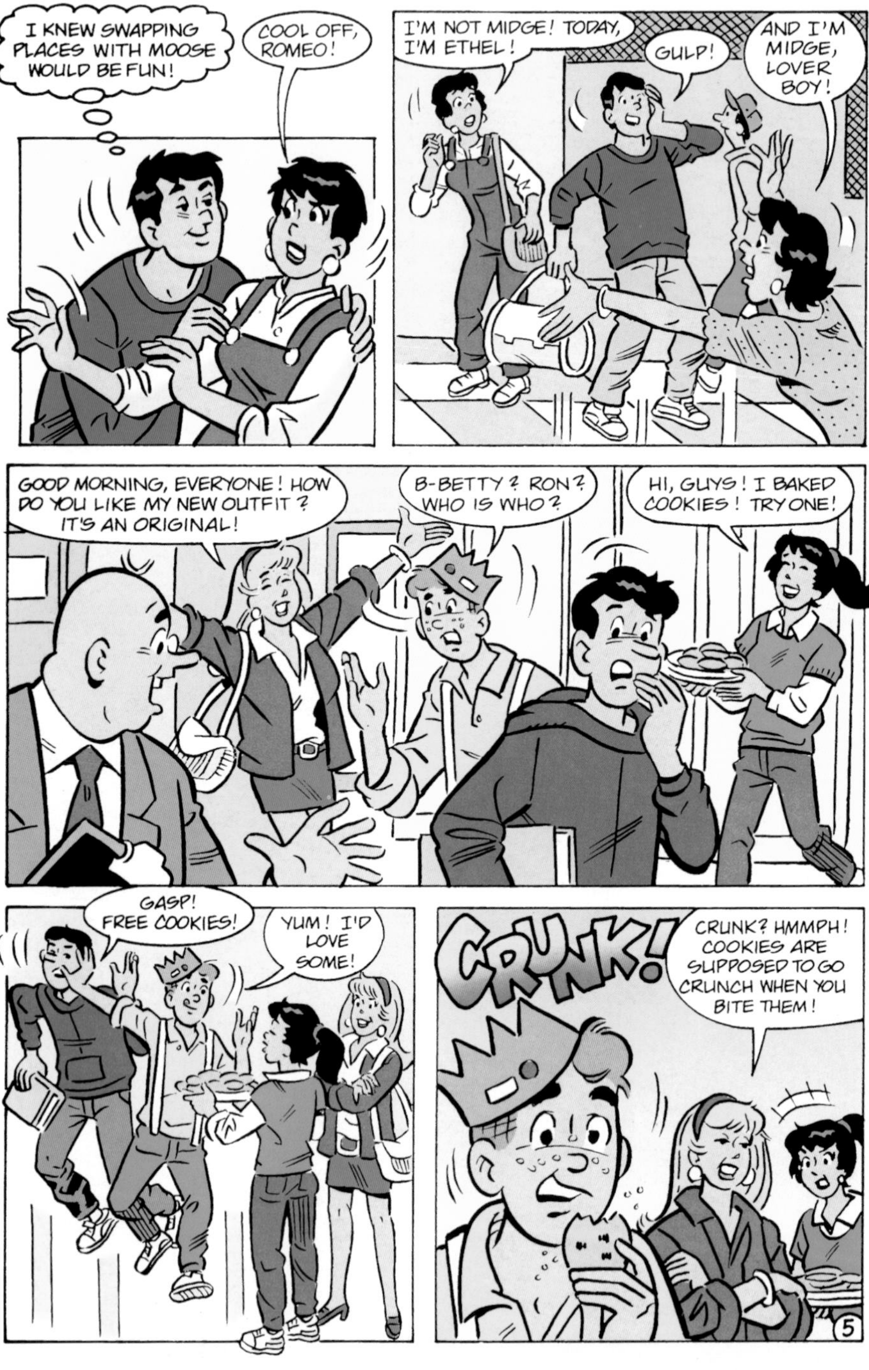
I KNEW SWAPPING PLACES WITH MOOSE WOULD BE FUN!
COOL OFF, ROMEO!
I'M NOT MIDGE! TODAY, I'M ETHEL!
GULP!
AND I'M MIDGE, LOVER BOY!
GOOD MORNING, EVERYONE! HOW DO YOU LIKE MY NEW OUTFIT? IT'S AN ORIGINAL!
B-BETTY? RON? WHO IS WHO?
HI, GUYS! I BAKED COOKIES! TRY ONE!
GASP! FREE COOKIES!
YUM! I'D LOVE SOME!
CRUNK!
CRUNK? HMMPH! COOKIES ARE SUPPOSED TO GO CRUNCH WHEN YOU BITE THEM!
5

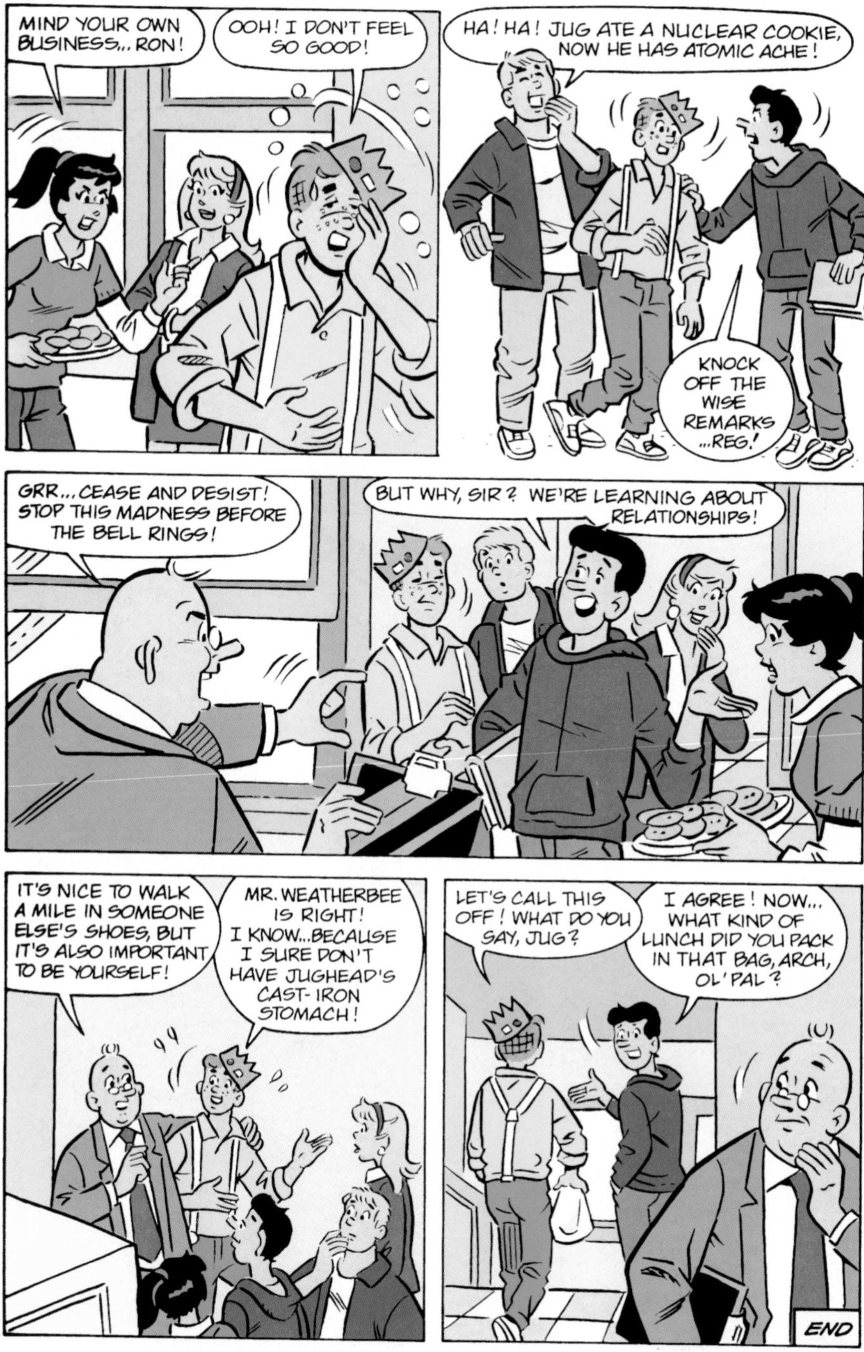
MIND YOUR OWN BUSINESS... RON!
OOH! I DON'T FEEL SO GOOD!
HA! HA! JUG ATE A NUCLEAR COOKIE, NOW HE HAS ATOMIC ACHE!
KNOCK OFF THE WISE REMARKS ...REG!
GRR... CEASE AND DESIST! STOP THIS MADNESS BEFORE THE BELL RINGS!
BUT WHY, SIR? WE'RE LEARNING ABOUT RELATIONSHIPS!
IT'S NICE TO WALK A MILE IN SOMEONE ELSE'S SHOES, BUT IT'S ALSO IMPORTANT TO BE YOURSELF!
MR. WEATHERBEE IS RIGHT! I KNOW...BECAUSE I SURE DON'T HAVE JUGHEAD'S CAST-IRON STOMACH!
LET'S CALL THIS OFF! WHAT DO YOU SAY, JUG?
I AGREE! NOW... WHAT KIND OF LUNCH DID YOU PACK IN THAT BAG, ARCH, OL' PAL?
END

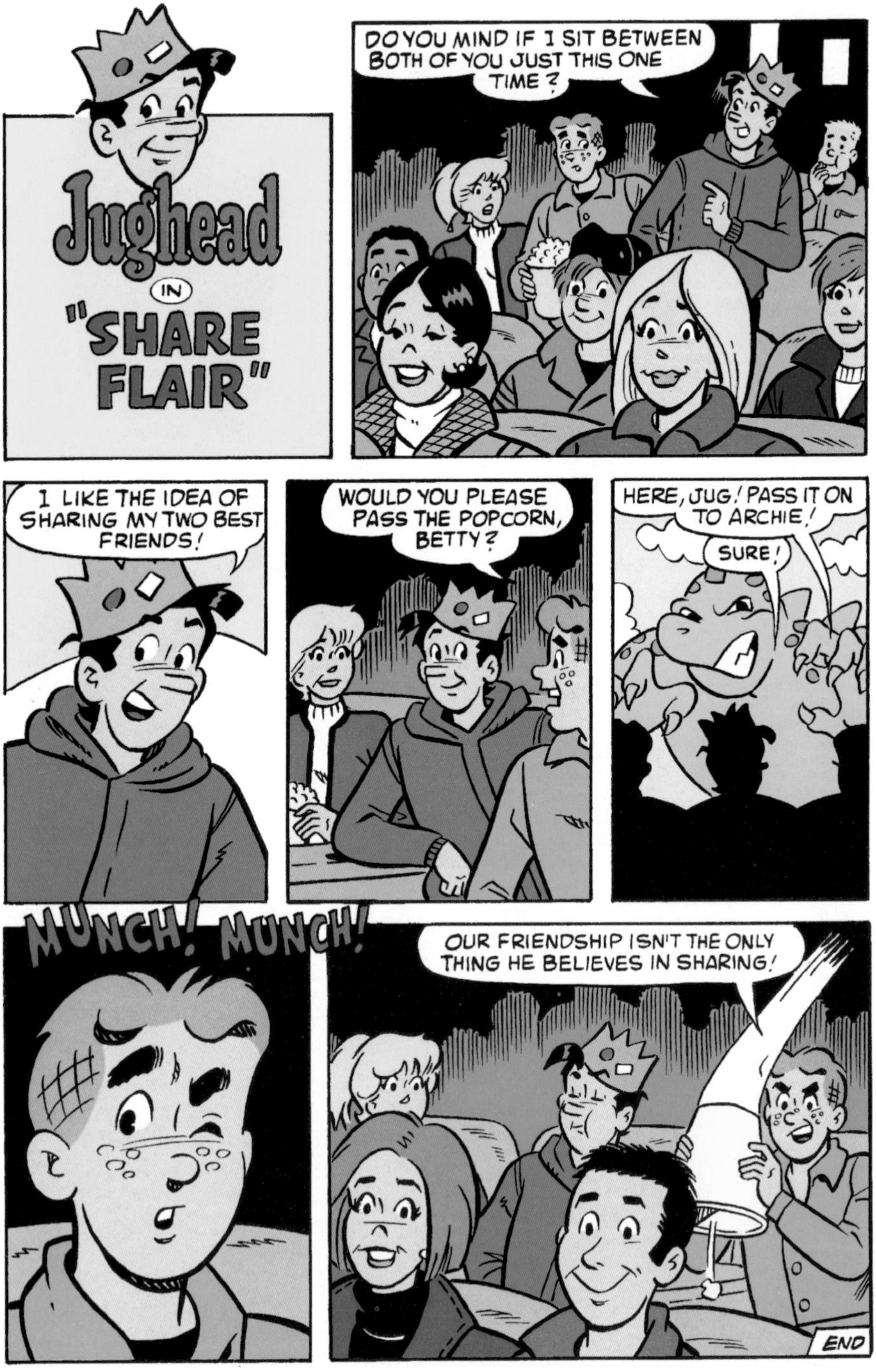
Jughead
IN
"SHARE FLAIR"
DO YOU MIND IF I SIT BETWEEN BOTH OF YOU JUST THIS ONE TIME?
I LIKE THE IDEA OF SHARING MY TWO BEST FRIENDS!
WOULD YOU PLEASE PASS THE POPCORN, BETTY?
HERE, JUG! PASS IT ON TO ARCHIE!
SURE!
MUNCH! MUNCH!
OUR FRIENDSHIP ISN'T THE ONLY THING HE BELIEVES IN SHARING!
END

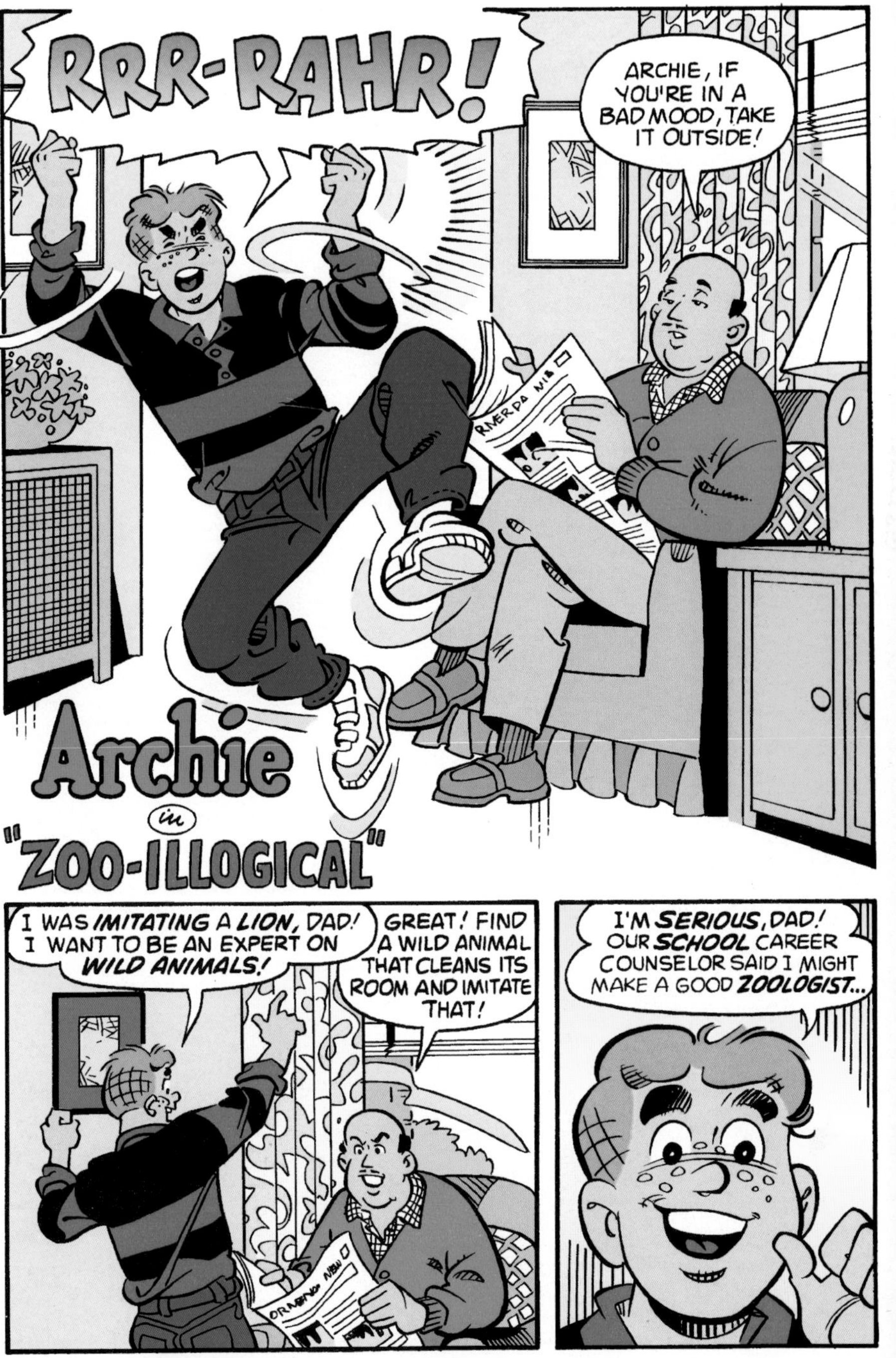
RRR-RAHR!
ARCHIE, IF YOU'RE IN A BAD MOOD, TAKE IT OUTSIDE!
Archie in "ZOO-ILLOGICAL"
I WAS IMITATING A LION, DAD! I WANT TO BE AN EXPERT ON WILD ANIMALS!
GREAT! FIND A WILD ANIMAL THAT CLEANS ITS ROOM AND IMITATE THAT!
I'M SERIOUS, DAD! OUR SCHOOL CAREER COUNSELOR SAID I MIGHT MAKE A GOOD ZOOLOGIST...

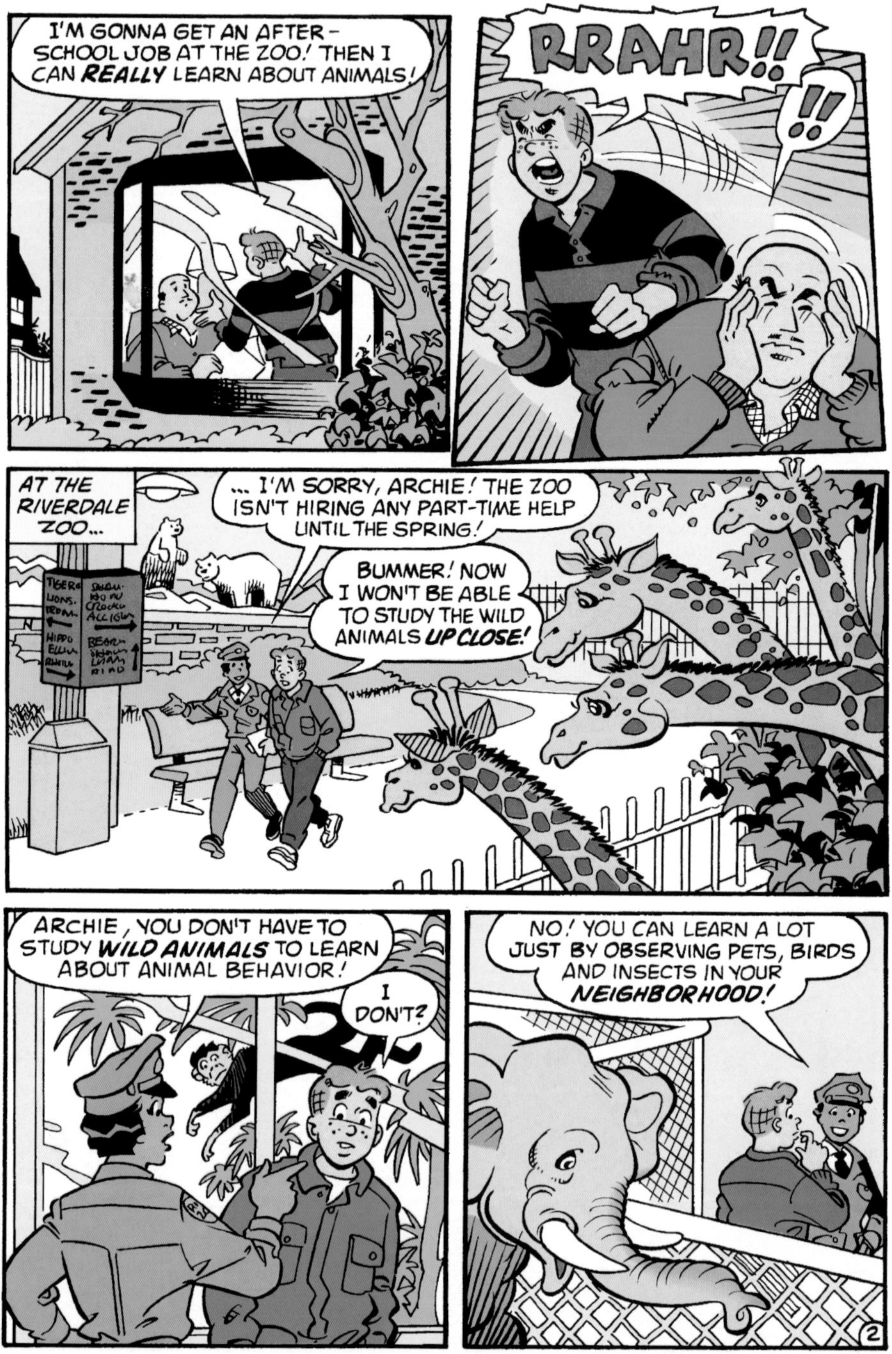
I'M GONNA GET AN AFTER-SCHOOL JOB AT THE ZOO! THEN I CAN REALLY LEARN ABOUT ANIMALS!
RRAHR!!
!!
AT THE RIVERDALE ZOO...
... I'M SORRY, ARCHIE! THE ZOO ISN'T HIRING ANY PART-TIME HELP UNTIL THE SPRING!
BUMMER! NOW I WON'T BE ABLE TO STUDY THE WILD ANIMALS UP CLOSE!
ARCHIE, YOU DON'T HAVE TO STUDY WILD ANIMALS TO LEARN ABOUT ANIMAL BEHAVIOR!
I DON'T?
NO! YOU CAN LEARN A LOT JUST BY OBSERVING PETS, BIRDS AND INSECTS IN YOUR NEIGHBORHOOD!
2

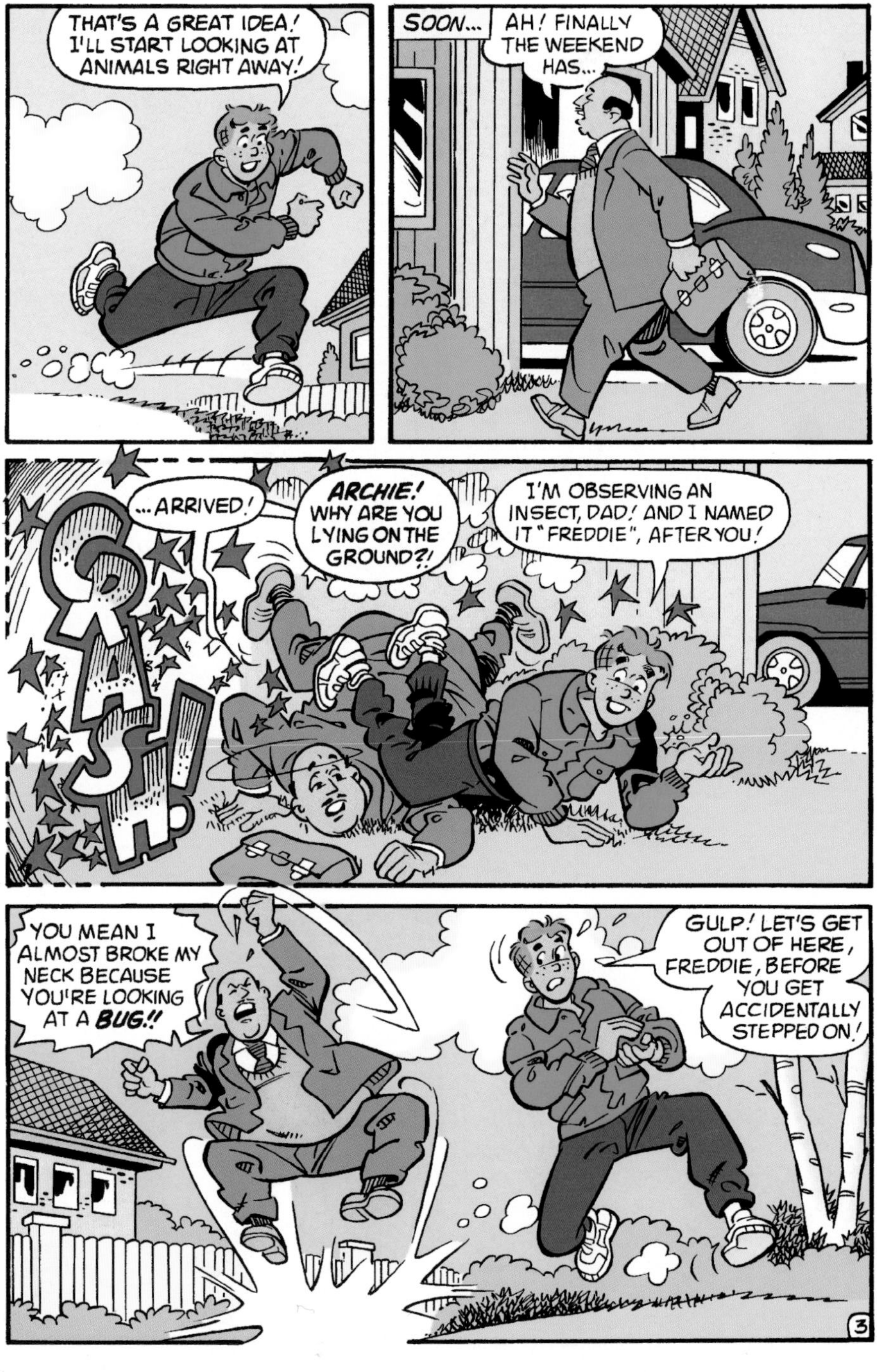
THAT'S A GREAT IDEA! I'LL START LOOKING AT ANIMALS RIGHT AWAY!
SOON...
AH! FINALLY THE WEEKEND HAS...
CRASH!
...ARRIVED!
ARCHIE! WHY ARE YOU LYING ON THE GROUND?!
I'M OBSERVING AN INSECT, DAD! AND I NAMED IT "FREDDIE", AFTER YOU!
YOU MEAN I ALMOST BROKE MY NECK BECAUSE YOU'RE LOOKING AT A BUG!!
GULP! LET'S GET OUT OF HERE, FREDDIE, BEFORE YOU GET ACCIDENTALLY STEPPED ON!
3

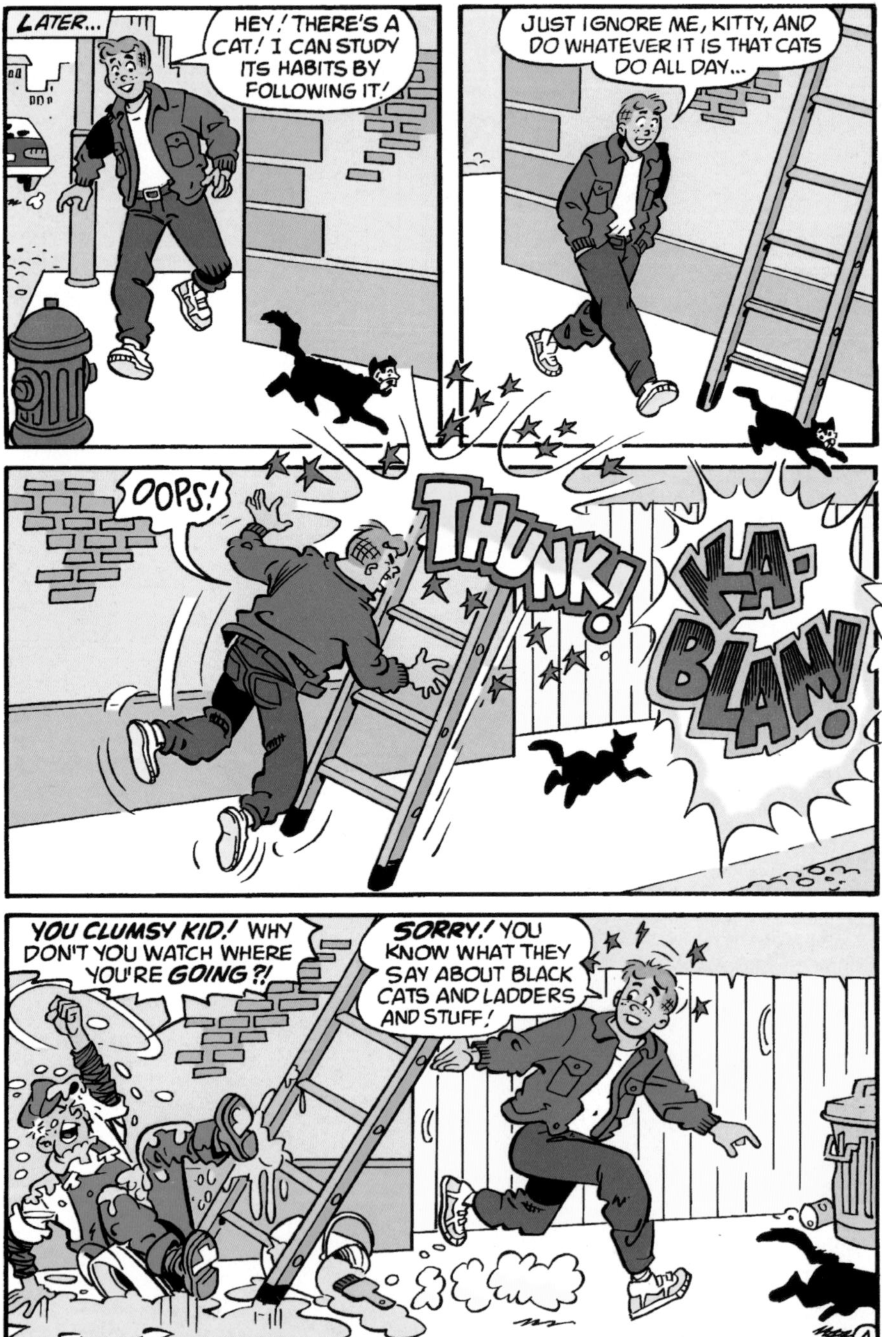
LATER...
HEY! THERE'S A CAT! I CAN STUDY ITS HABITS BY FOLLOWING IT!
JUST IGNORE ME, KITTY, AND DO WHATEVER IT IS THAT CATS DO ALL DAY...
OOPS!
THUNK!
KLA-BLAM!
YOU CLUMSY KID! WHY DON'T YOU WATCH WHERE YOU'RE GOING?!
SORRY! YOU KNOW WHAT THEY SAY ABOUT BLACK CATS AND LADDERS AND STUFF!
4

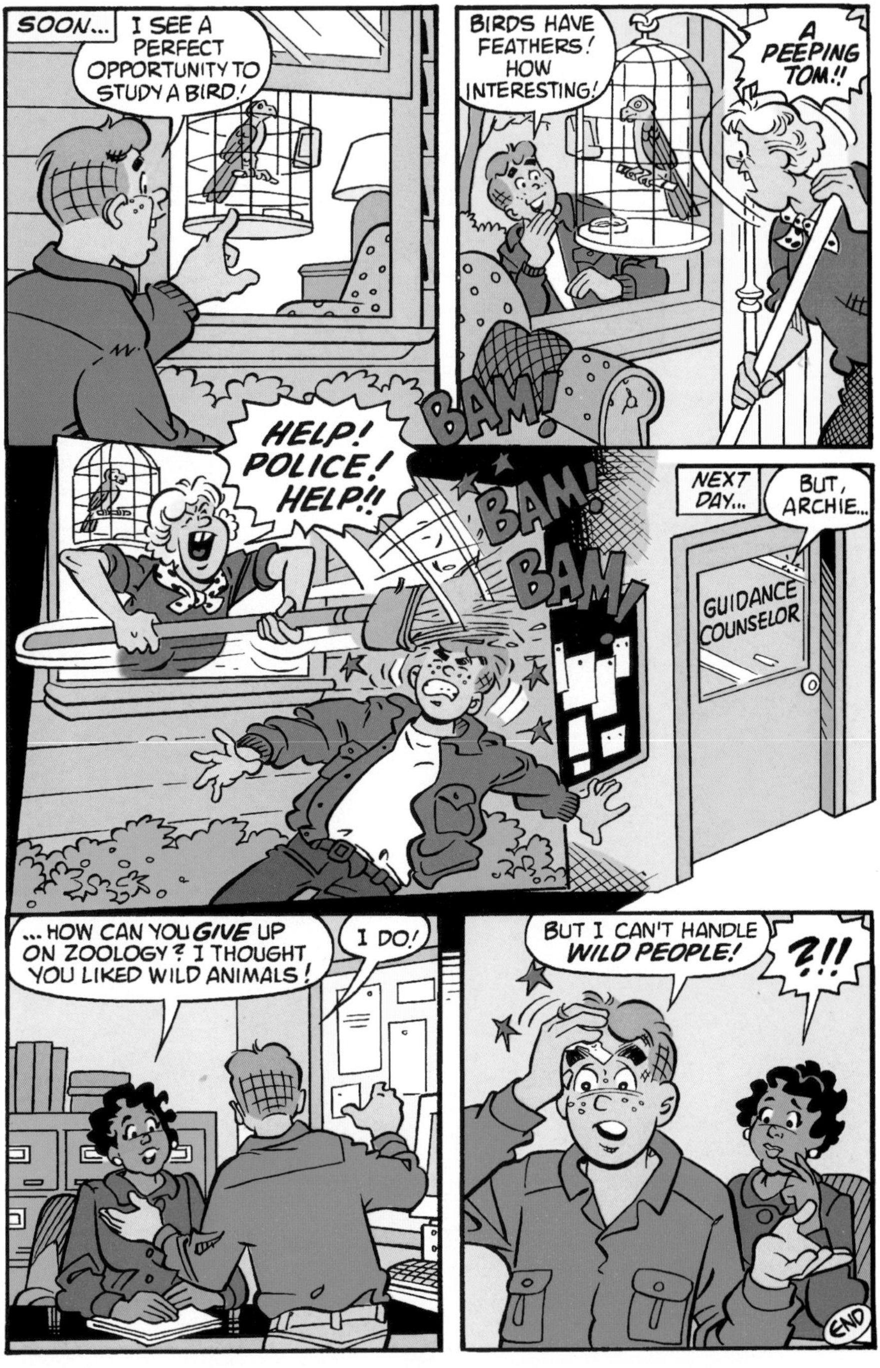
SOON...
I SEE A PERFECT OPPORTUNITY TO STUDY A BIRD!
BIRDS HAVE FEATHERS! HOW INTERESTING!
A PEEPING TOM!!
BAM!
HELP! POLICE! HELP!!
BAM!
BAM!
NEXT DAY...
BUT, ARCHIE...
GUIDANCE COUNSELOR
...HOW CAN YOU GIVE UP ON ZOOLOGY? I THOUGHT YOU LIKED WILD ANIMALS!
I DO!
BUT I CAN'T HANDLE WILD PEOPLE!
?!!
END

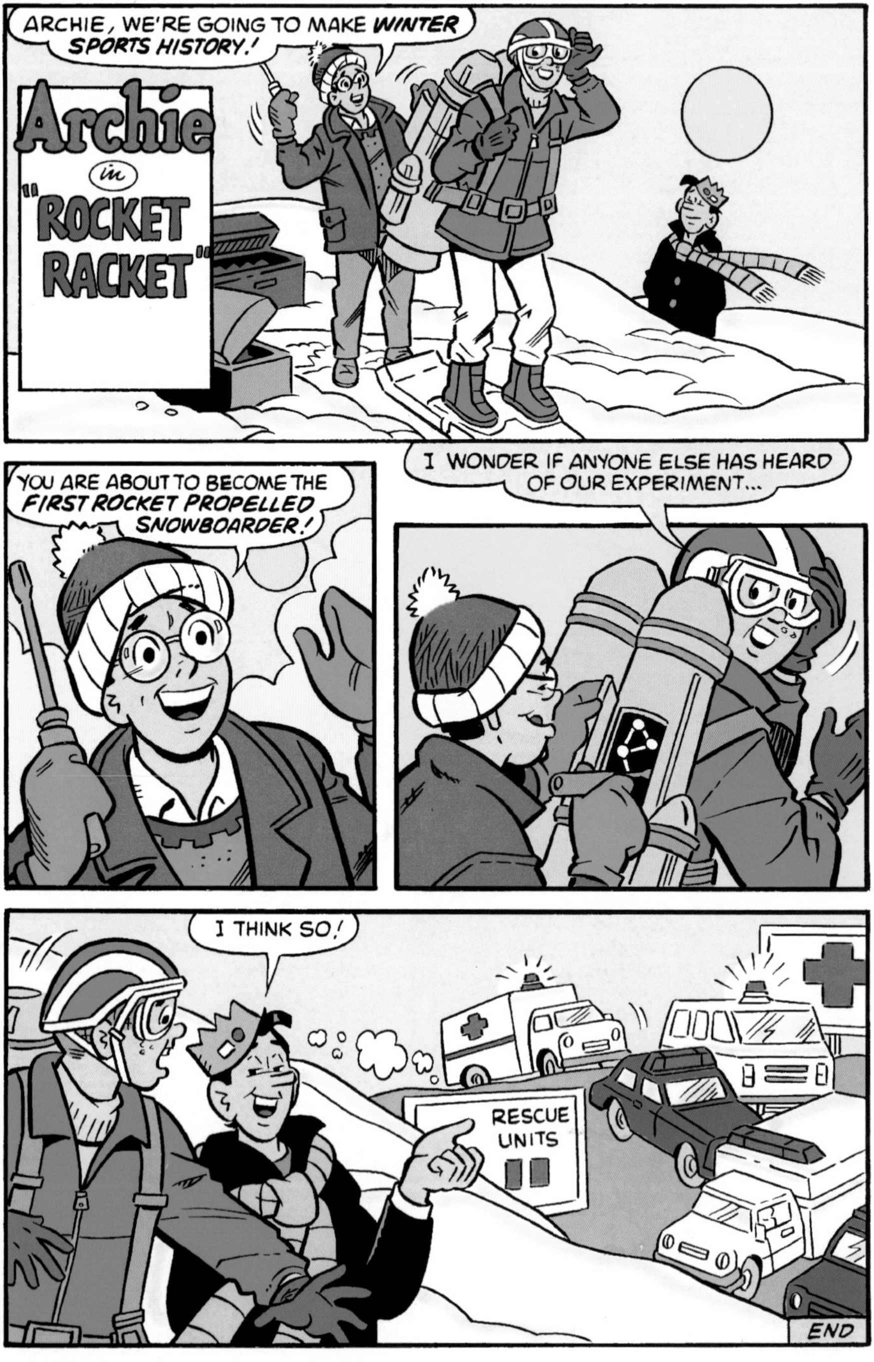
ARCHIE, WE'RE GOING TO MAKE WINTER SPORTS HISTORY!
Archie in "ROCKET RACKET"
YOU ARE ABOUT TO BECOME THE FIRST ROCKET PROPELLED SNOWBOARDER!
I WONDER IF ANYONE ELSE HAS HEARD OF OUR EXPERIMENT...
I THINK SO!
RESCUE UNITS
END

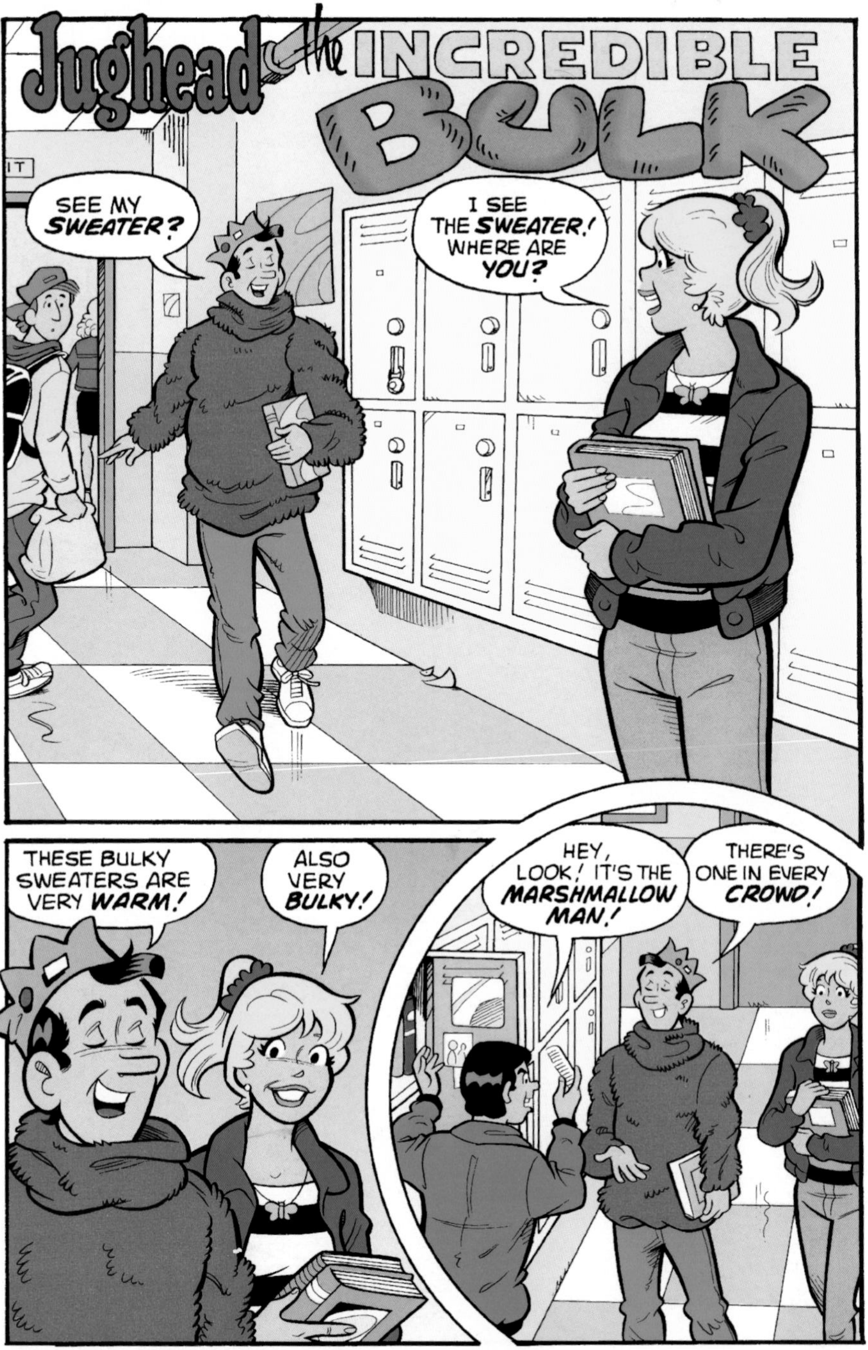
Jughead the INCREDIBLE BULK
IT
SEE MY SWEATER?
I SEE THE SWEATER! WHERE ARE YOU?
THESE BULKY SWEATERS ARE VERY WARM!
ALSO VERY BULKY!
HEY, LOOK! IT'S THE MARSHMALLOW MAN!
THERE'S ONE IN EVERY CROWD!

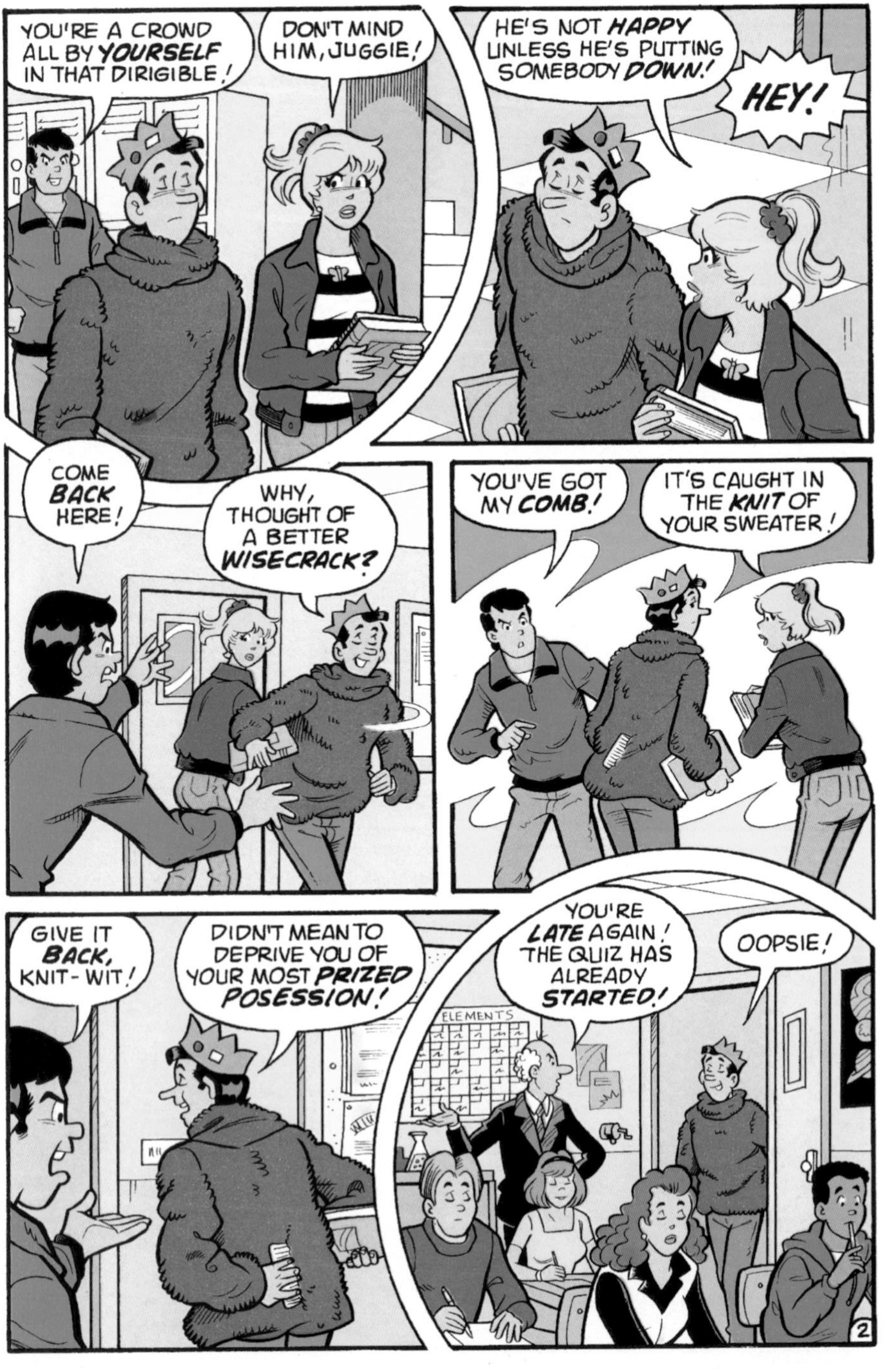

YOU'RE A CROWD ALL BY YOURSELF IN THAT DIRIGIBLE!
DON'T MIND HIM, JUGGIE!
HE'S NOT HAPPY UNLESS HE'S PUTTING SOMEBODY DOWN!
HEY!
COME BACK HERE!
WHY, THOUGHT OF A BETTER WISECRACK?
YOU'VE GOT MY COMB!
IT'S CAUGHT IN THE KNIT OF YOUR SWEATER!
GIVE IT BACK, KNIT-WIT!
DIDN'T MEAN TO DEPRIVE YOU OF YOUR MOST PRIZED POSESSION!
YOU'RE LATE AGAIN! THE QUIZ HAS ALREADY STARTED!
OOPSIE!
ELEMENTS
2

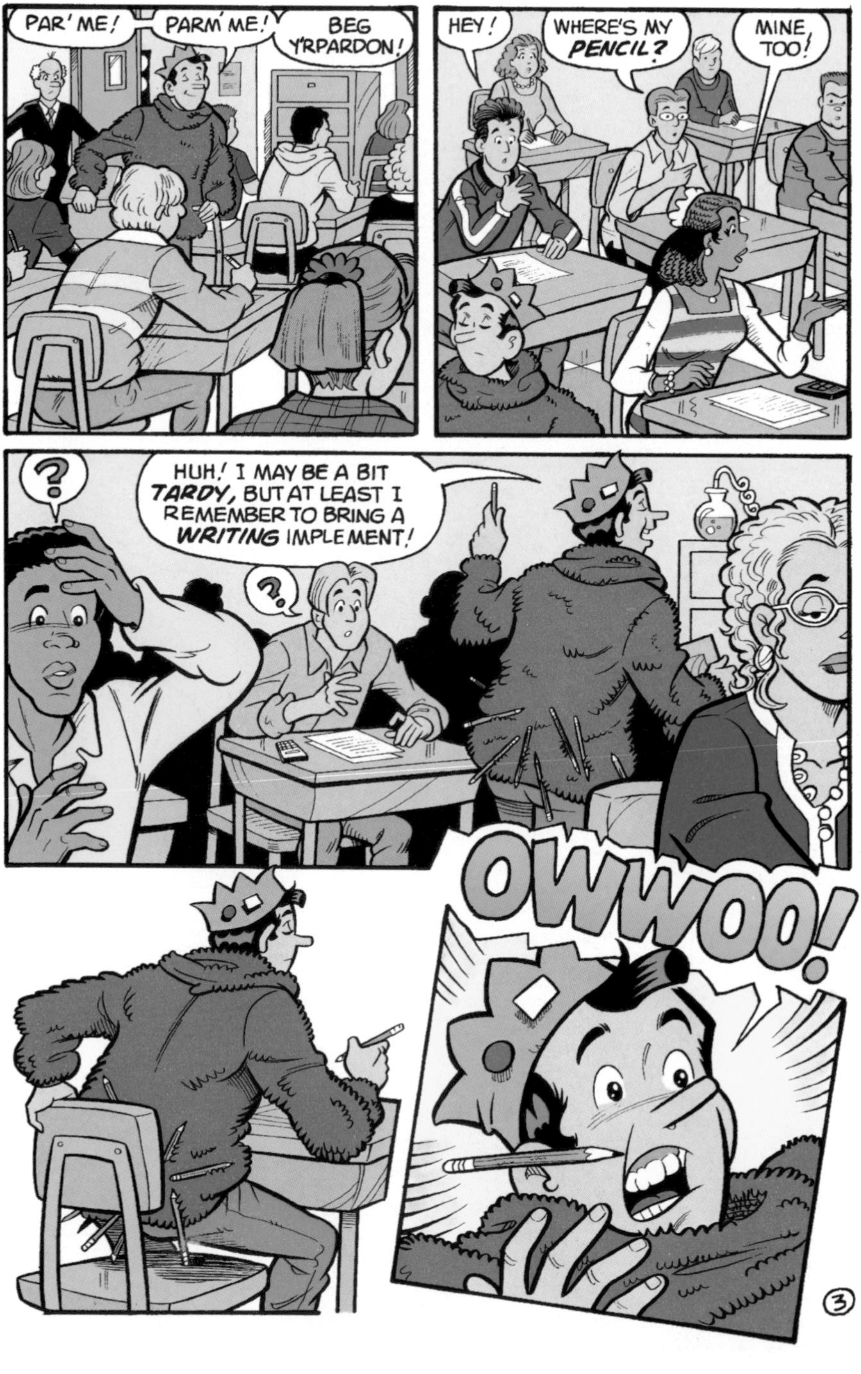
PAR' ME!
PARM' ME!
BEG Y'RPARDON!
HEY!
WHERE'S MY PENCIL?
MINE, TOO!
?
HUH! I MAY BE A BIT TARDY, BUT AT LEAST I REMEMBER TO BRING A WRITING IMPLEMENT!
?
OWWOO!
3

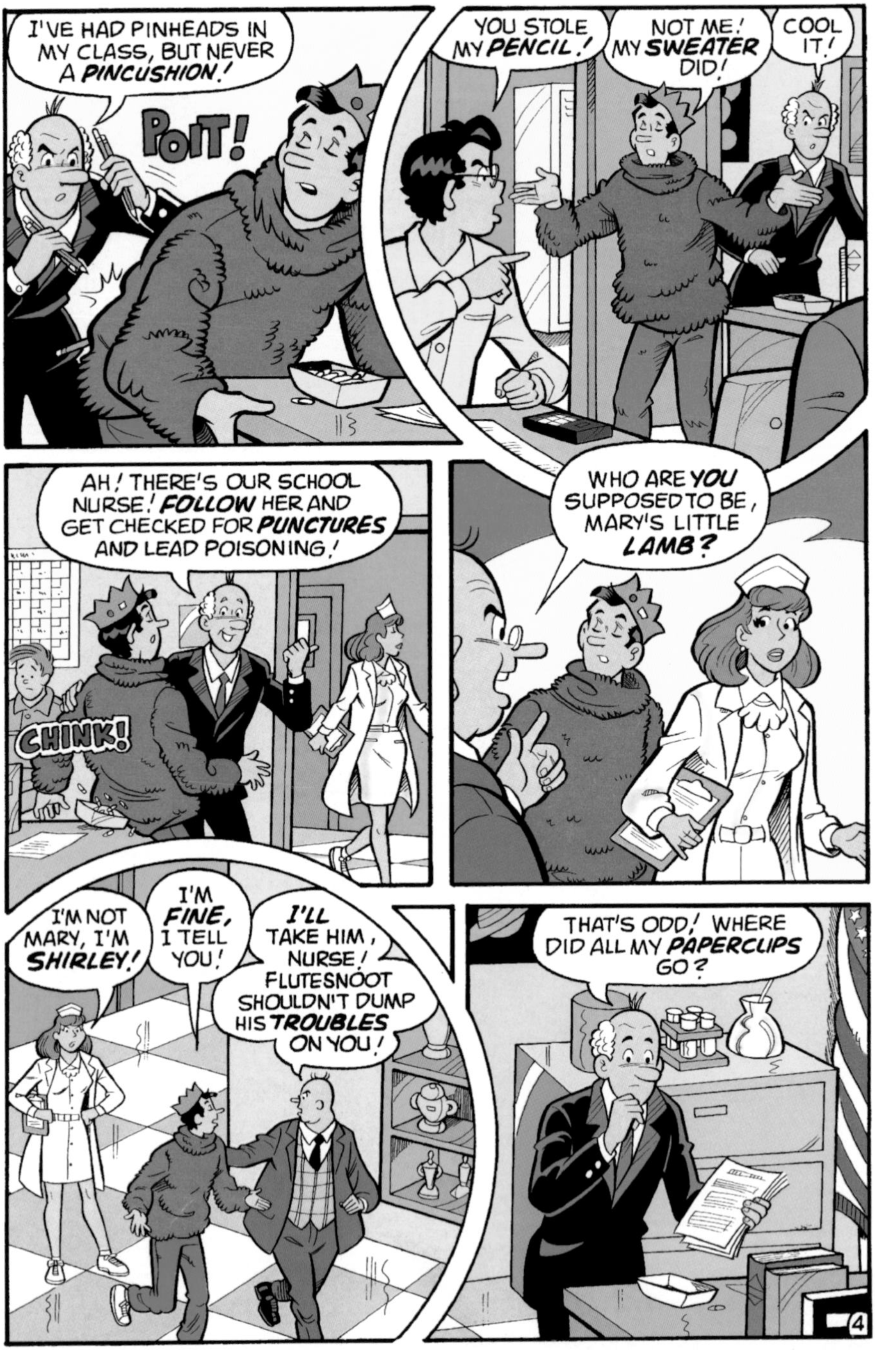
I'VE HAD PINHEADS IN MY CLASS, BUT NEVER A PINCUSHION!
POIT!
YOU STOLE MY PENCIL!
NOT ME! MY SWEATER DID!
COOL IT!
AH! THERE'S OUR SCHOOL NURSE! FOLLOW HER AND GET CHECKED FOR PUNCTURES AND LEAD POISONING!
CHINK!
WHO ARE YOU SUPPOSED TO BE, MARY'S LITTLE LAMB?
I'M NOT MARY, I'M SHIRLEY!
I'M FINE, I TELL YOU!
I'LL TAKE HIM, NURSE! FLUTESNOOT SHOULDN'T DUMP HIS TROUBLES ON YOU!
THAT'S ODD! WHERE DID ALL MY PAPERCLIPS GO?
4

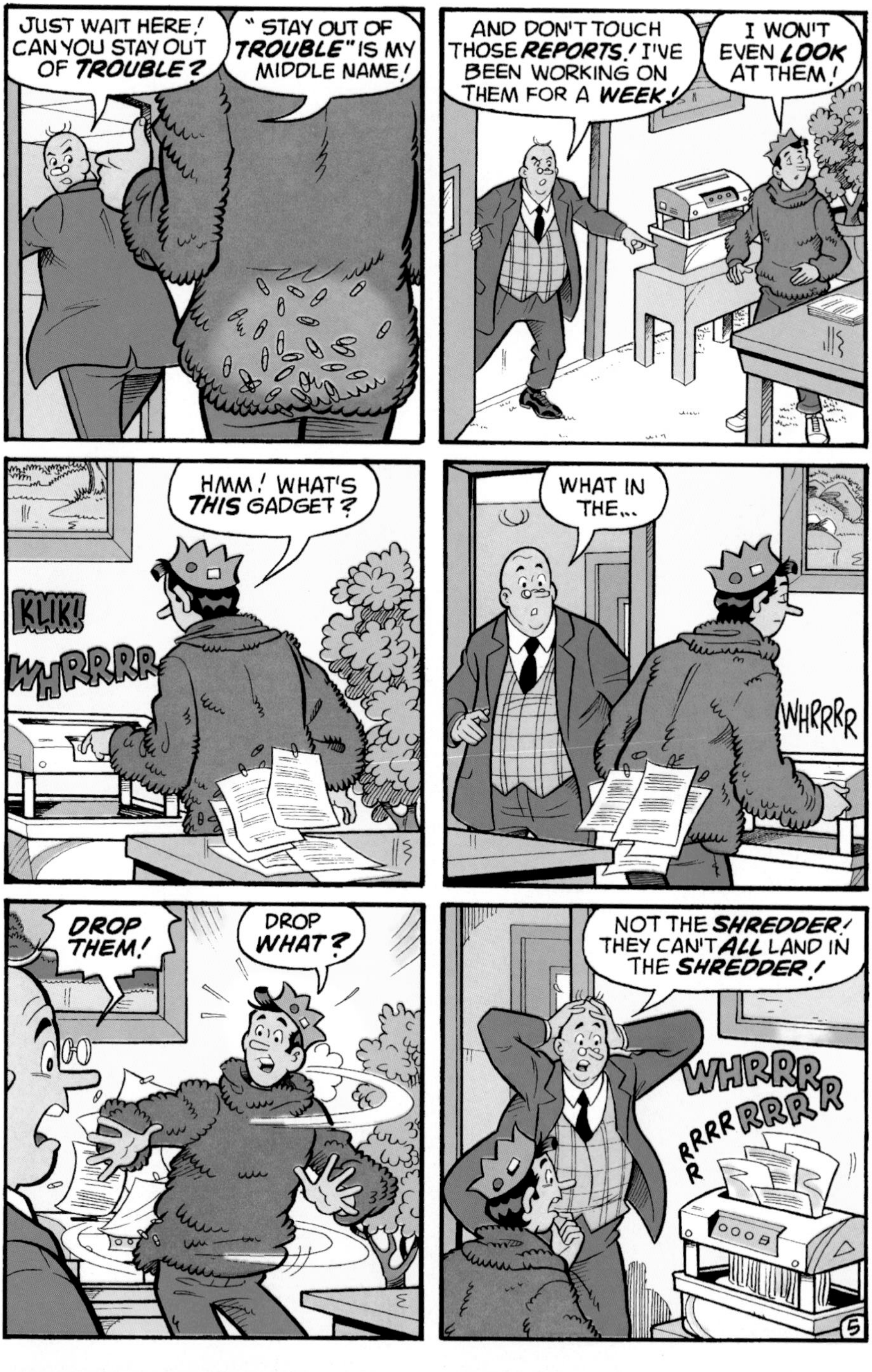
JUST WAIT HERE! CAN YOU STAY OUT OF TROUBLE?
"STAY OUT OF TROUBLE" IS MY MIDDLE NAME!
AND DON'T TOUCH THOSE REPORTS! I'VE BEEN WORKING ON THEM FOR A WEEK!
I WON'T EVEN LOOK AT THEM!
KLIK!
WHRRRR
HMM! WHAT'S THIS GADGET?
WHAT IN THE...
WHRRRR
DROP THEM!
DROP WHAT?
NOT THE SHREDDER! THEY CAN'T ALL LAND IN THE SHREDDER!
WHRRRRR
RRRRRRRR
5

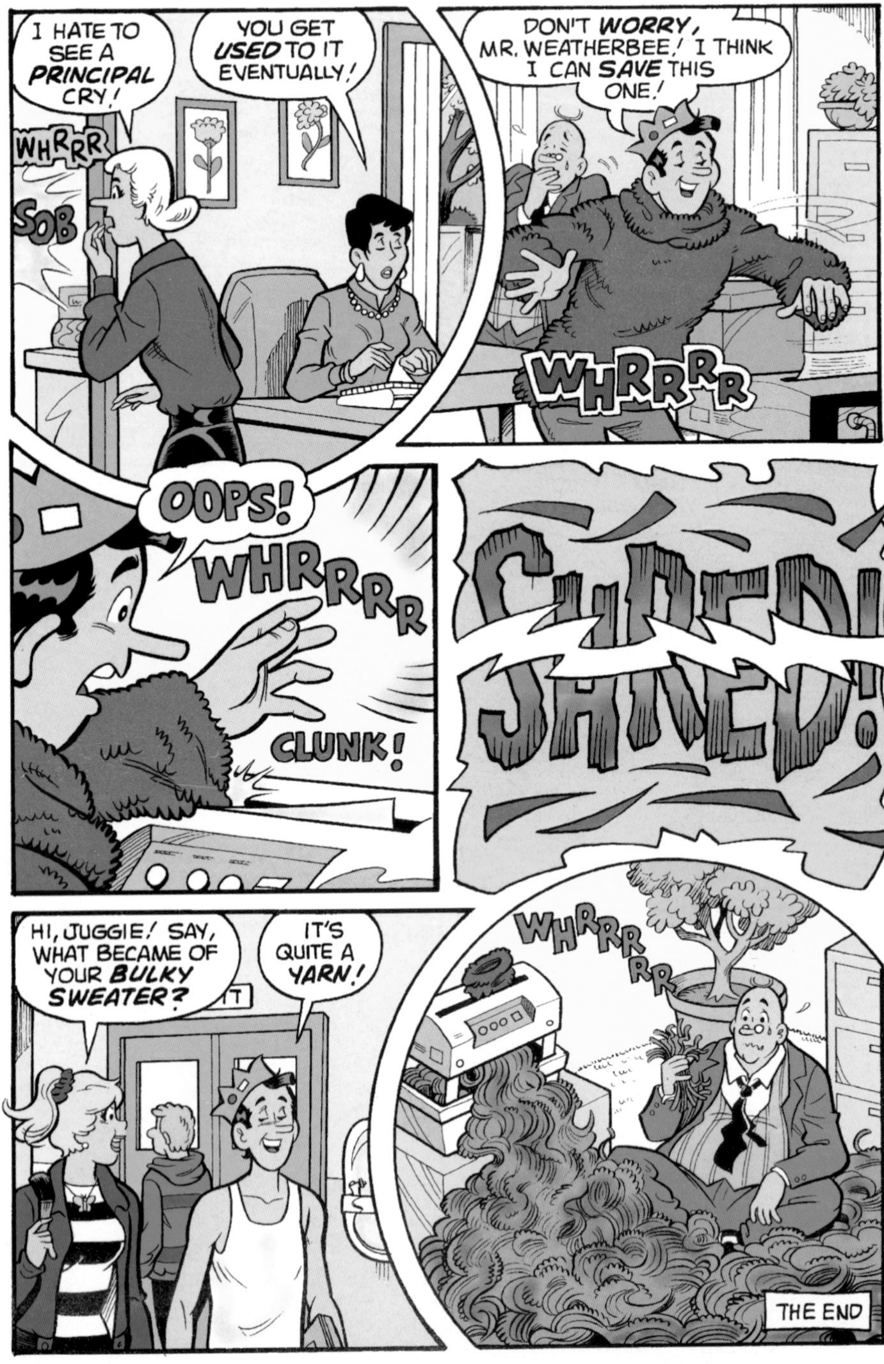
I HATE TO SEE A PRINCIPAL CRY!
YOU GET USED TO IT EVENTUALLY!
WHRRR
SOB
DON'T WORRY, MR. WEATHERBEE! I THINK I CAN SAVE THIS ONE!
WHRRRRR
OOPS!
WHRRRRR
CLUNK!
SHRED SHRED!
HI, JUGGIE! SAY, WHAT BECAME OF YOUR BULKY SWEATER?
IT'S QUITE A YARN!
WHRRRRR
THE END

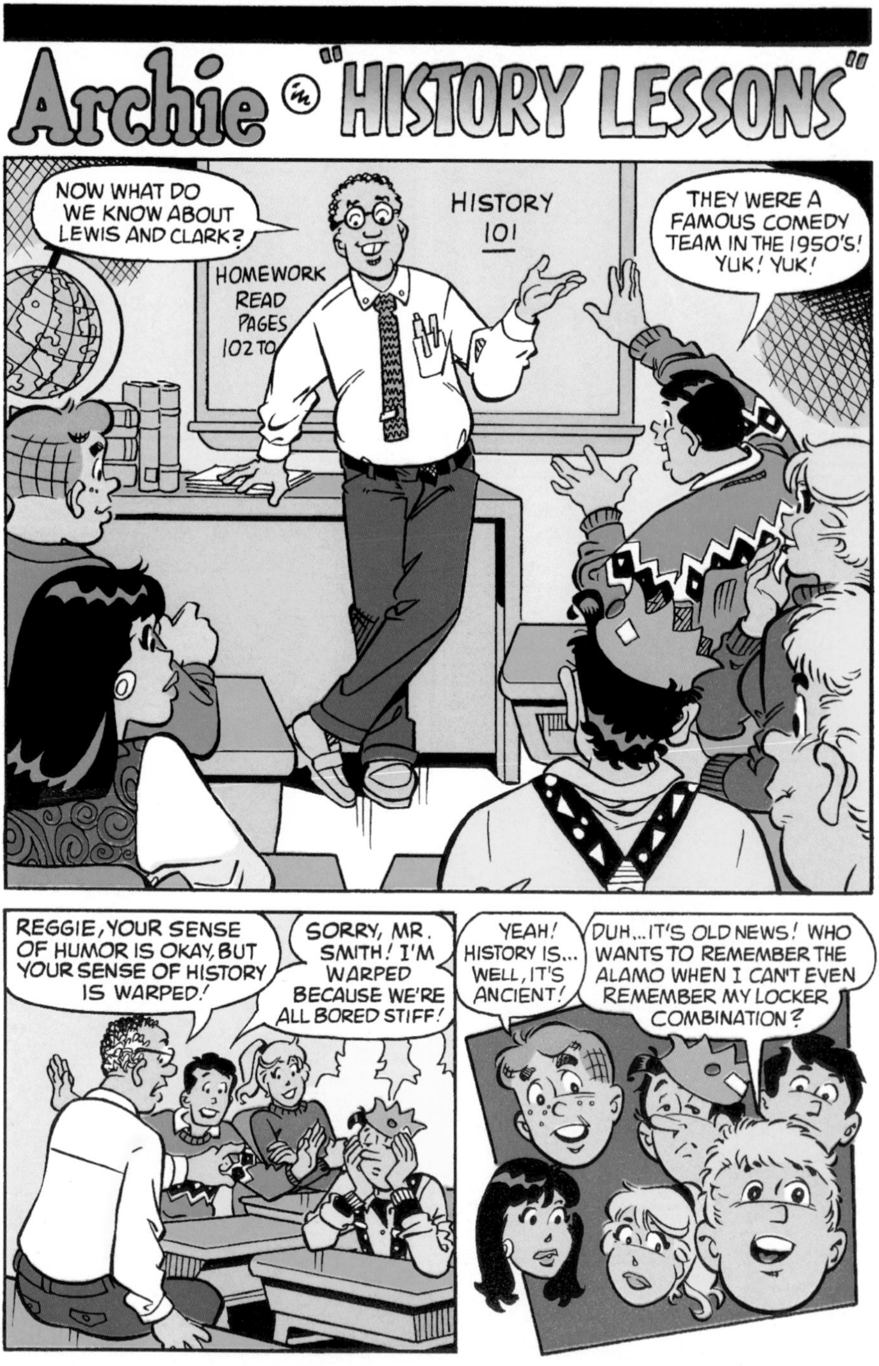
Archie in "HISTORY LESSONS"
NOW WHAT DO WE KNOW ABOUT LEWIS AND CLARK?
HISTORY 101
HOMEWORK READ PAGES 102 TO
THEY WERE A FAMOUS COMEDY TEAM IN THE 1950'S! YUK! YUK!
REGGIE, YOUR SENSE OF HUMOR IS OKAY, BUT YOUR SENSE OF HISTORY IS WARPED!
SORRY, MR. SMITH! I'M WARPED BECAUSE WE'RE ALL BORED STIFF!
YEAH! HISTORY IS... WELL, IT'S ANCIENT!
DUH...IT'S OLD NEWS! WHO WANTS TO REMEMBER THE ALAMO WHEN I CAN'T EVEN REMEMBER MY LOCKER COMBINATION?

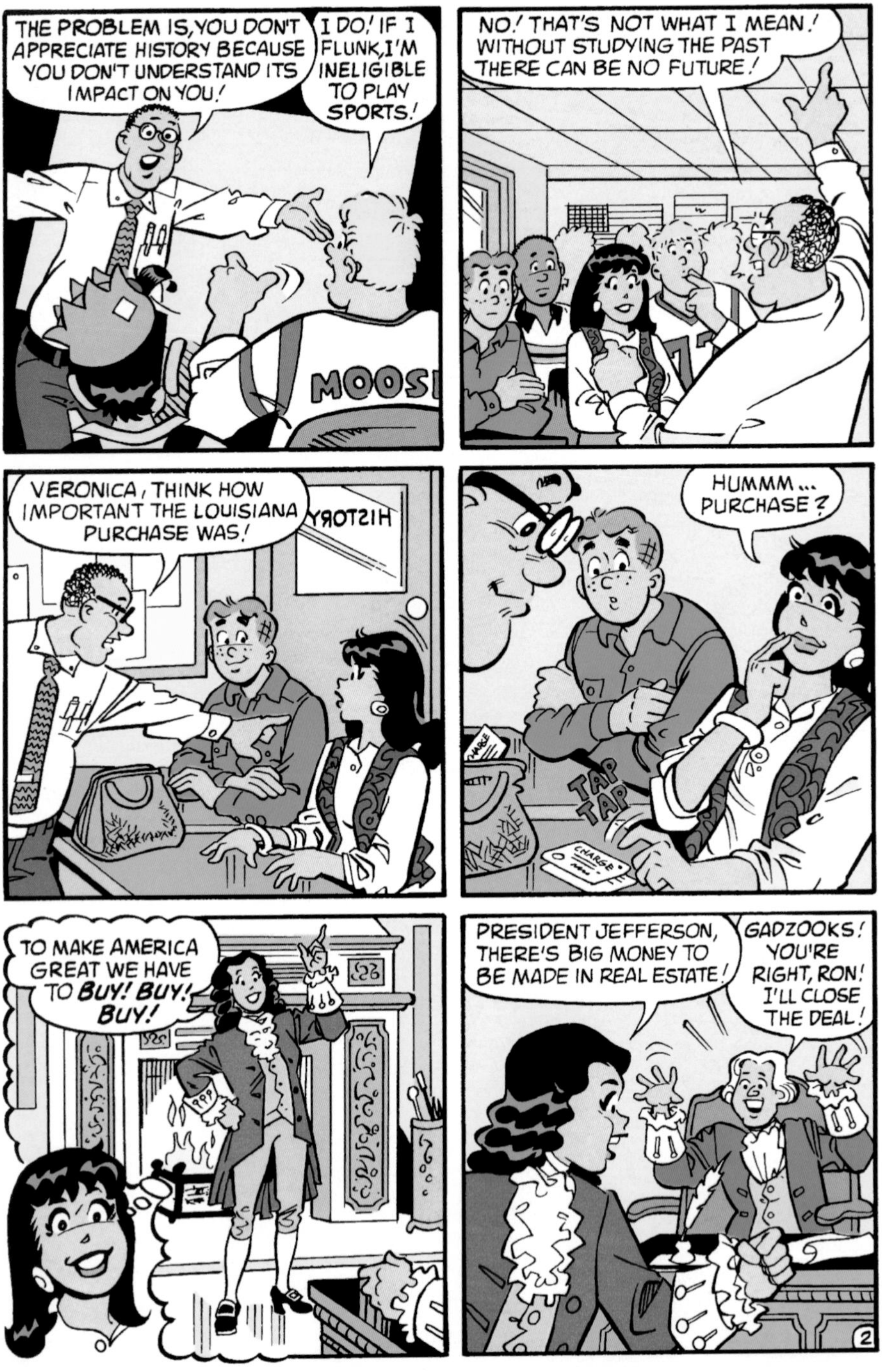
THE PROBLEM IS, YOU DON'T APPRECIATE HISTORY BECAUSE YOU DON'T UNDERSTAND ITS IMPACT ON YOU!
I DO! IF I FLUNK, I'M INELIGIBLE TO PLAY SPORTS!
NO! THAT'S NOT WHAT I MEAN! WITHOUT STUDYING THE PAST THERE CAN BE NO FUTURE!
VERONICA, THINK HOW IMPORTANT THE LOUISIANA PURCHASE WAS!
HISTORY
HUMMM... PURCHASE?
TAP TAP
CHARGE
TO MAKE AMERICA GREAT WE HAVE TO BUY! BUY! BUY!
PRESIDENT JEFFERSON, THERE'S BIG MONEY TO BE MADE IN REAL ESTATE!
GADZOOKS! YOU'RE RIGHT, RON! I'LL CLOSE THE DEAL!
2

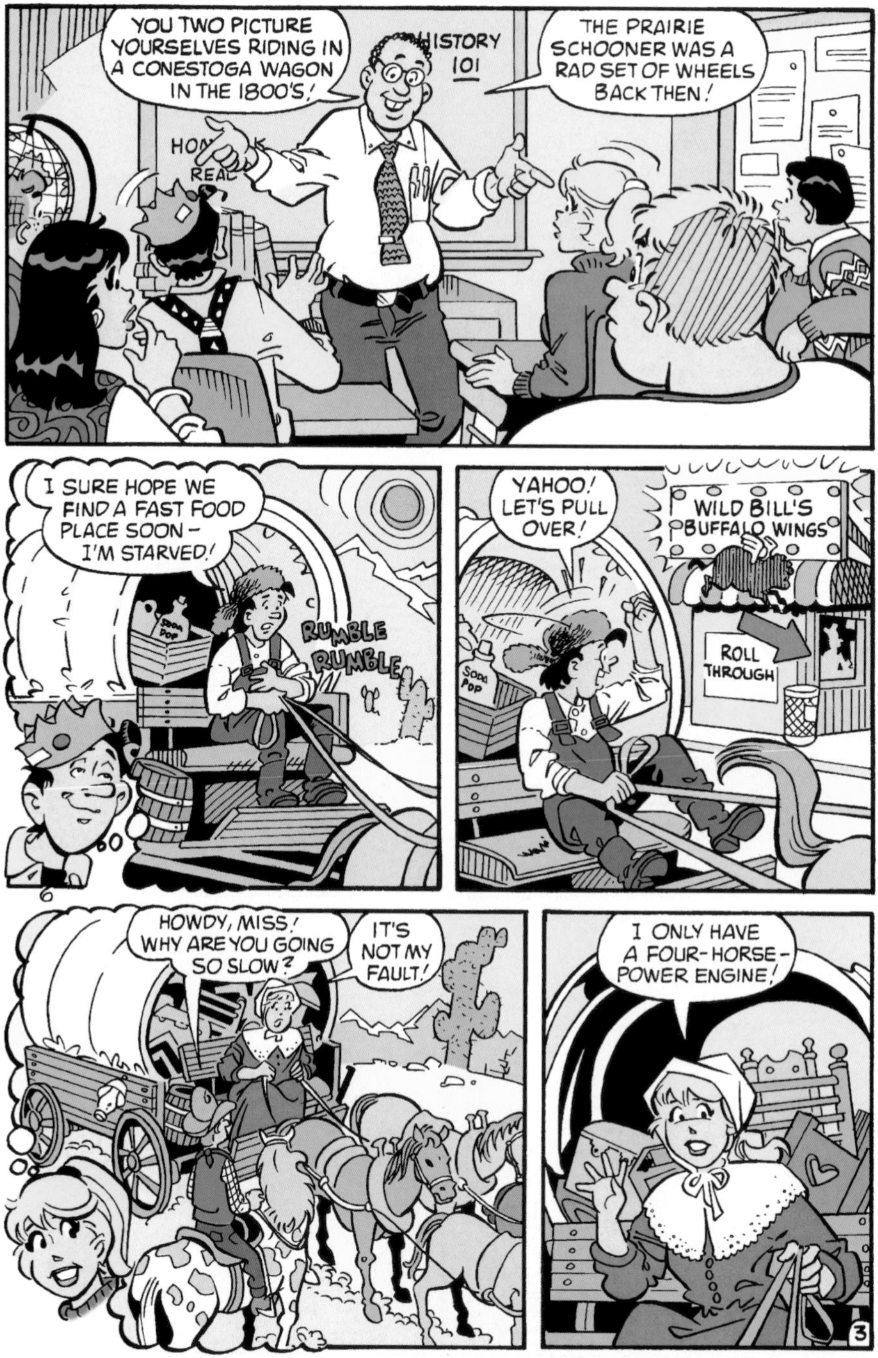
YOU TWO PICTURE YOURSELVES RIDING IN A CONESTOGA WAGON IN THE 1800'S!
HISTORY 101
THE PRAIRIE SCHOONER WAS A RAD SET OF WHEELS BACK THEN!
I SURE HOPE WE FIND A FAST FOOD PLACE SOON – I'M STARVED!
SODA POP
RUMBLE RUMBLE
YAHOO! LET'S PULL OVER!
WILD BILL'S BUFFALO WINGS
ROLL THROUGH
SODA POP
HOWDY, MISS! WHY ARE YOU GOING SO SLOW?
IT'S NOT MY FAULT!
I ONLY HAVE A FOUR-HORSE-POWER ENGINE!
3

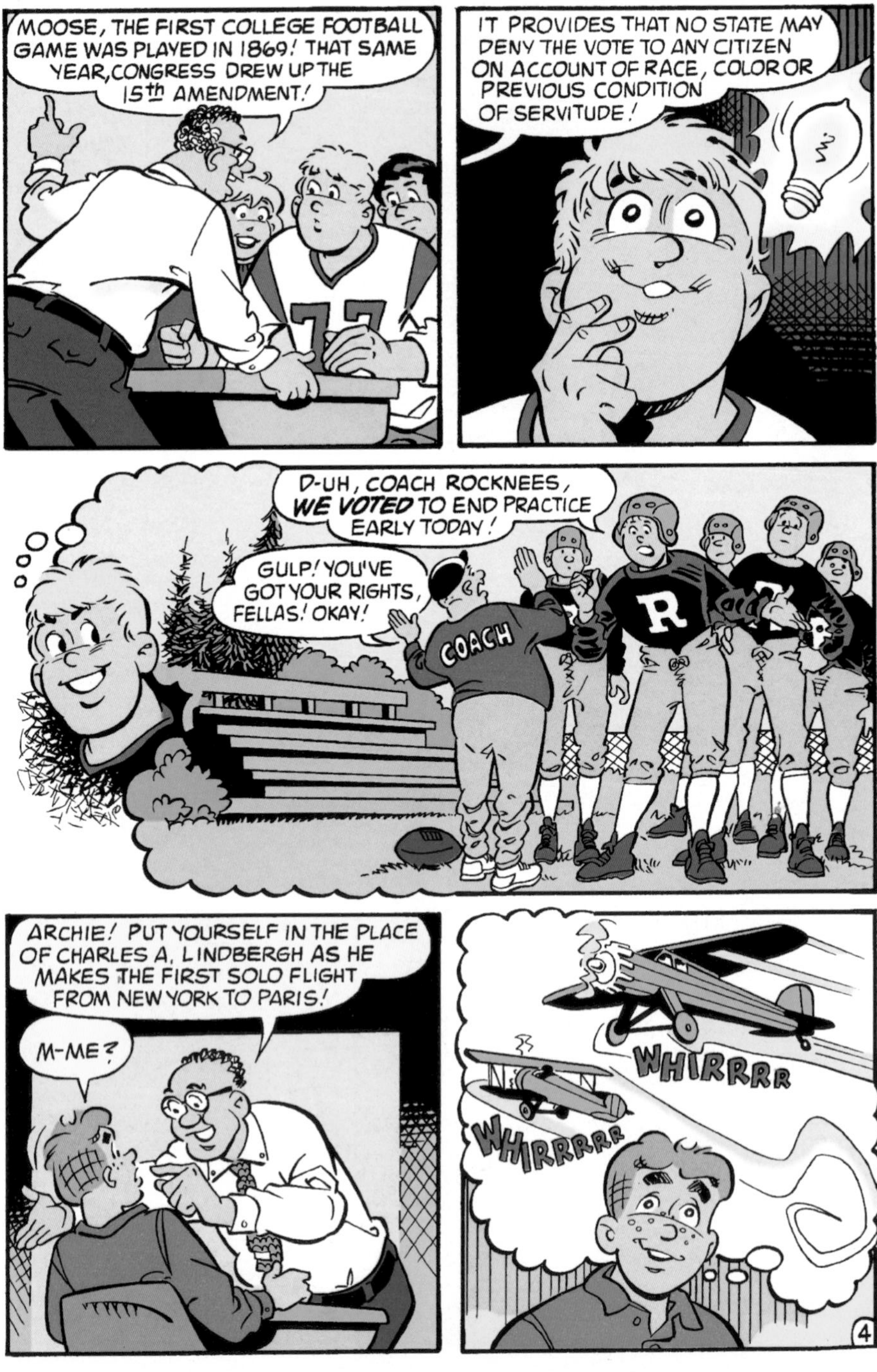
MOOSE, THE FIRST COLLEGE FOOTBALL GAME WAS PLAYED IN 1869! THAT SAME YEAR, CONGRESS DREW UP THE 15th AMENDMENT!
77
IT PROVIDES THAT NO STATE MAY DENY THE VOTE TO ANY CITIZEN ON ACCOUNT OF RACE, COLOR OR PREVIOUS CONDITION OF SERVITUDE!
D-UH, COACH ROCKNEES, WE VOTED TO END PRACTICE EARLY TODAY!
GULP! YOU'VE GOT YOUR RIGHTS, FELLAS! OKAY!
COACH
R
ARCHIE! PUT YOURSELF IN THE PLACE OF CHARLES A. LINDBERGH AS HE MAKES THE FIRST SOLO FLIGHT FROM NEW YORK TO PARIS!
M-ME?
WHIRRRR
WHIRRRRR
4

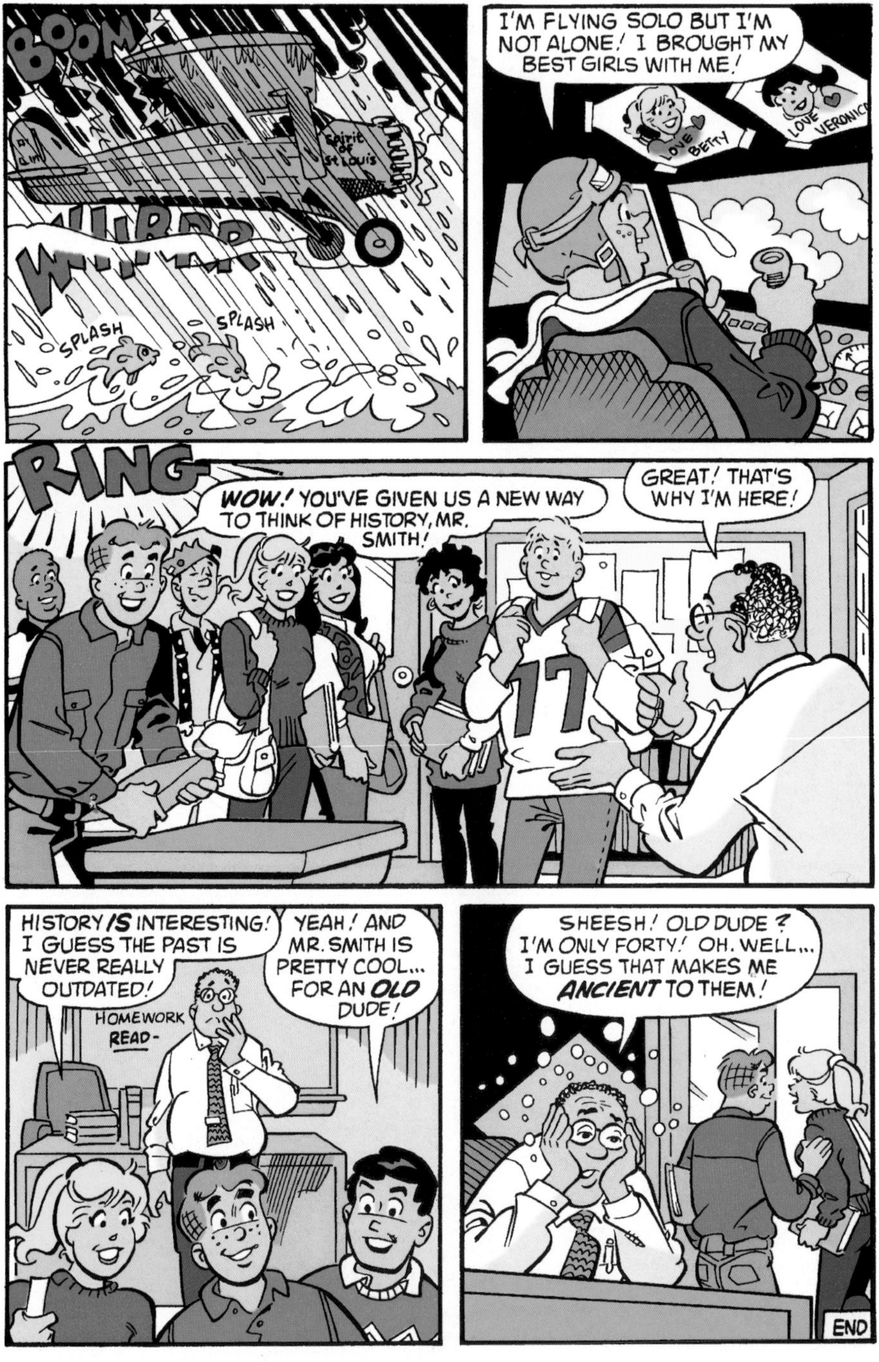
BOOM
Spirit of St Louis
WHIRRR
SPLASH
SPLASH
I'M FLYING SOLO BUT I'M NOT ALONE! I BROUGHT MY BEST GIRLS WITH ME!
LOVE BETTY
LOVE VERONICA
RING
WOW! YOU'VE GIVEN US A NEW WAY TO THINK OF HISTORY, MR. SMITH!
GREAT! THAT'S WHY I'M HERE!
HISTORY IS INTERESTING! I GUESS THE PAST IS NEVER REALLY OUTDATED!
YEAH! AND MR. SMITH IS PRETTY COOL... FOR AN OLD DUDE!
HOMEWORK READ-
SHEESH! OLD DUDE? I'M ONLY FORTY! OH, WELL... I GUESS THAT MAKES ME ANCIENT TO THEM!
END

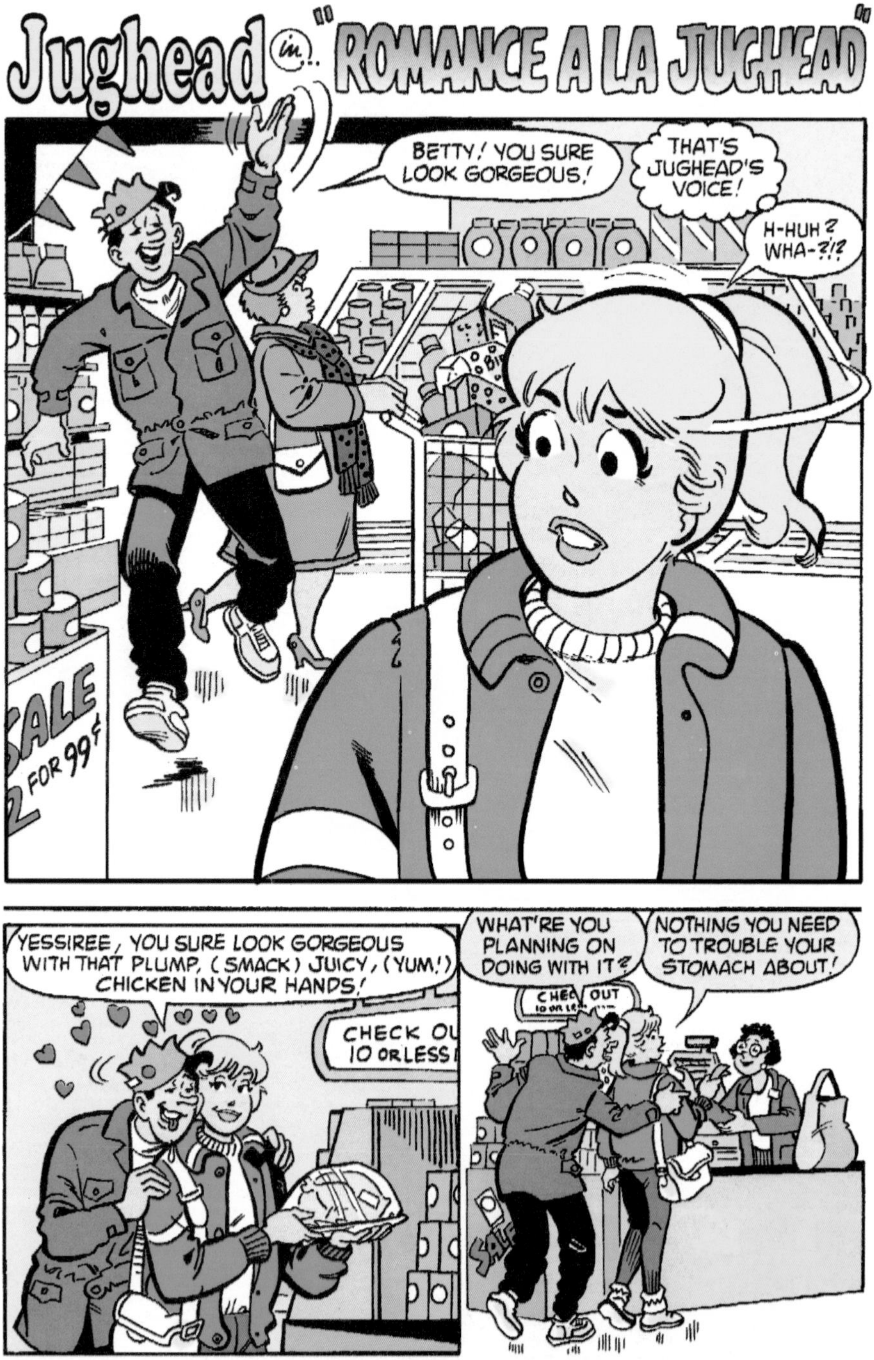
Jughead in... "ROMANCE A LA JUGHEAD"
BETTY! YOU SURE LOOK GORGEOUS!
THAT'S JUGHEAD'S VOICE!
H-HUH? WHA-?!?
SALE 2 FOR 99¢
YESSIREE, YOU SURE LOOK GORGEOUS WITH THAT PLUMP, (SMACK) JUICY, (YUM!) CHICKEN IN YOUR HANDS!
CHECK OU 10 OR LESS
WHAT'RE YOU PLANNING ON DOING WITH IT?
NOTHING YOU NEED TO TROUBLE YOUR STOMACH ABOUT!
CHECK OUT

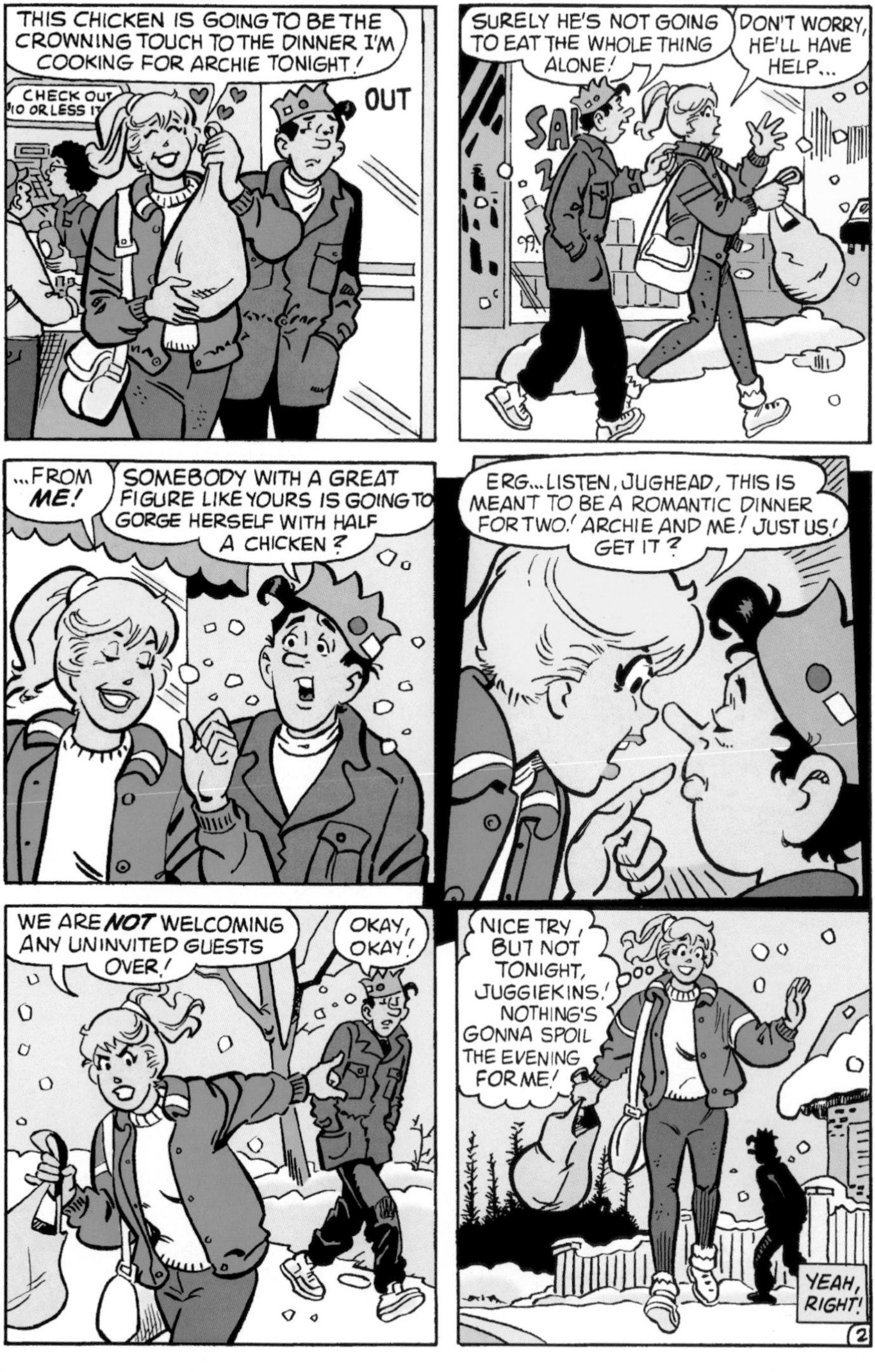
THIS CHICKEN IS GOING TO BE THE CROWNING TOUCH TO THE DINNER I'M COOKING FOR ARCHIE TONIGHT!
CHECK OUT 10 OR LESS IT
OUT
SURELY HE'S NOT GOING TO EAT THE WHOLE THING ALONE!
DON'T WORRY, HE'LL HAVE HELP...
...FROM ME!
SOMEBODY WITH A GREAT FIGURE LIKE YOURS IS GOING TO GORGE HERSELF WITH HALF A CHICKEN?
ERG... LISTEN, JUGHEAD, THIS IS MEANT TO BE A ROMANTIC DINNER FOR TWO! ARCHIE AND ME! JUST US! GET IT?
WE ARE NOT WELCOMING ANY UNINVITED GUESTS OVER!
OKAY, OKAY!
NICE TRY, BUT NOT TONIGHT, JUGGIEKINS! NOTHING'S GONNA SPOIL THE EVENING FOR ME!
YEAH, RIGHT!
2

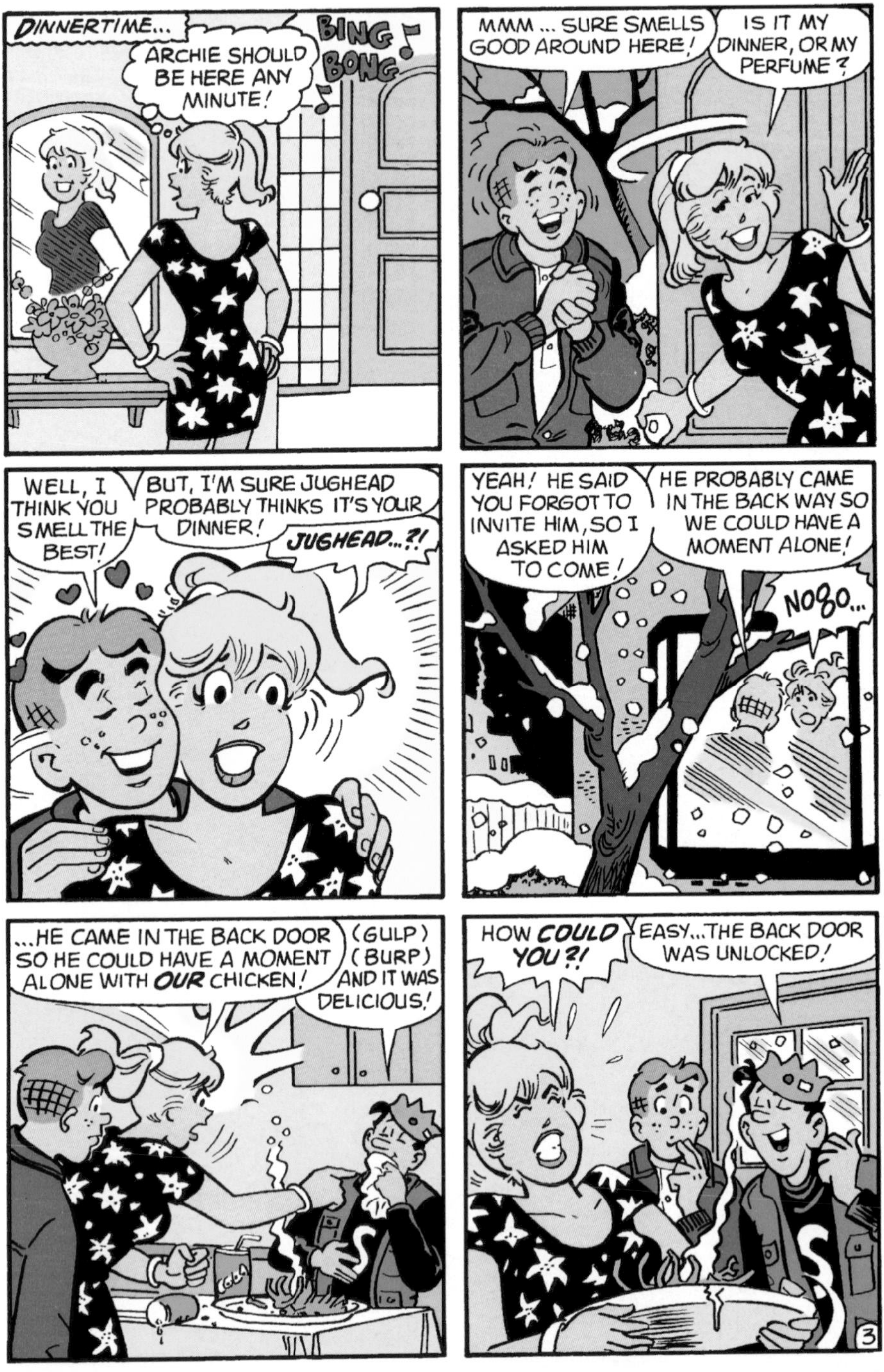
DINNERTIME...
ARCHIE SHOULD BE HERE ANY MINUTE!
BING BONG
MMM ... SURE SMELLS GOOD AROUND HERE!
IS IT MY DINNER, OR MY PERFUME?
WELL, I THINK YOU SMELL THE BEST!
BUT, I'M SURE JUGHEAD PROBABLY THINKS IT'S YOUR DINNER!
JUGHEAD...?!
YEAH! HE SAID YOU FORGOT TO INVITE HIM, SO I ASKED HIM TO COME!
HE PROBABLY CAME IN THE BACK WAY SO WE COULD HAVE A MOMENT ALONE!
NOSO...
...HE CAME IN THE BACK DOOR SO HE COULD HAVE A MOMENT ALONE WITH OUR CHICKEN!
(GULP) (BURP) AND IT WAS DELICIOUS!
HOW COULD YOU?!
EASY...THE BACK DOOR WAS UNLOCKED!
3

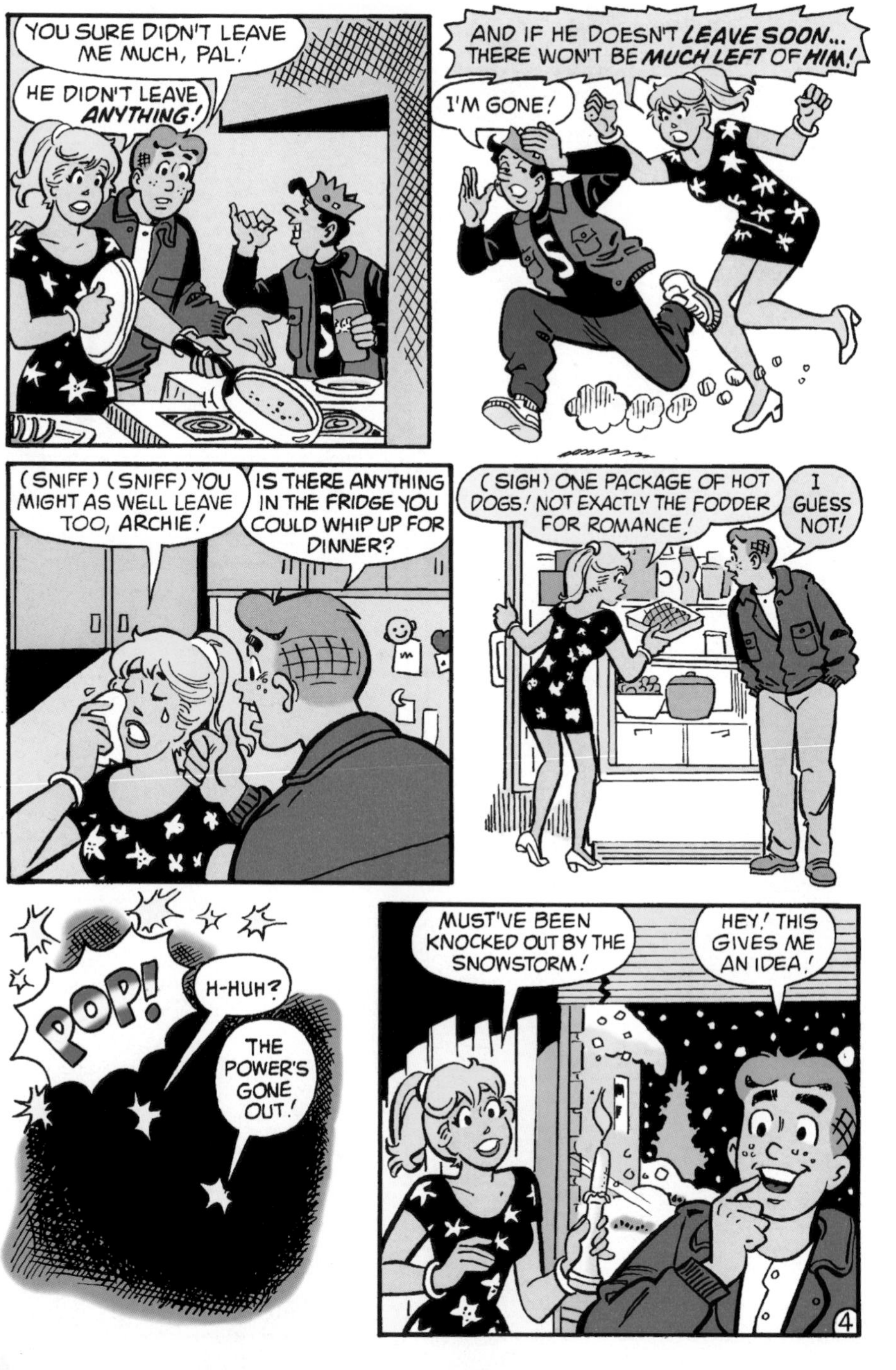
YOU SURE DIDN'T LEAVE ME MUCH, PAL!
HE DIDN'T LEAVE ANYTHING!
AND IF HE DOESN'T LEAVE SOON... THERE WON'T BE MUCH LEFT OF HIM!
I'M GONE!
(SNIFF) (SNIFF) YOU MIGHT AS WELL LEAVE TOO, ARCHIE!
IS THERE ANYTHING IN THE FRIDGE YOU COULD WHIP UP FOR DINNER?
(SIGH) ONE PACKAGE OF HOT DOGS! NOT EXACTLY THE FODDER FOR ROMANCE!
I GUESS NOT!
POP!
H-HUH?
THE POWER'S GONE OUT!
MUST'VE BEEN KNOCKED OUT BY THE SNOWSTORM!
HEY! THIS GIVES ME AN IDEA!
4

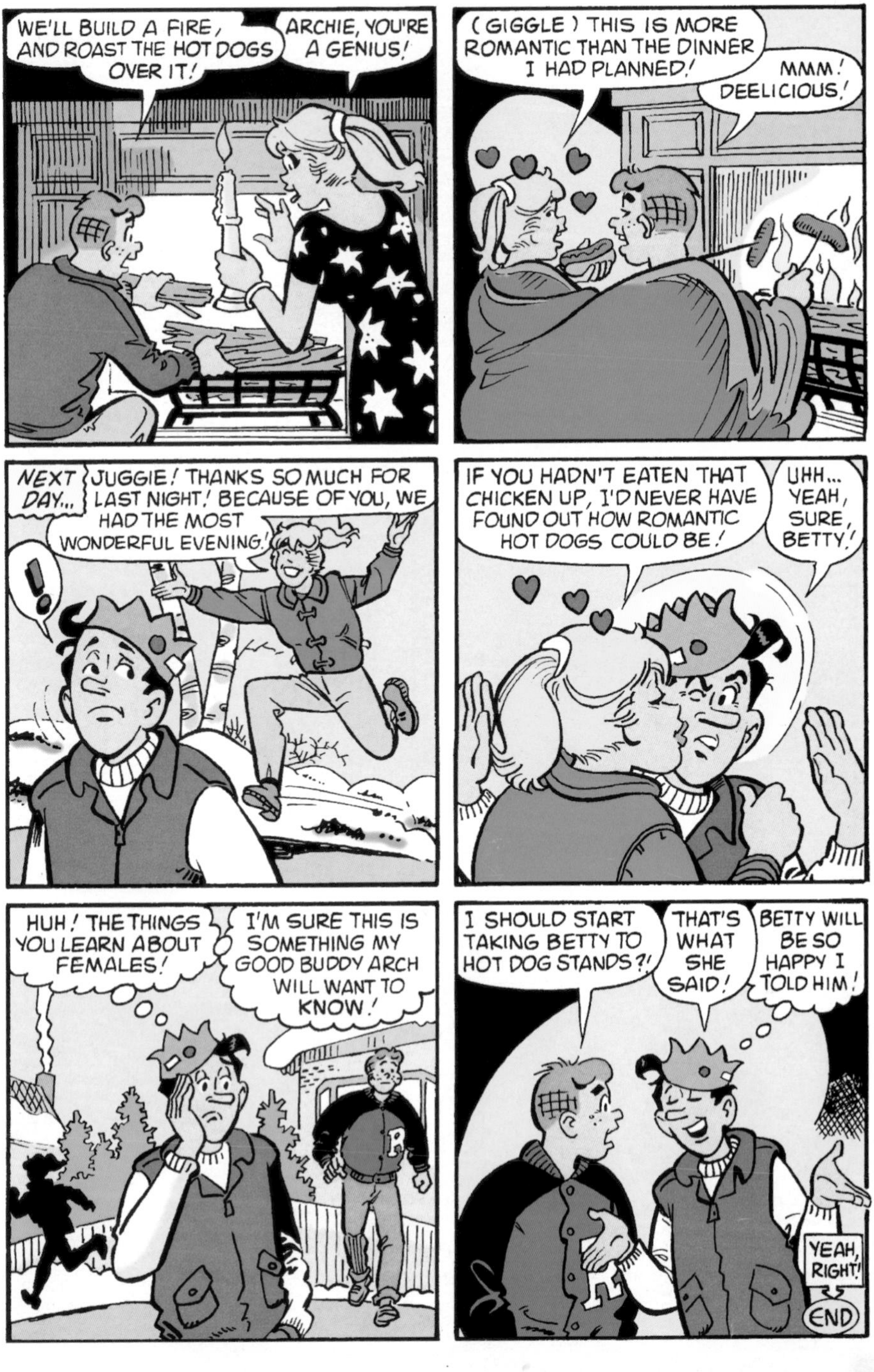
WE'LL BUILD A FIRE, AND ROAST THE HOT DOGS OVER IT!
ARCHIE, YOU'RE A GENIUS!
(GIGGLE) THIS IS MORE ROMANTIC THAN THE DINNER I HAD PLANNED!
MMM! DEELICIOUS!
NEXT DAY...
JUGGIE! THANKS SO MUCH FOR LAST NIGHT! BECAUSE OF YOU, WE HAD THE MOST WONDERFUL EVENING!
!
IF YOU HADN'T EATEN THAT CHICKEN UP, I'D NEVER HAVE FOUND OUT HOW ROMANTIC HOT DOGS COULD BE!
UHH... YEAH, SURE, BETTY!
HUH! THE THINGS YOU LEARN ABOUT FEMALES!
I'M SURE THIS IS SOMETHING MY GOOD BUDDY ARCH WILL WANT TO KNOW!
I SHOULD START TAKING BETTY TO HOT DOG STANDS?!
THAT'S WHAT SHE SAID!
BETTY WILL BE SO HAPPY I TOLD HIM!
YEAH, RIGHT!
END

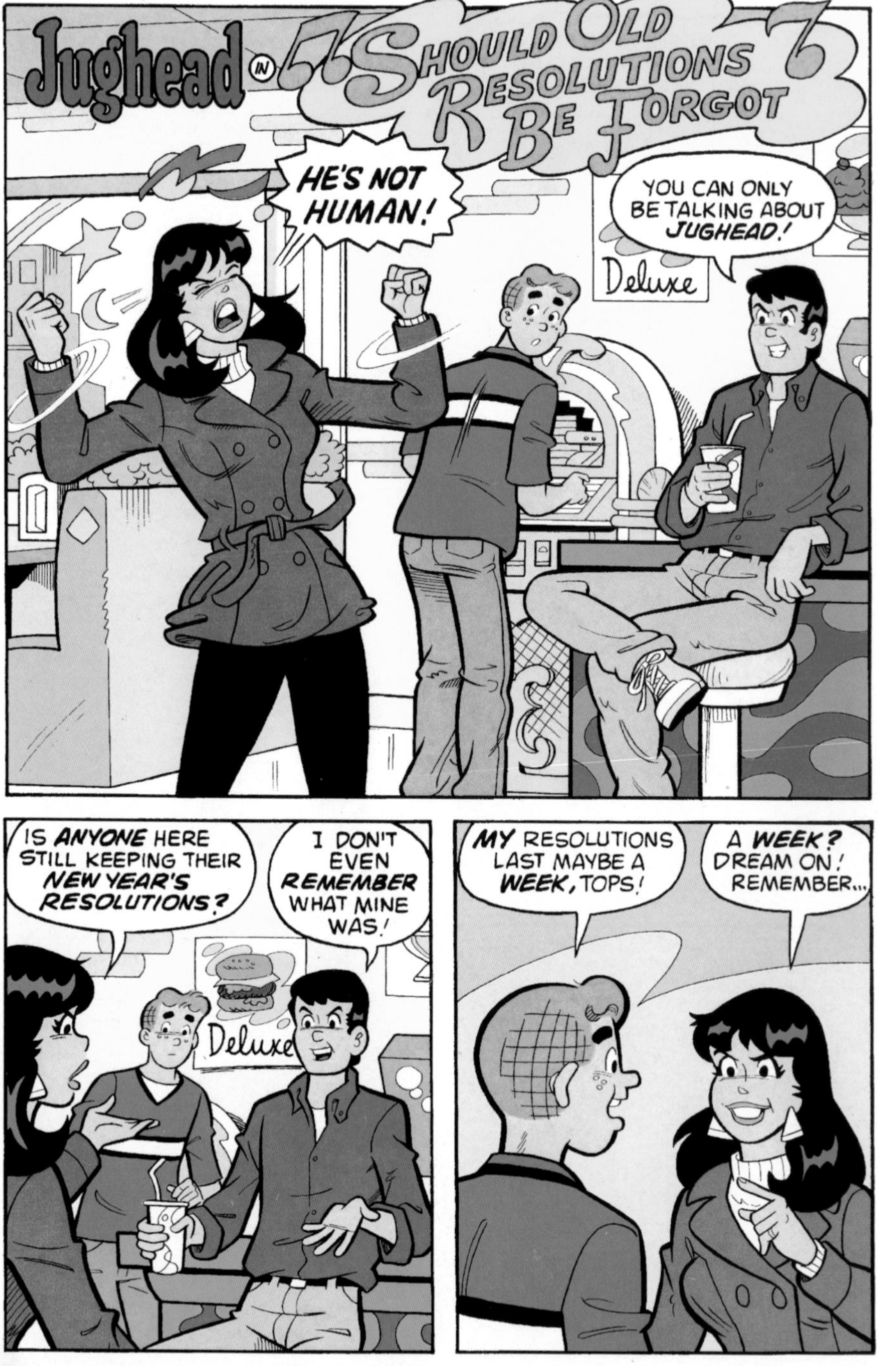
Jughead in "Should Old Resolutions Be Forgot"
HE'S NOT HUMAN!
YOU CAN ONLY BE TALKING ABOUT JUGHEAD!
Deluxe
IS ANYONE HERE STILL KEEPING THEIR NEW YEAR'S RESOLUTIONS?
I DON'T EVEN REMEMBER WHAT MINE WAS!
Deluxe
MY RESOLUTIONS LAST MAYBE A WEEK, TOPS!
A WEEK? DREAM ON! REMEMBER...

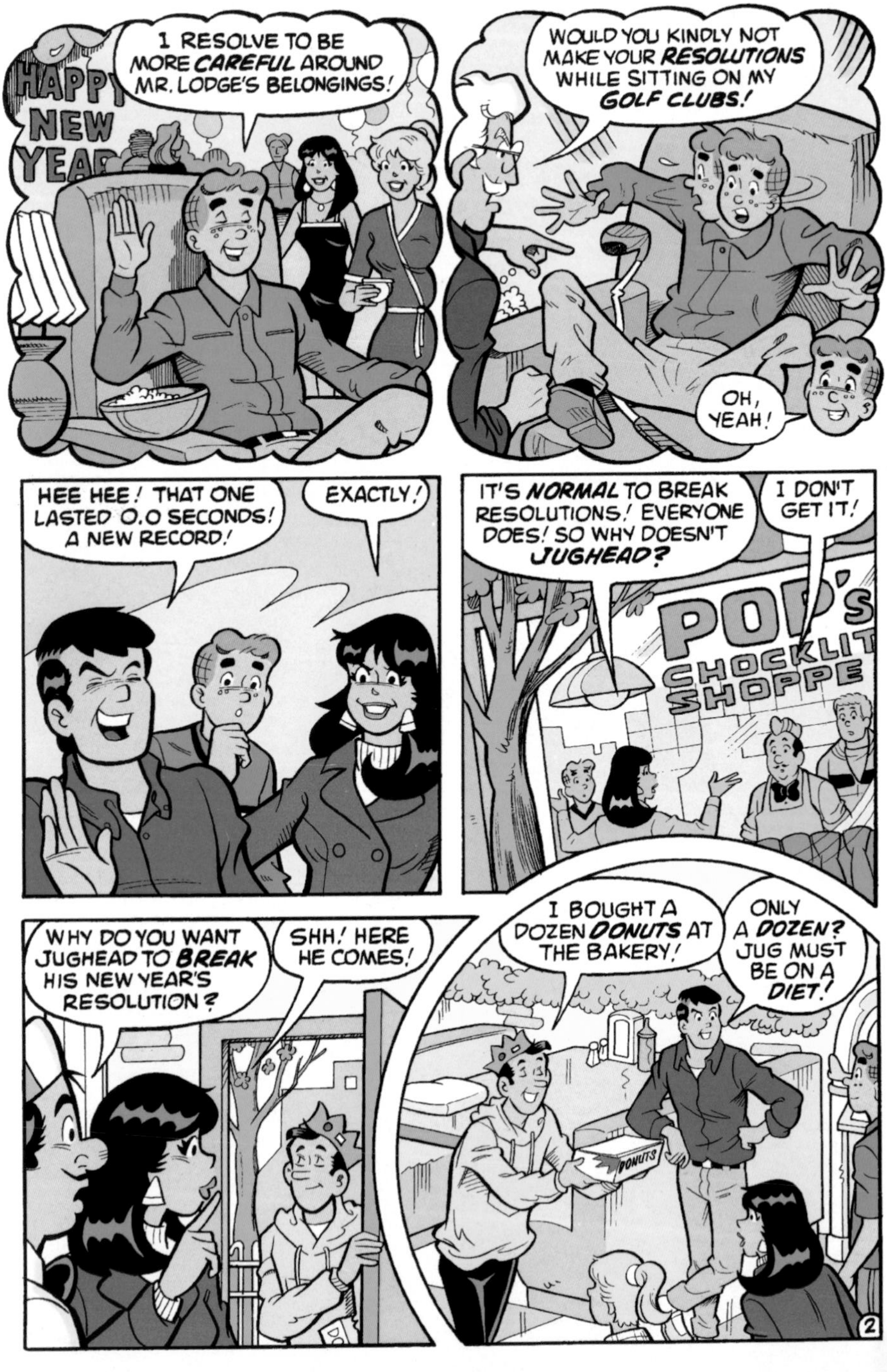

HAPPY NEW YEAR
I RESOLVE TO BE MORE *CAREFUL* AROUND MR. LODGE'S BELONGINGS!
WOULD YOU KINDLY NOT MAKE YOUR *RESOLUTIONS* WHILE SITTING ON MY *GOLF CLUBS!*
OH, YEAH!
HEE HEE! THAT ONE LASTED 0.0 SECONDS! A NEW RECORD!
EXACTLY!
IT'S *NORMAL* TO BREAK RESOLUTIONS! EVERYONE DOES! SO WHY DOESN'T *JUGHEAD?*
I DON'T GET IT!
POP'S CHOCKLIT SHOPPE
WHY DO YOU WANT JUGHEAD TO *BREAK* HIS NEW YEAR'S RESOLUTION?
SHH! HERE HE COMES!
I BOUGHT A DOZEN *DONUTS* AT THE BAKERY!
ONLY A *DOZEN?* JUG MUST BE ON A *DIET!*
DONUTS
2

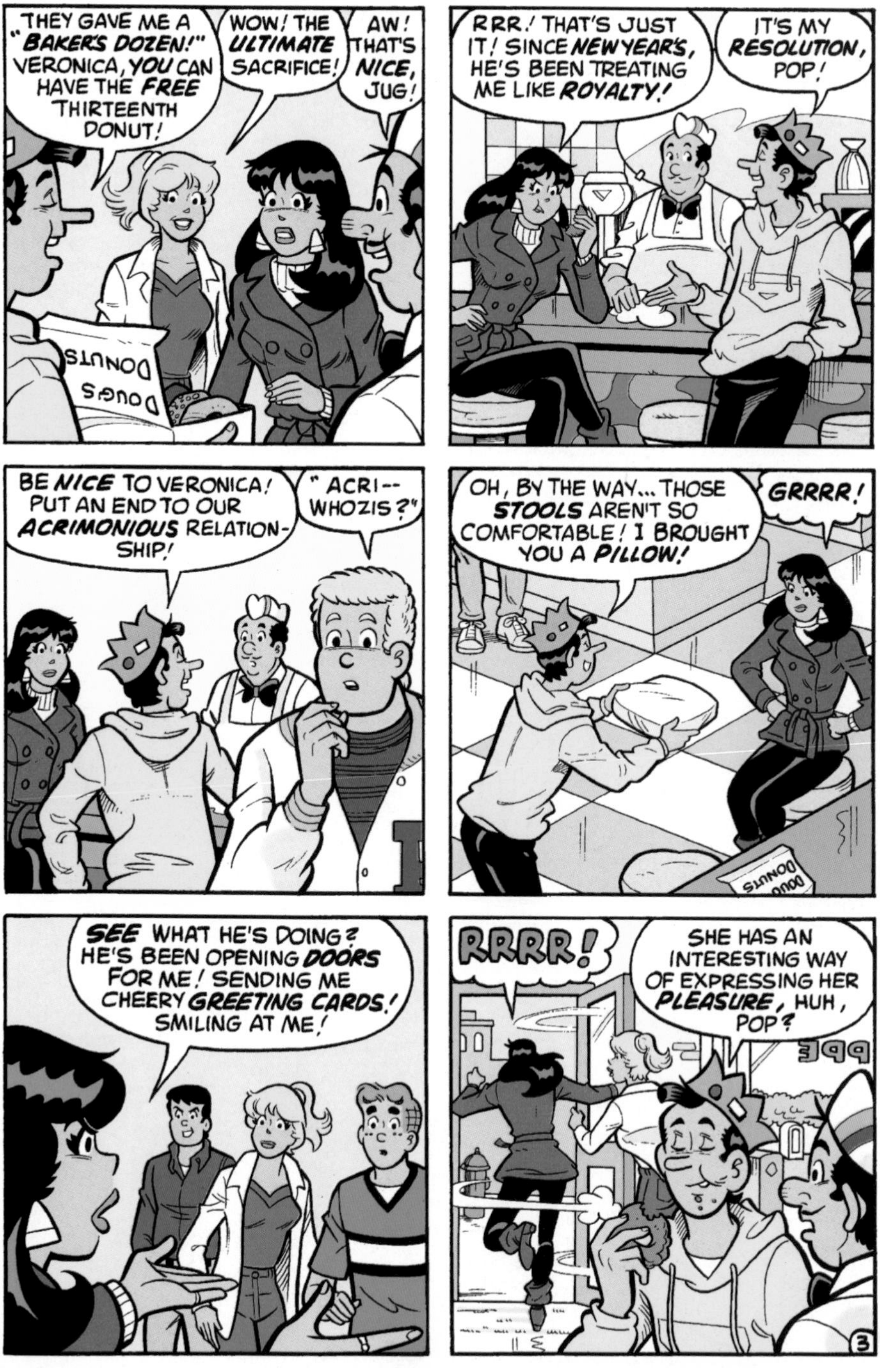
THEY GAVE ME A "BAKER'S DOZEN!" VERONICA, YOU CAN HAVE THE FREE THIRTEENTH DONUT!
WOW! THE ULTIMATE SACRIFICE!
AW! THAT'S NICE, JUG!
DOUG'S DONUTS
RRR! THAT'S JUST IT! SINCE NEW YEAR'S, HE'S BEEN TREATING ME LIKE ROYALTY!
IT'S MY RESOLUTION, POP!
BE NICE TO VERONICA! PUT AN END TO OUR ACRIMONIOUS RELATION-SHIP!
"ACRI--WHOZIS?"
OH, BY THE WAY... THOSE STOOLS AREN'T SO COMFORTABLE! I BROUGHT YOU A PILLOW!
GRRRR!
DOUG'S DONUTS
SEE WHAT HE'S DOING? HE'S BEEN OPENING DOORS FOR ME! SENDING ME CHEERY GREETING CARDS! SMILING AT ME!
RRRR!
SHE HAS AN INTERESTING WAY OF EXPRESSING HER PLEASURE, HUH, POP?
3

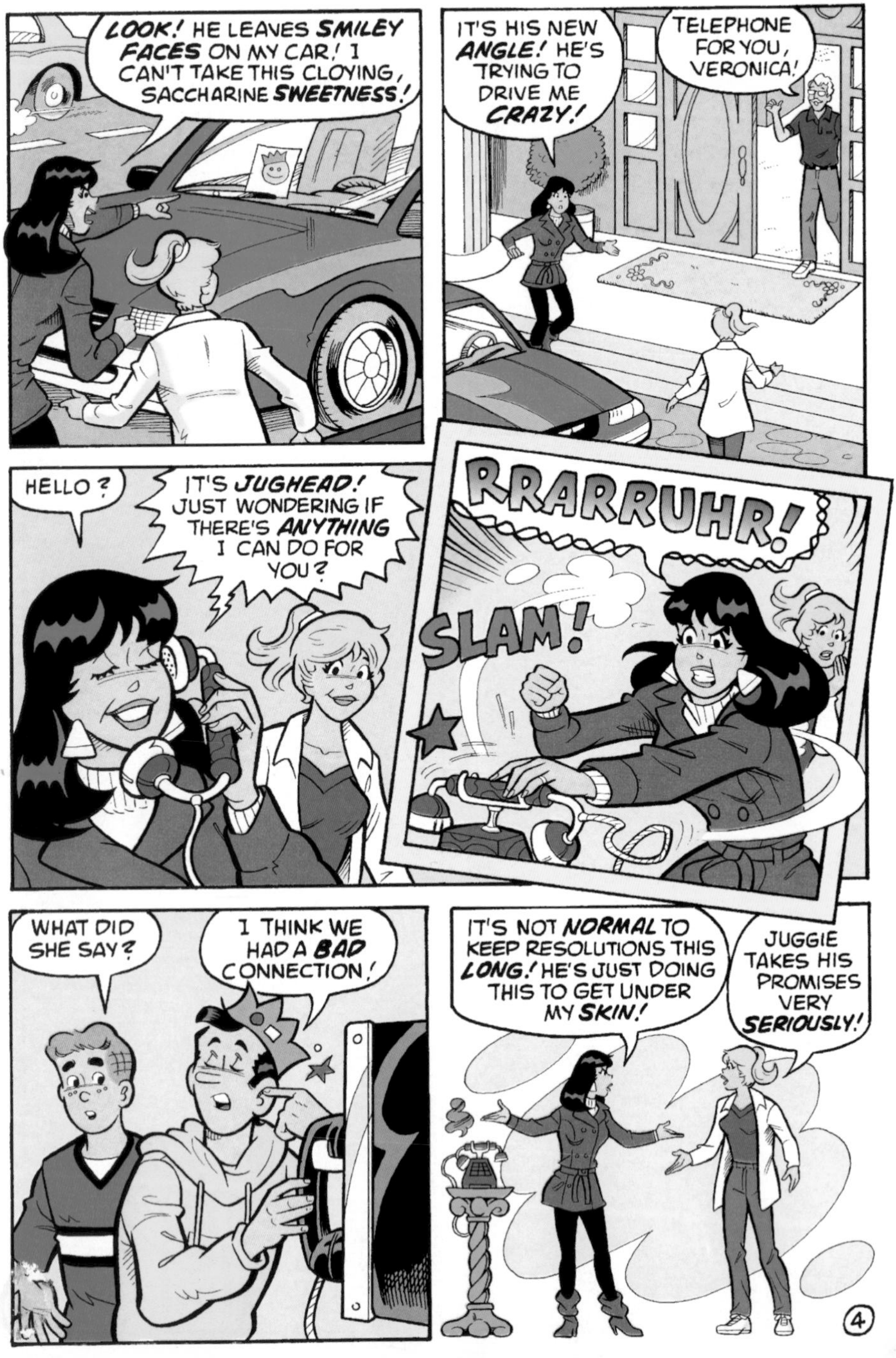
LOOK! HE LEAVES SMILEY FACES ON MY CAR! I CAN'T TAKE THIS CLOYING, SACCHARINE SWEETNESS!
IT'S HIS NEW ANGLE! HE'S TRYING TO DRIVE ME CRAZY!
TELEPHONE FOR YOU, VERONICA!
HELLO?
IT'S JUGHEAD! JUST WONDERING IF THERE'S ANYTHING I CAN DO FOR YOU?
RRARRUHR!
SLAM!
WHAT DID SHE SAY?
I THINK WE HAD A BAD CONNECTION!
IT'S NOT NORMAL TO KEEP RESOLUTIONS THIS LONG! HE'S JUST DOING THIS TO GET UNDER MY SKIN!
JUGGIE TAKES HIS PROMISES VERY SERIOUSLY!
4

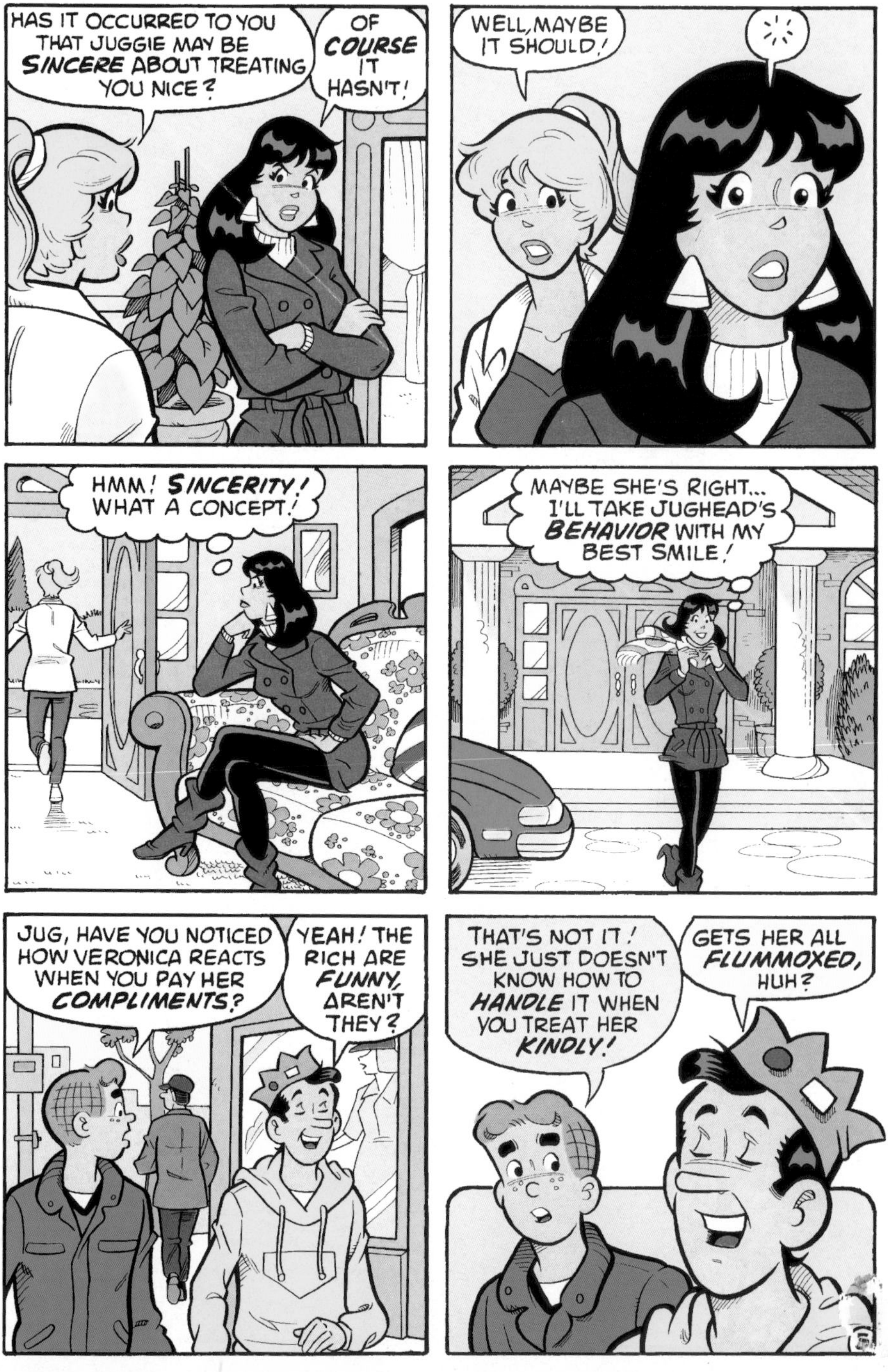
HAS IT OCCURRED TO YOU THAT JUGGIE MAY BE SINCERE ABOUT TREATING YOU NICE?
OF COURSE IT HASN'T!
WELL, MAYBE IT SHOULD!
HMM! SINCERITY! WHAT A CONCEPT!
MAYBE SHE'S RIGHT... I'LL TAKE JUGHEAD'S BEHAVIOR WITH MY BEST SMILE!
JUG, HAVE YOU NOTICED HOW VERONICA REACTS WHEN YOU PAY HER COMPLIMENTS?
YEAH! THE RICH ARE FUNNY, AREN'T THEY?
THAT'S NOT IT! SHE JUST DOESN'T KNOW HOW TO HANDLE IT WHEN YOU TREAT HER KINDLY!
GETS HER ALL FLUMMOXED, HUH?

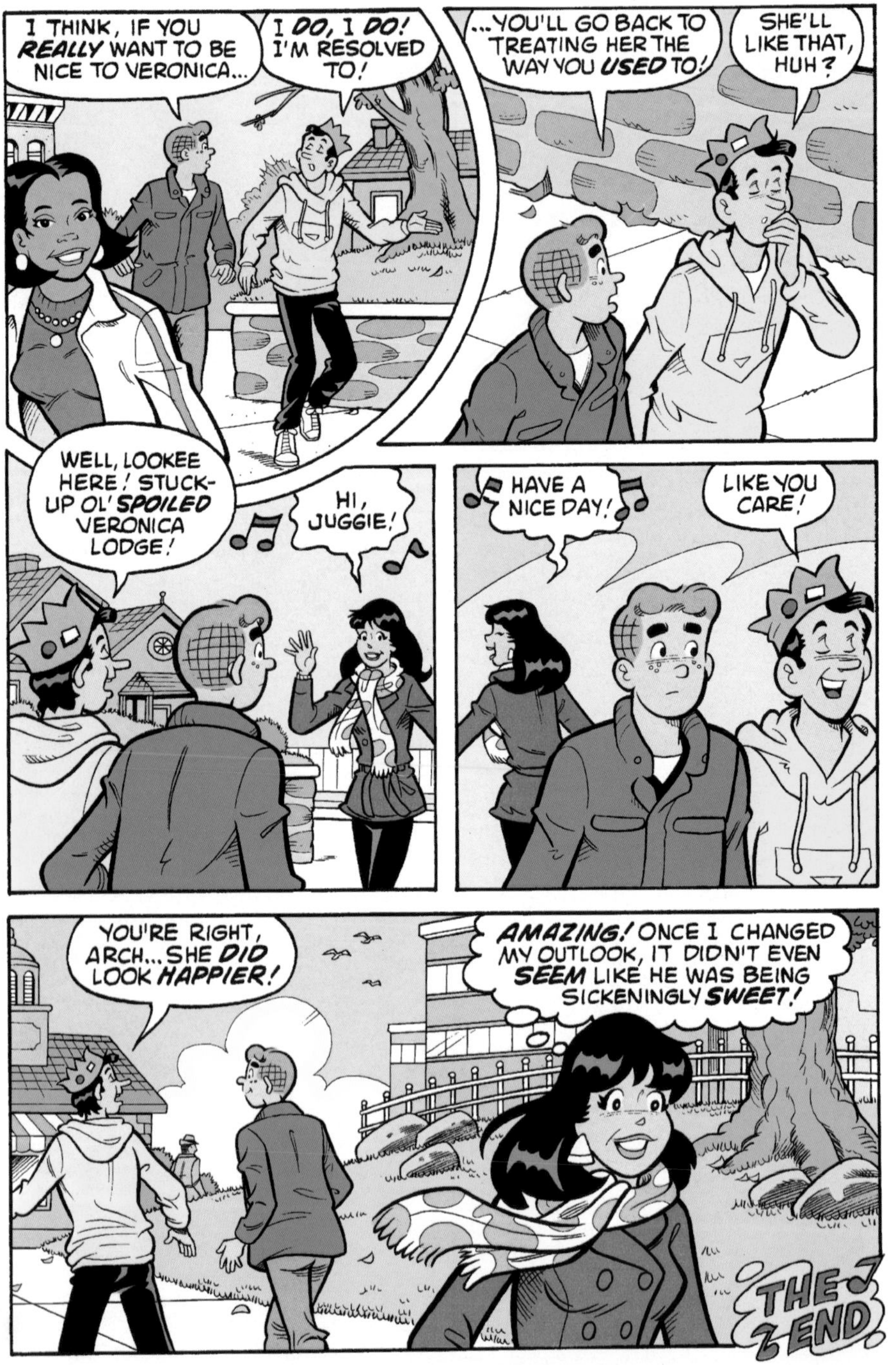
I THINK, IF YOU REALLY WANT TO BE NICE TO VERONICA...
I DO, I DO! I'M RESOLVED TO!
...YOU'LL GO BACK TO TREATING HER THE WAY YOU USED TO!
SHE'LL LIKE THAT, HUH?
WELL, LOOKEE HERE! STUCK-UP OL' SPOILED VERONICA LODGE!
HI, JUGGIE!
HAVE A NICE DAY!
LIKE YOU CARE!
YOU'RE RIGHT, ARCH... SHE DID LOOK HAPPIER!
AMAZING! ONCE I CHANGED MY OUTLOOK, IT DIDN'T EVEN SEEM LIKE HE WAS BEING SICKENINGLY SWEET!
THE END

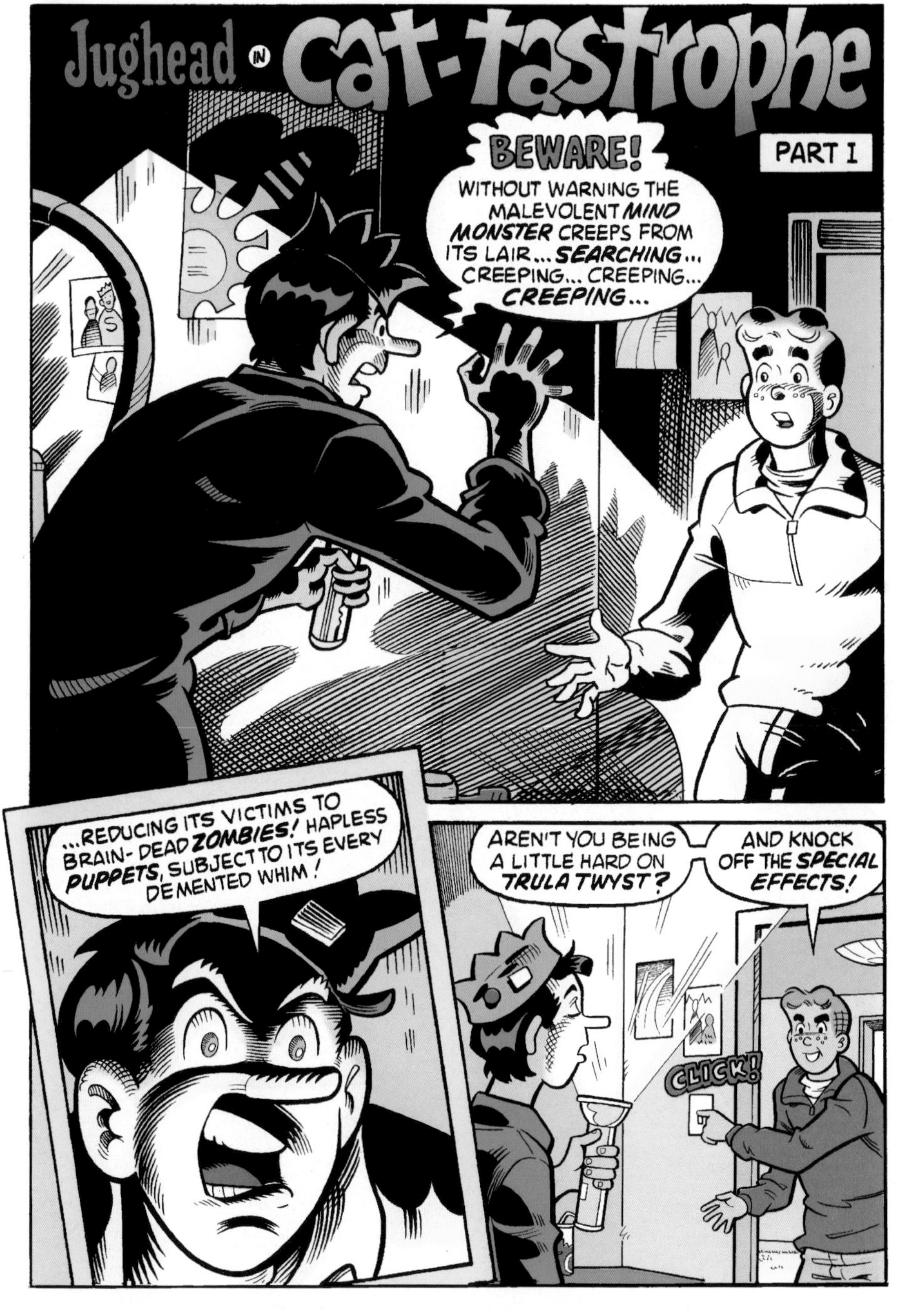
Jughead in Cat-tastrophe
PART 1
BEWARE! WITHOUT WARNING THE MALEVOLENT MIND MONSTER CREEPS FROM ITS LAIR... SEARCHING... CREEPING... CREEPING... CREEPING...
...REDUCING ITS VICTIMS TO BRAIN-DEAD ZOMBIES! HAPLESS PUPPETS, SUBJECT TO ITS EVERY DEMENTED WHIM!
AREN'T YOU BEING A LITTLE HARD ON TRULA TWYST?
AND KNOCK OFF THE SPECIAL EFFECTS!
CLICK!

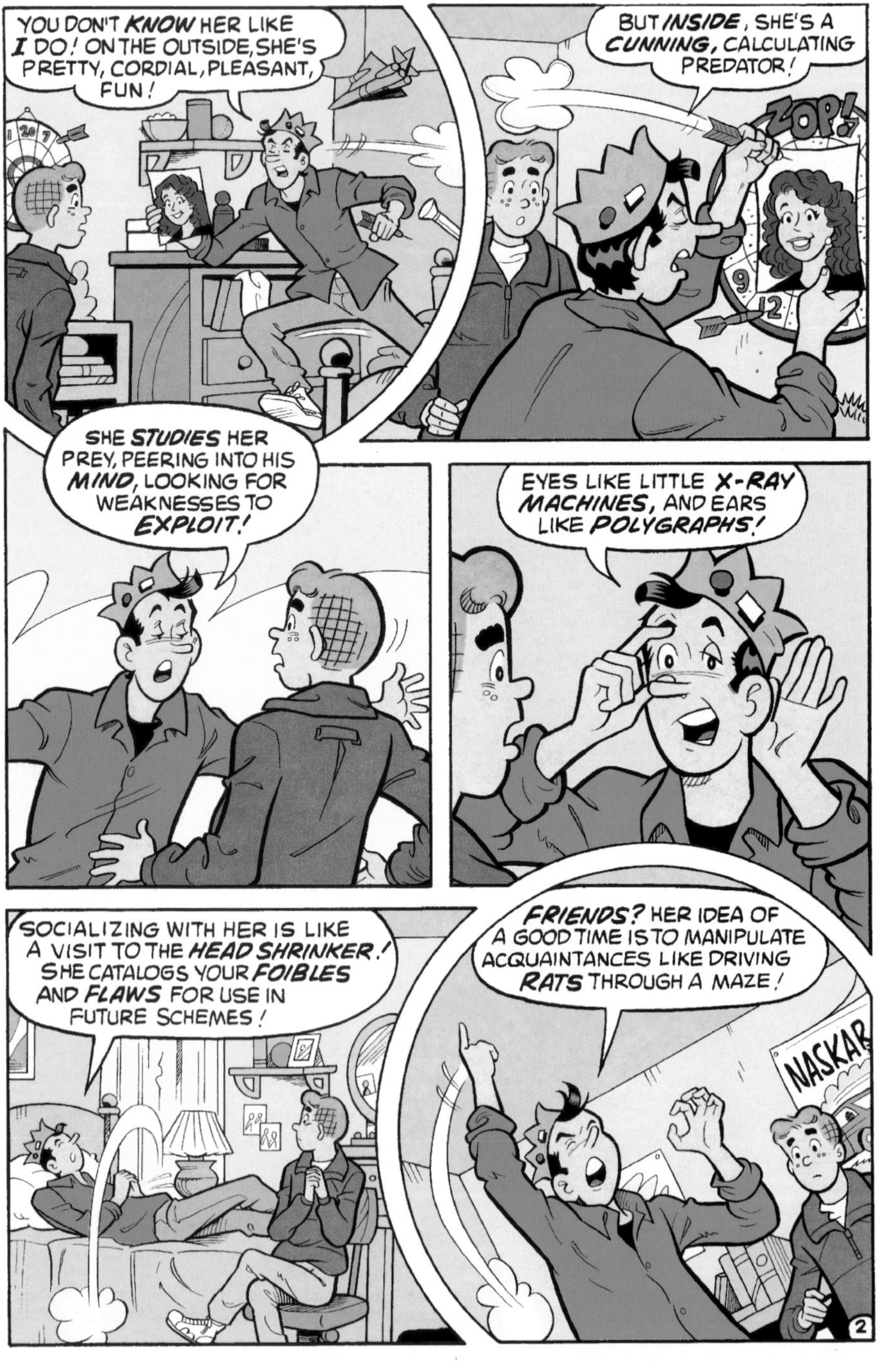
YOU DON'T KNOW HER LIKE I DO! ON THE OUTSIDE, SHE'S PRETTY, CORDIAL, PLEASANT, FUN!
BUT INSIDE, SHE'S A CUNNING, CALCULATING PREDATOR!
ZOP!
SHE STUDIES HER PREY, PEERING INTO HIS MIND, LOOKING FOR WEAKNESSES TO EXPLOIT!
EYES LIKE LITTLE X-RAY MACHINES, AND EARS LIKE POLYGRAPHS!
SOCIALIZING WITH HER IS LIKE A VISIT TO THE HEAD SHRINKER! SHE CATALOGS YOUR FOIBLES AND FLAWS FOR USE IN FUTURE SCHEMES!
FRIENDS? HER IDEA OF A GOOD TIME IS TO MANIPULATE ACQUAINTANCES LIKE DRIVING RATS THROUGH A MAZE!
NASKAR
2

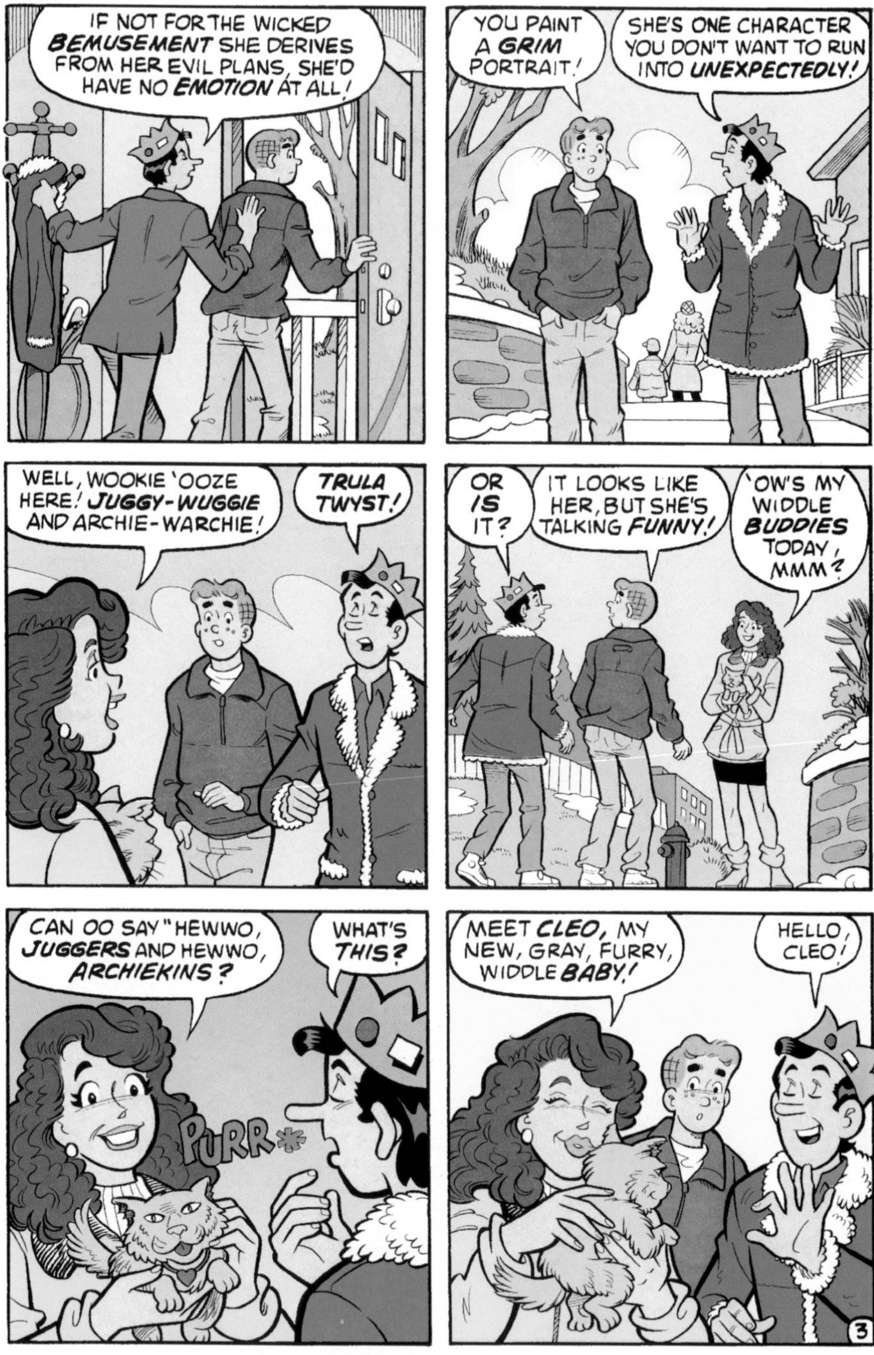
IF NOT FOR THE WICKED BEMUSEMENT SHE DERIVES FROM HER EVIL PLANS, SHE'D HAVE NO EMOTION AT ALL!
YOU PAINT A GRIM PORTRAIT!
SHE'S ONE CHARACTER YOU DON'T WANT TO RUN INTO UNEXPECTEDLY!
WELL, WOOKIE 'OOZE HERE! JUGGY-WUGGIE AND ARCHIE-WARCHIE!
TRULA TWYST!
OR IS IT?
IT LOOKS LIKE HER, BUT SHE'S TALKING FUNNY!
'OW'S MY WIDDLE BUDDIES TODAY, MMM?
CAN OO SAY "HEWWO, JUGGERS AND HEWWO, ARCHIEKINS?
WHAT'S THIS?
PURR*
MEET CLEO, MY NEW, GRAY, FURRY, WIDDLE BABY!
HELLO, CLEO!
3

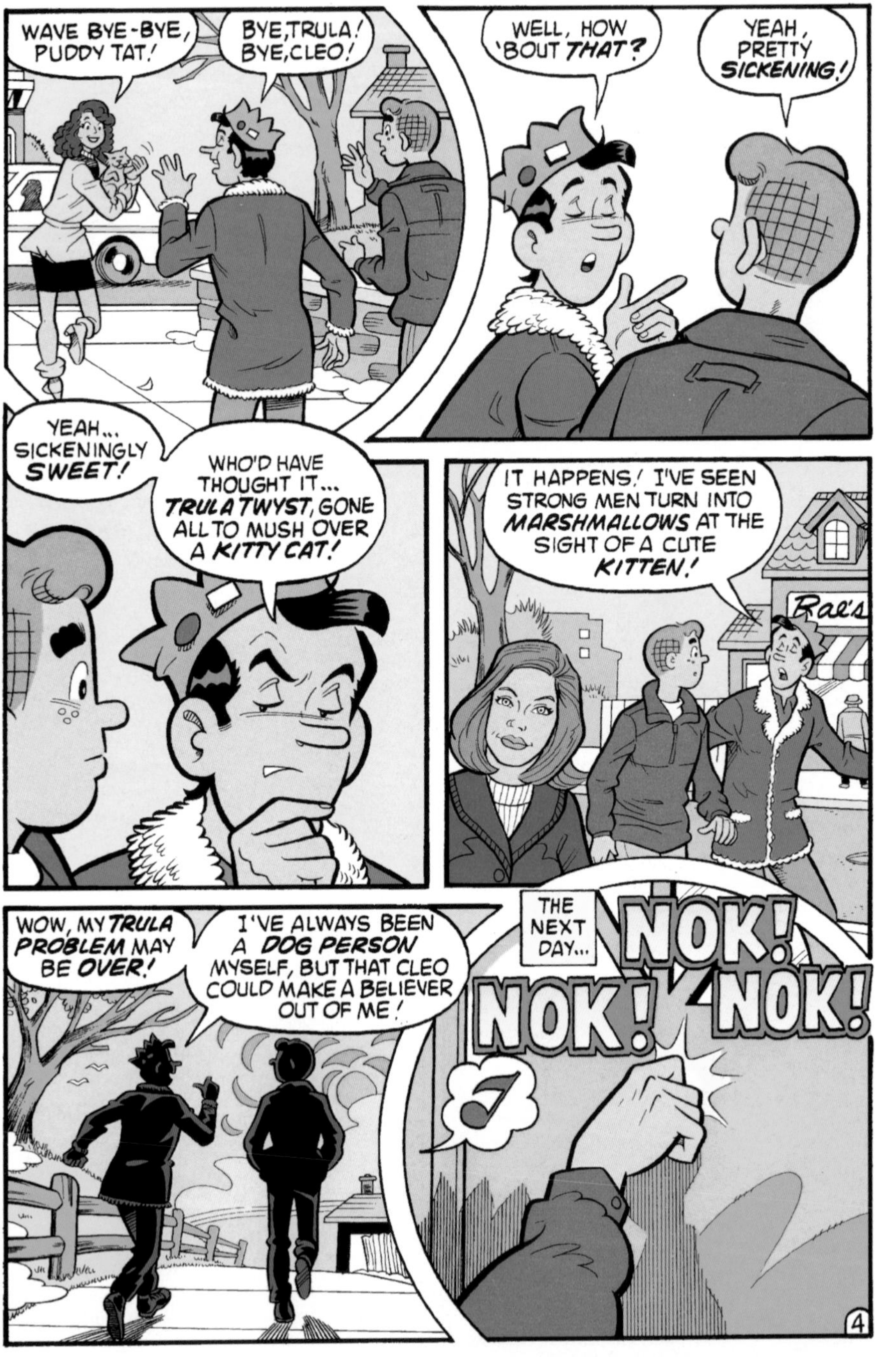
WAVE BYE-BYE, PUDDY TAT!
BYE, TRULA! BYE, CLEO!
WELL, HOW 'BOUT THAT?
YEAH, PRETTY SICKENING!
YEAH... SICKENINGLY SWEET!
WHO'D HAVE THOUGHT IT... TRULA TWYST, GONE ALL TO MUSH OVER A KITTY CAT!
IT HAPPENS! I'VE SEEN STRONG MEN TURN INTO MARSHMALLOWS AT THE SIGHT OF A CUTE KITTEN!
Rae's
WOW, MY TRULA PROBLEM MAY BE OVER!
I'VE ALWAYS BEEN A DOG PERSON MYSELF, BUT THAT CLEO COULD MAKE A BELIEVER OUT OF ME!
THE NEXT DAY...
NOK!
NOK!
NOK!
4

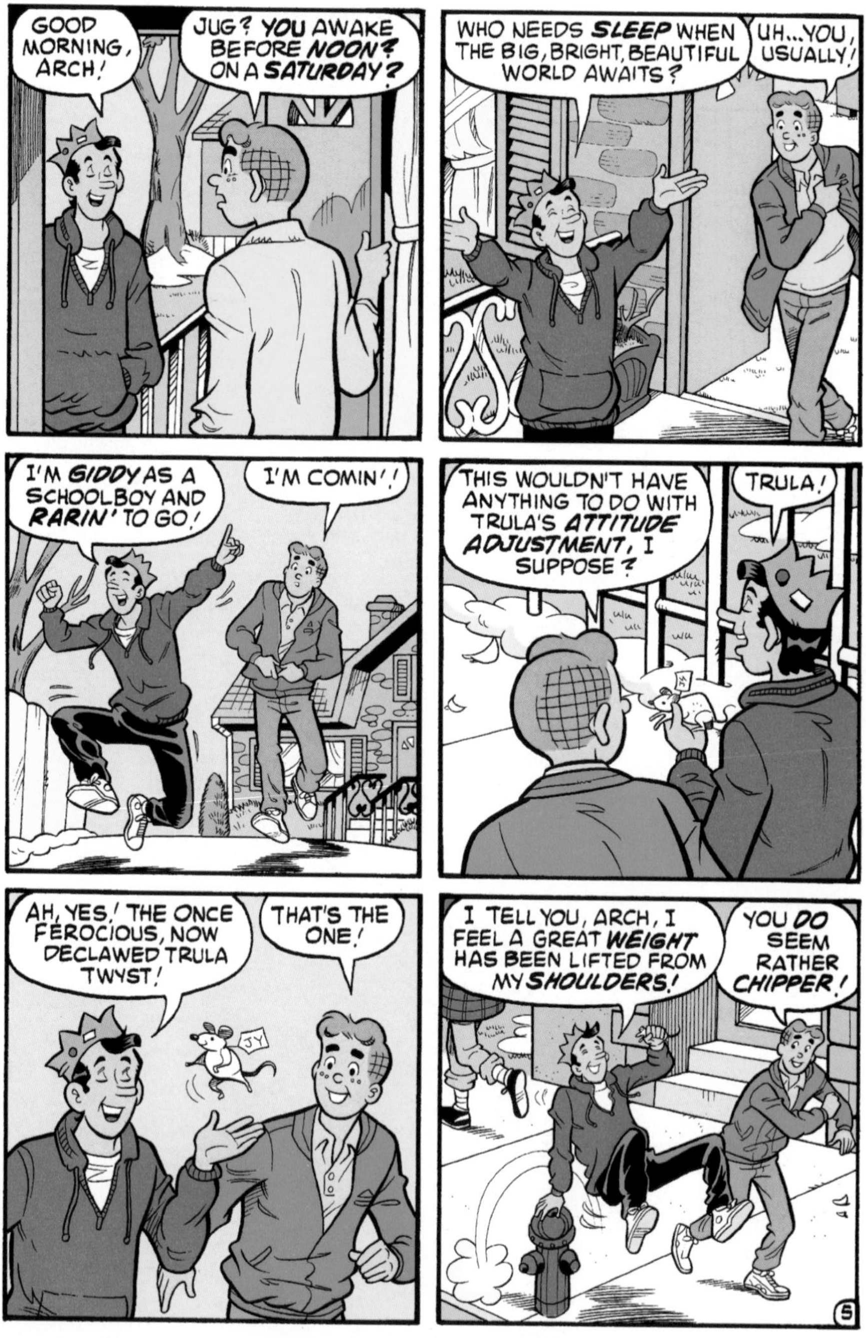
GOOD MORNING, ARCH!
JUG? YOU AWAKE BEFORE NOON? ON A SATURDAY?
WHO NEEDS SLEEP WHEN THE BIG, BRIGHT, BEAUTIFUL WORLD AWAITS?
UH...YOU, USUALLY!
I'M GIDDY AS A SCHOOLBOY AND RARIN' TO GO!
I'M COMIN'!
THIS WOULDN'T HAVE ANYTHING TO DO WITH TRULA'S ATTITUDE ADJUSTMENT, I SUPPOSE?
TRULA!
AH, YES! THE ONCE FEROCIOUS, NOW DECLAWED TRULA TWYST!
THAT'S THE ONE!
JY
I TELL YOU, ARCH, I FEEL A GREAT WEIGHT HAS BEEN LIFTED FROM MY SHOULDERS!
YOU DO SEEM RATHER CHIPPER!
5

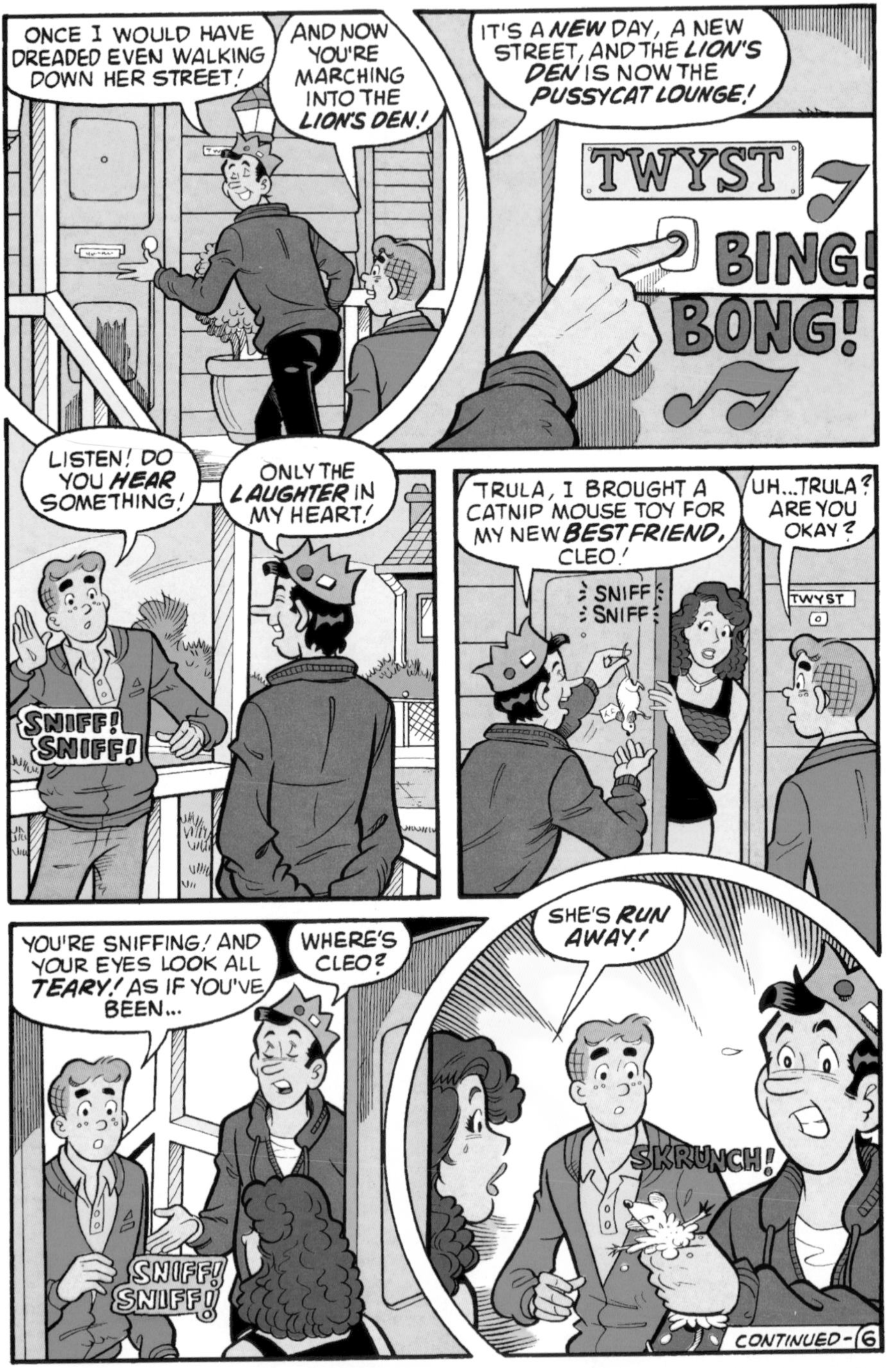
ONCE I WOULD HAVE DREADED EVEN WALKING DOWN HER STREET!
AND NOW YOU'RE MARCHING INTO THE LION'S DEN!
IT'S A NEW DAY, A NEW STREET, AND THE LION'S DEN IS NOW THE PUSSYCAT LOUNGE!
TWYST
BING!
BONG!
LISTEN! DO YOU HEAR SOMETHING!
ONLY THE LAUGHTER IN MY HEART!
SNIFF! SNIFF!
TRULA, I BROUGHT A CATNIP MOUSE TOY FOR MY NEW BEST FRIEND, CLEO!
UH...TRULA? ARE YOU OKAY?
SNIFF
SNIFF
TWYST
YOU'RE SNIFFING! AND YOUR EYES LOOK ALL TEARY! AS IF YOU'VE BEEN...
WHERE'S CLEO?
SNIFF! SNIFF!
SHE'S RUN AWAY!
SKRUNCH!
CONTINUED-6

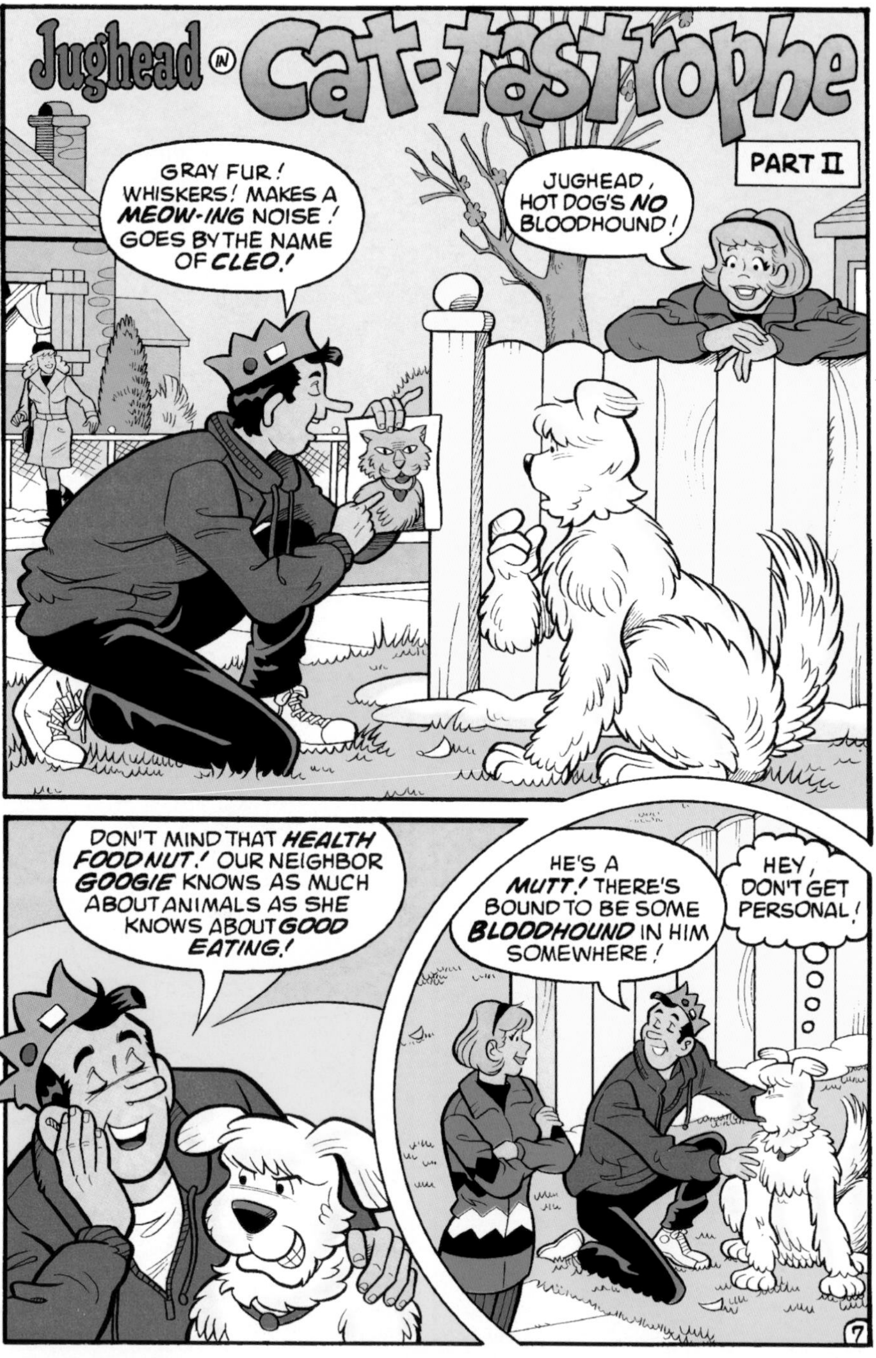
Jughead in Cat-tastrophe
PART II
GRAY FUR! WHISKERS! MAKES A MEOW-ING NOISE! GOES BY THE NAME OF CLEO!
JUGHEAD, HOT DOG'S NO BLOODHOUND!
DON'T MIND THAT HEALTH FOOD NUT! OUR NEIGHBOR GOOGIE KNOWS AS MUCH ABOUT ANIMALS AS SHE KNOWS ABOUT GOOD EATING!
HE'S A MUTT! THERE'S BOUND TO BE SOME BLOODHOUND IN HIM SOMEWHERE!
HEY, DON'T GET PERSONAL!
7

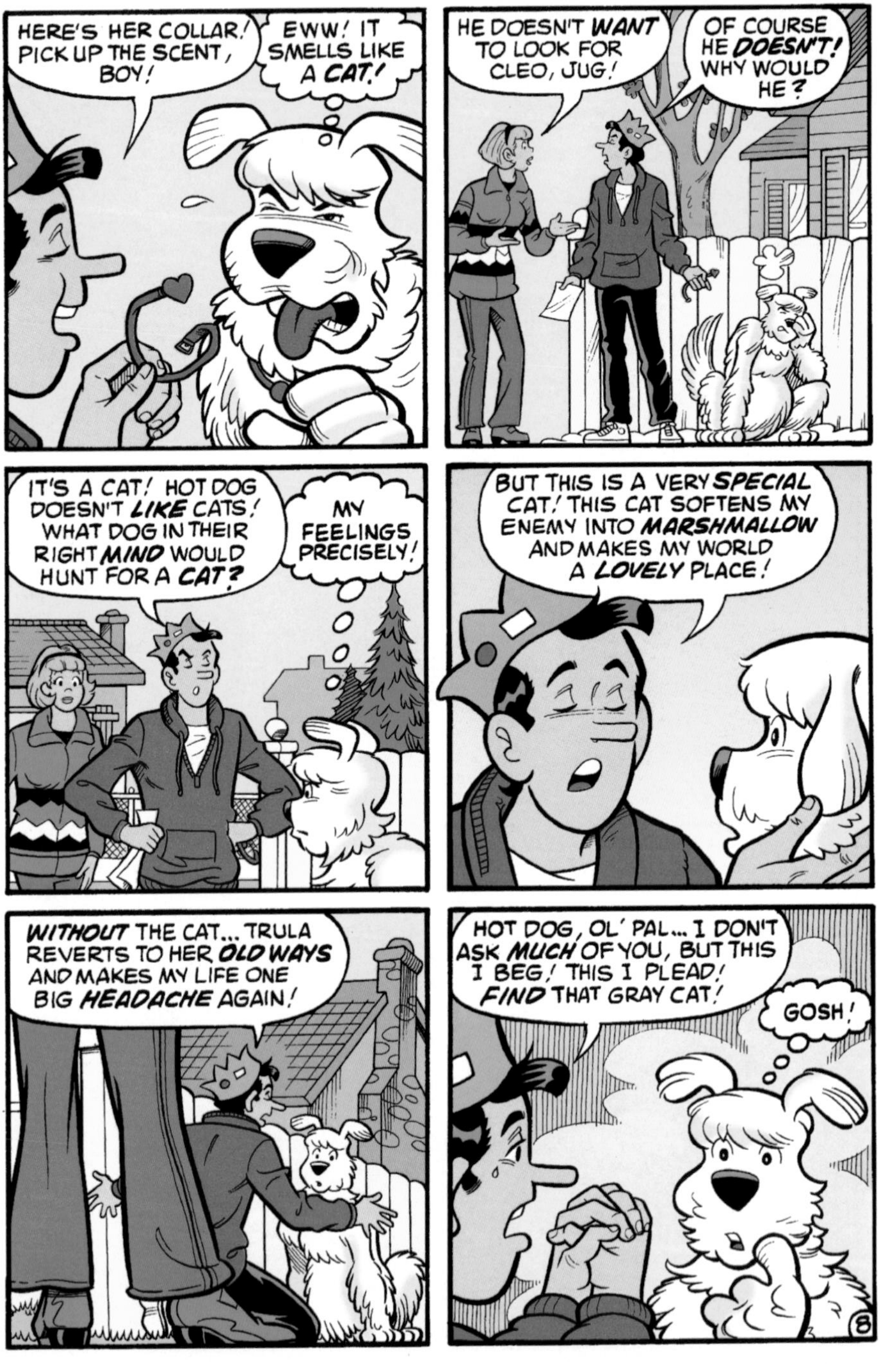
HERE'S HER COLLAR! PICK UP THE SCENT, BOY!
EWW! IT SMELLS LIKE A CAT!
HE DOESN'T WANT TO LOOK FOR CLEO, JUG!
OF COURSE HE DOESN'T! WHY WOULD HE?
IT'S A CAT! HOT DOG DOESN'T LIKE CATS! WHAT DOG IN THEIR RIGHT MIND WOULD HUNT FOR A CAT?
MY FEELINGS PRECISELY!
BUT THIS IS A VERY SPECIAL CAT! THIS CAT SOFTENS MY ENEMY INTO MARSHMALLOW AND MAKES MY WORLD A LOVELY PLACE!
WITHOUT THE CAT... TRULA REVERTS TO HER OLD WAYS AND MAKES MY LIFE ONE BIG HEADACHE AGAIN!
HOT DOG, OL' PAL... I DON'T ASK MUCH OF YOU, BUT THIS I BEG! THIS I PLEAD! FIND THAT GRAY CAT!
GOSH!
8

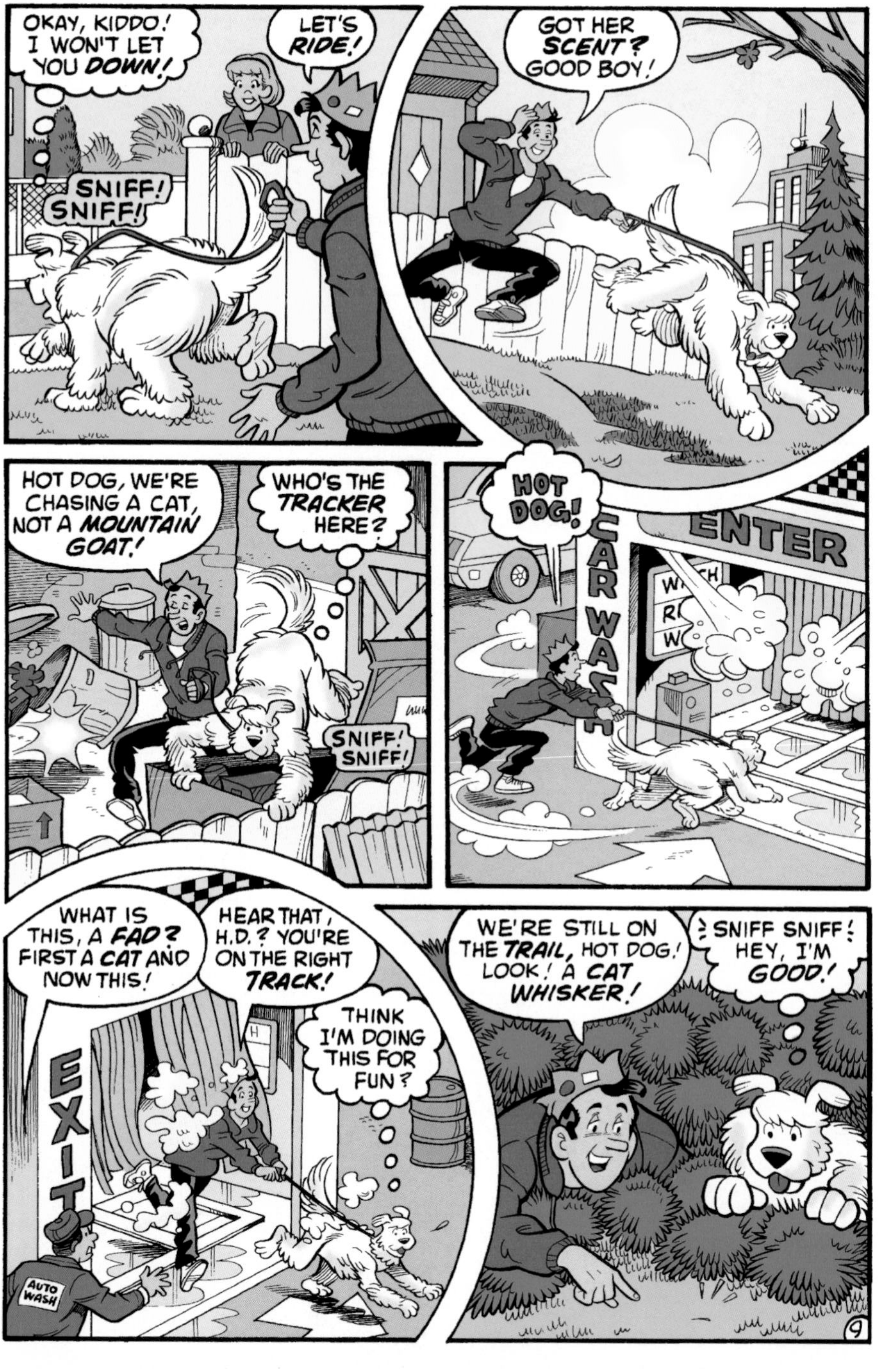
OKAY, KIDDO! I WON'T LET YOU DOWN!
LET'S RIDE!
SNIFF! SNIFF!
GOT HER SCENT? GOOD BOY!
HOT DOG, WE'RE CHASING A CAT, NOT A MOUNTAIN GOAT!
WHO'S THE TRACKER HERE?
SNIFF! SNIFF!
HOT DOG!
CAR WASH
ENTER
WHAT IS THIS, A FAD? FIRST A CAT AND NOW THIS!
HEAR THAT, H.D.? YOU'RE ON THE RIGHT TRACK!
THINK I'M DOING THIS FOR FUN?
EXIT
AUTO WASH
WE'RE STILL ON THE TRAIL, HOT DOG! LOOK! A CAT WHISKER!
SNIFF SNIFF! HEY, I'M GOOD!
9

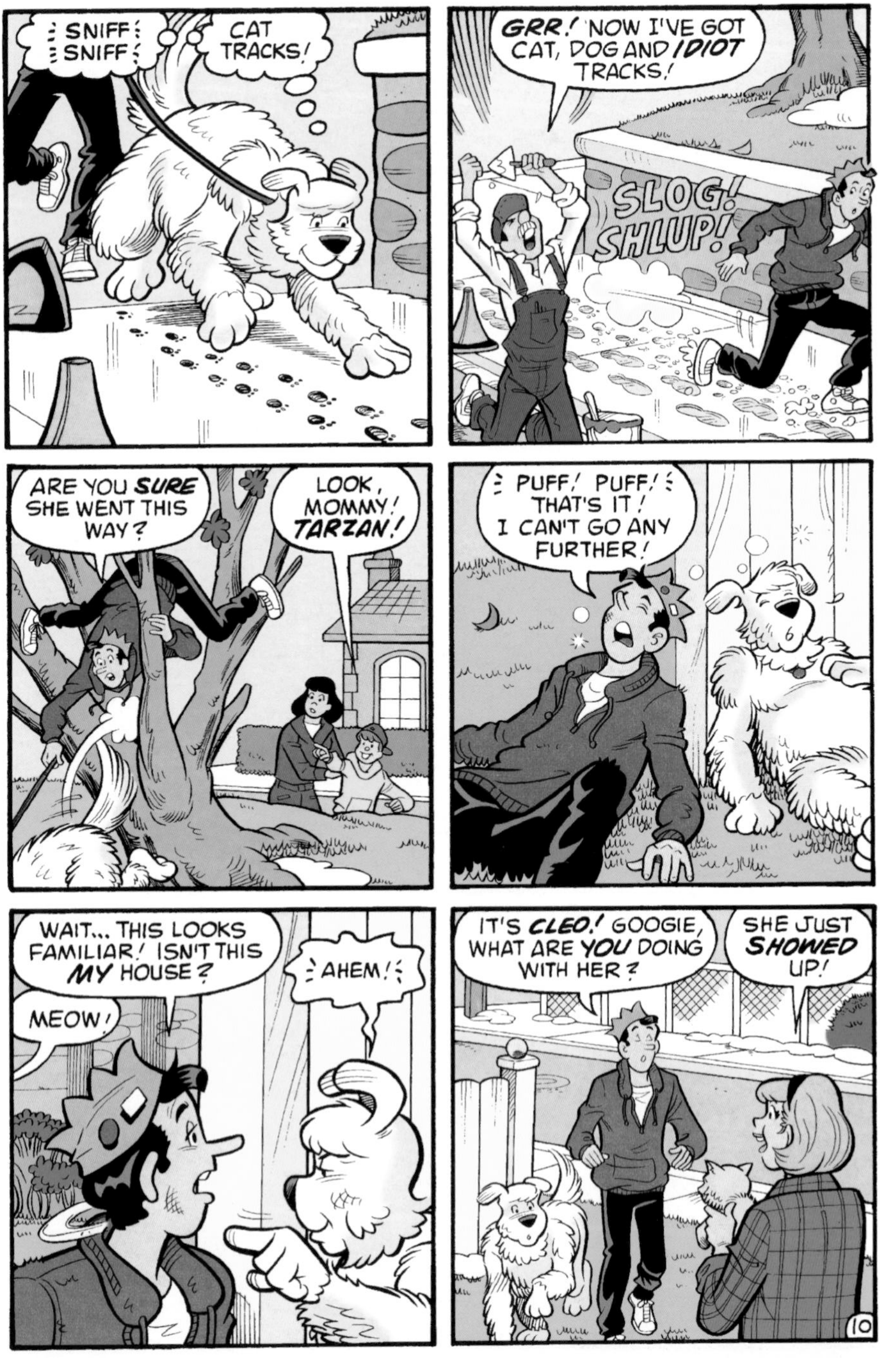
SNIFF SNIFF
CAT TRACKS!
GRR! NOW I'VE GOT CAT, DOG AND IDIOT TRACKS!
SLOG! SHLUP!
ARE YOU SURE SHE WENT THIS WAY?
LOOK, MOMMY! TARZAN!
PUFF! PUFF! THAT'S IT! I CAN'T GO ANY FURTHER!
WAIT... THIS LOOKS FAMILIAR! ISN'T THIS MY HOUSE?
MEOW!
AHEM!
IT'S CLEO! GOOGIE, WHAT ARE YOU DOING WITH HER?
SHE JUST SHOWED UP!
10

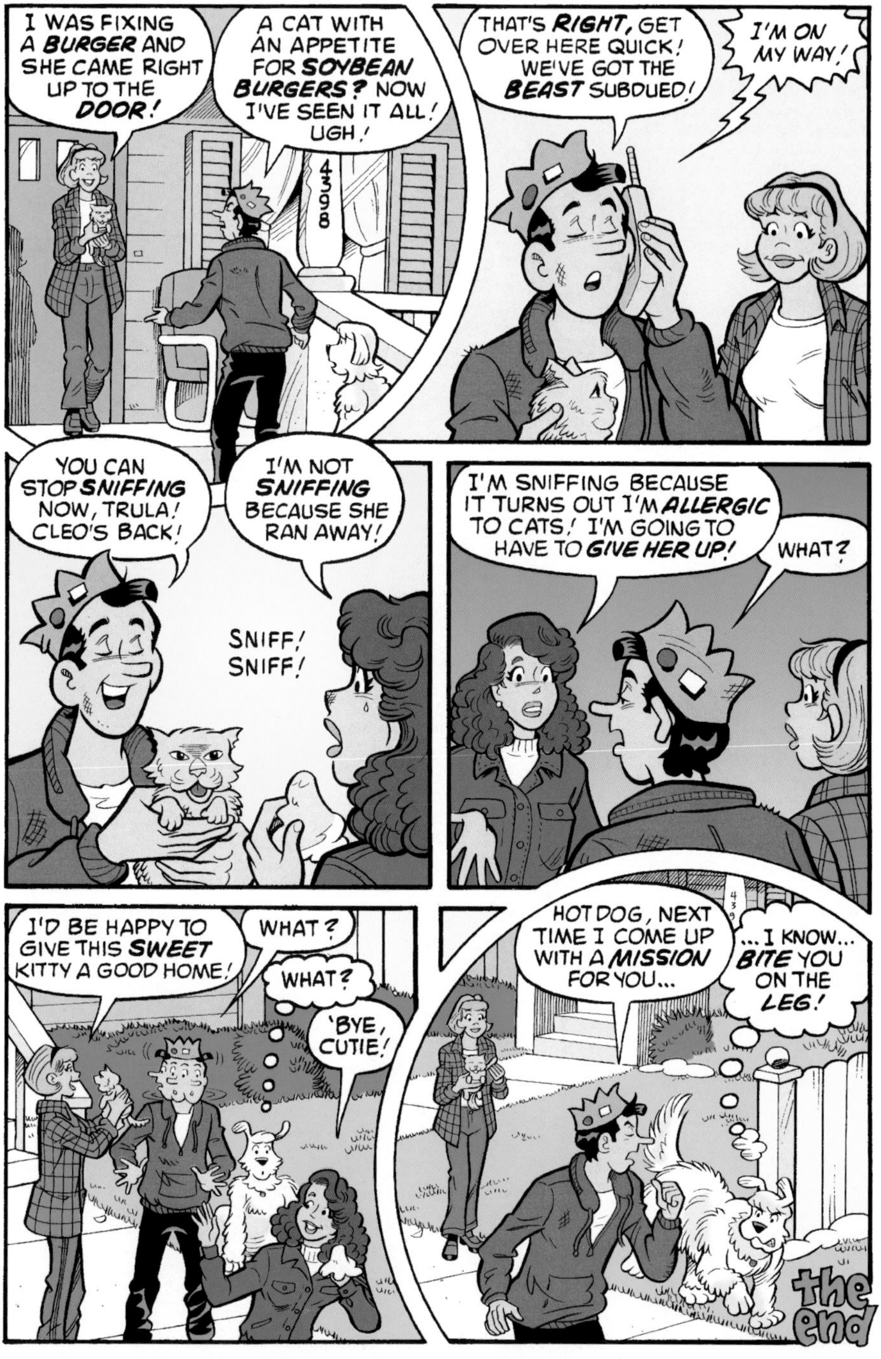
I WAS FIXING A BURGER AND SHE CAME RIGHT UP TO THE DOOR!
A CAT WITH AN APPETITE FOR SOYBEAN BURGERS? NOW I'VE SEEN IT ALL! UGH!
4398
THAT'S RIGHT, GET OVER HERE QUICK! WE'VE GOT THE BEAST SUBDUED!
I'M ON MY WAY!
YOU CAN STOP SNIFFING NOW, TRULA! CLEO'S BACK!
I'M NOT SNIFFING BECAUSE SHE RAN AWAY!
SNIFF! SNIFF!
I'M SNIFFING BECAUSE IT TURNS OUT I'M ALLERGIC TO CATS! I'M GOING TO HAVE TO GIVE HER UP!
WHAT?
I'D BE HAPPY TO GIVE THIS SWEET KITTY A GOOD HOME!
WHAT?
WHAT?
'BYE, CUTIE!
HOT DOG, NEXT TIME I COME UP WITH A MISSION FOR YOU...
...I KNOW... BITE YOU ON THE LEG!
the end

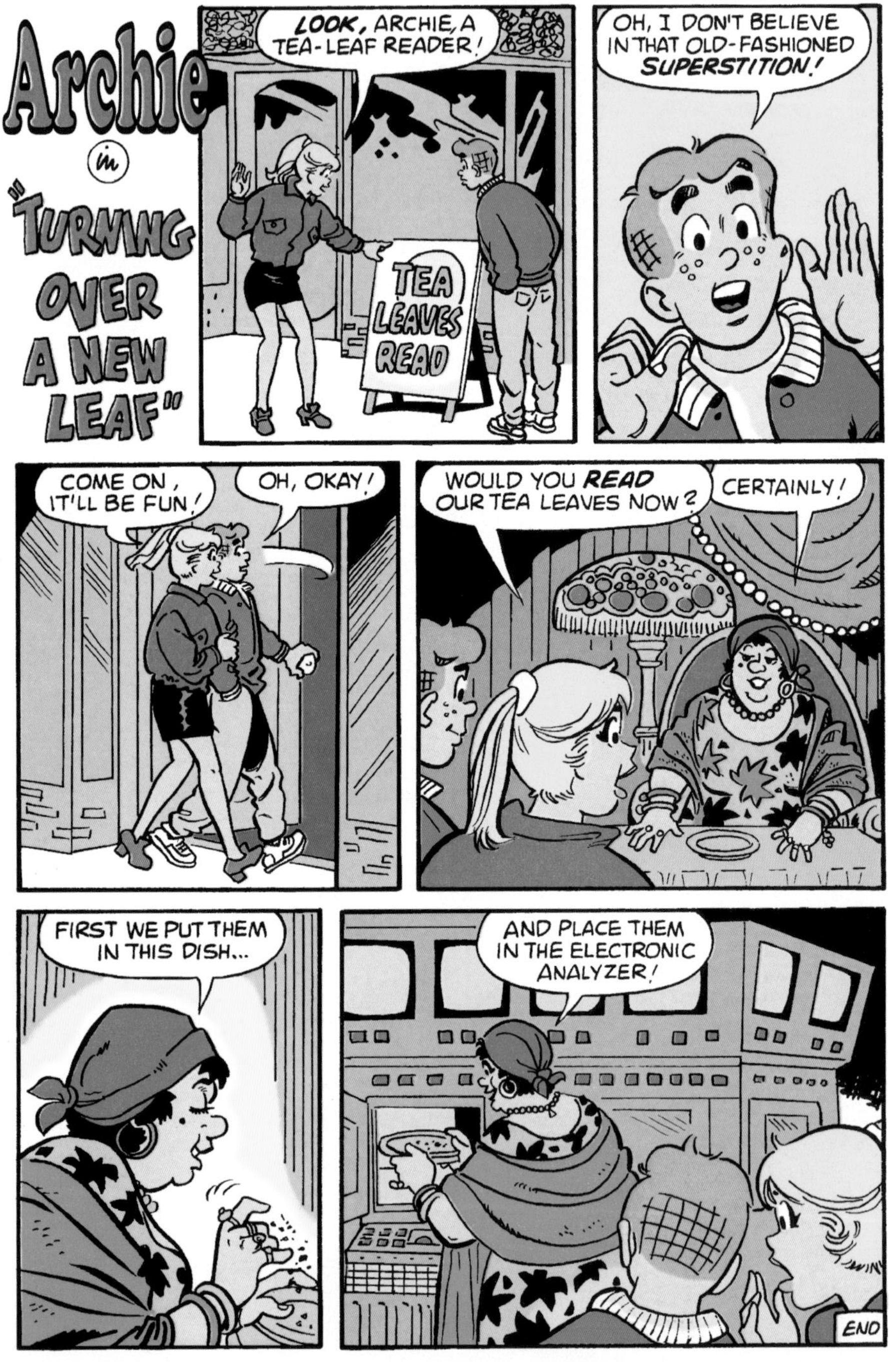
Archie
in
"TURNING OVER A NEW LEAF"
LOOK, ARCHIE, A TEA-LEAF READER!
TEA LEAVES READ
OH, I DON'T BELIEVE IN THAT OLD-FASHIONED SUPERSTITION!
COME ON, IT'LL BE FUN!
OH, OKAY!
WOULD YOU READ OUR TEA LEAVES NOW?
CERTAINLY!
FIRST WE PUT THEM IN THIS DISH...
AND PLACE THEM IN THE ELECTRONIC ANALYZER!
END

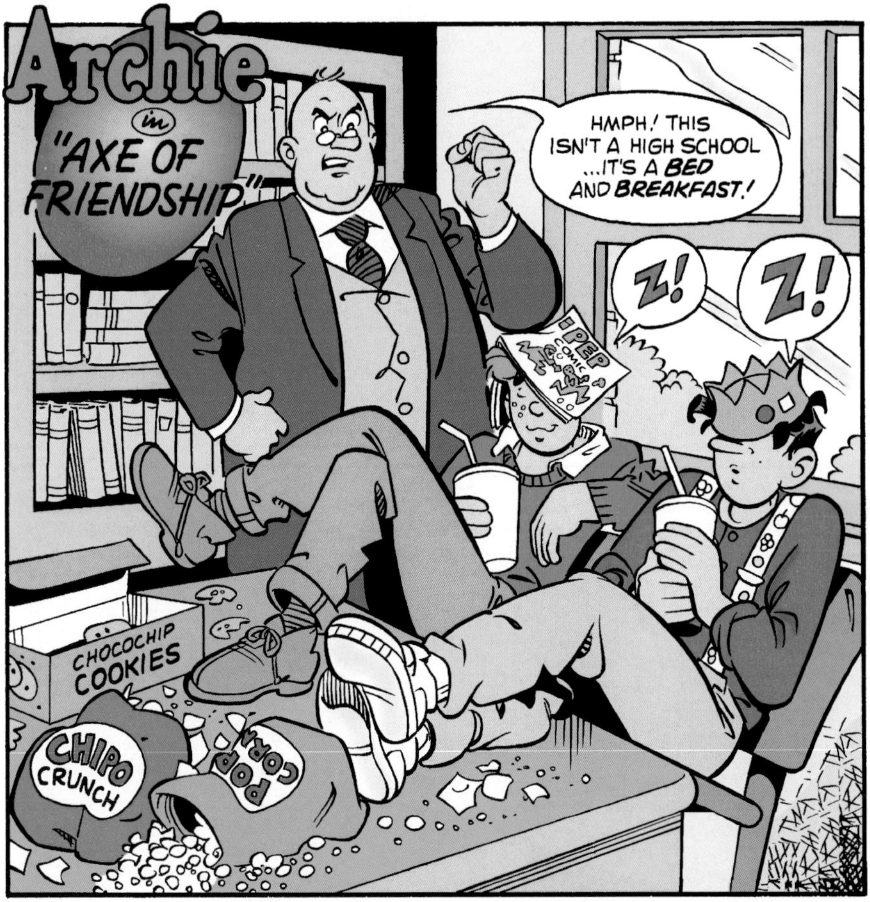
Archie
in
"AXE OF FRIENDSHIP"
HMPH! THIS ISN'T A HIGH SCHOOL ...IT'S A BED AND BREAKFAST!
Z!
Z!
PEP COMIC
CHOCOCHIP COOKIES
CHIPO CRUNCH
POP CORN

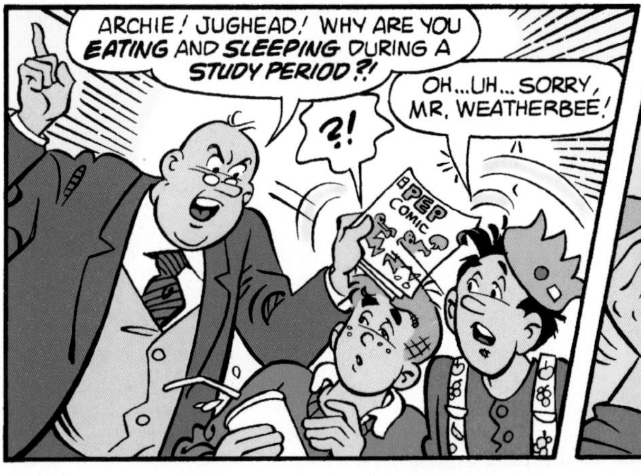
ARCHIE! JUGHEAD! WHY ARE YOU EATING AND SLEEPING DURING A STUDY PERIOD?!
?!
OH...UH... SORRY, MR. WEATHERBEE!
PEP COMIC

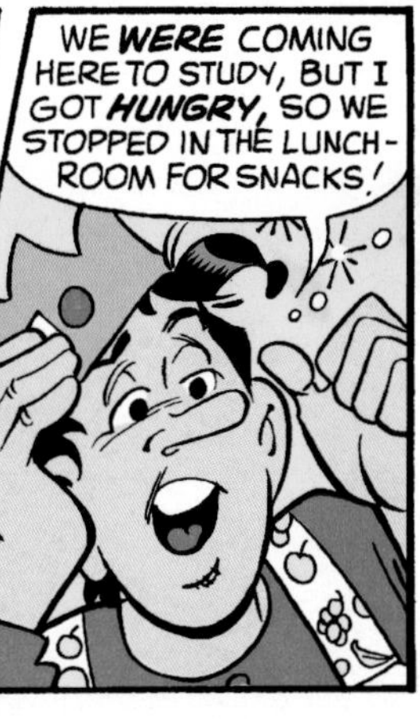
WE WERE COMING HERE TO STUDY, BUT I GOT HUNGRY, SO WE STOPPED IN THE LUNCH-ROOM FOR SNACKS!

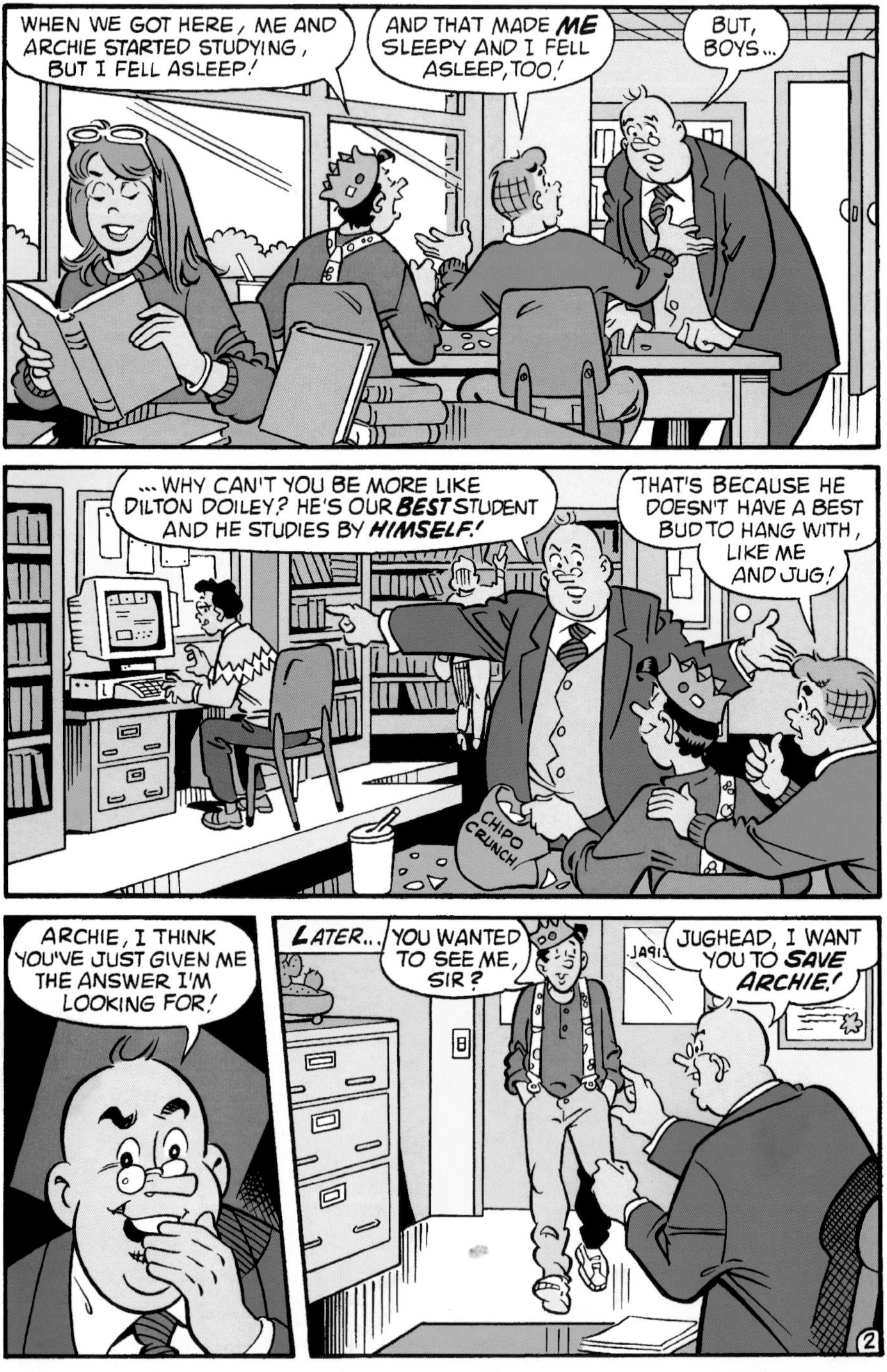
WHEN WE GOT HERE, ME AND ARCHIE STARTED STUDYING, BUT I FELL ASLEEP!
AND THAT MADE **ME** SLEEPY AND I FELL ASLEEP, TOO!
BUT, BOYS...
...WHY CAN'T YOU BE MORE LIKE DILTON DOILEY? HE'S OUR **BEST** STUDENT AND HE STUDIES BY **HIMSELF!**
THAT'S BECAUSE HE DOESN'T HAVE A BEST BUD TO HANG WITH, LIKE ME AND JUG!
CHIPO CRUNCH
ARCHIE, I THINK YOU'VE JUST GIVEN ME THE ANSWER I'M LOOKING FOR!
LATER...
YOU WANTED TO SEE ME, SIR?
JUGHEAD, I WANT YOU TO **SAVE ARCHIE!**
2

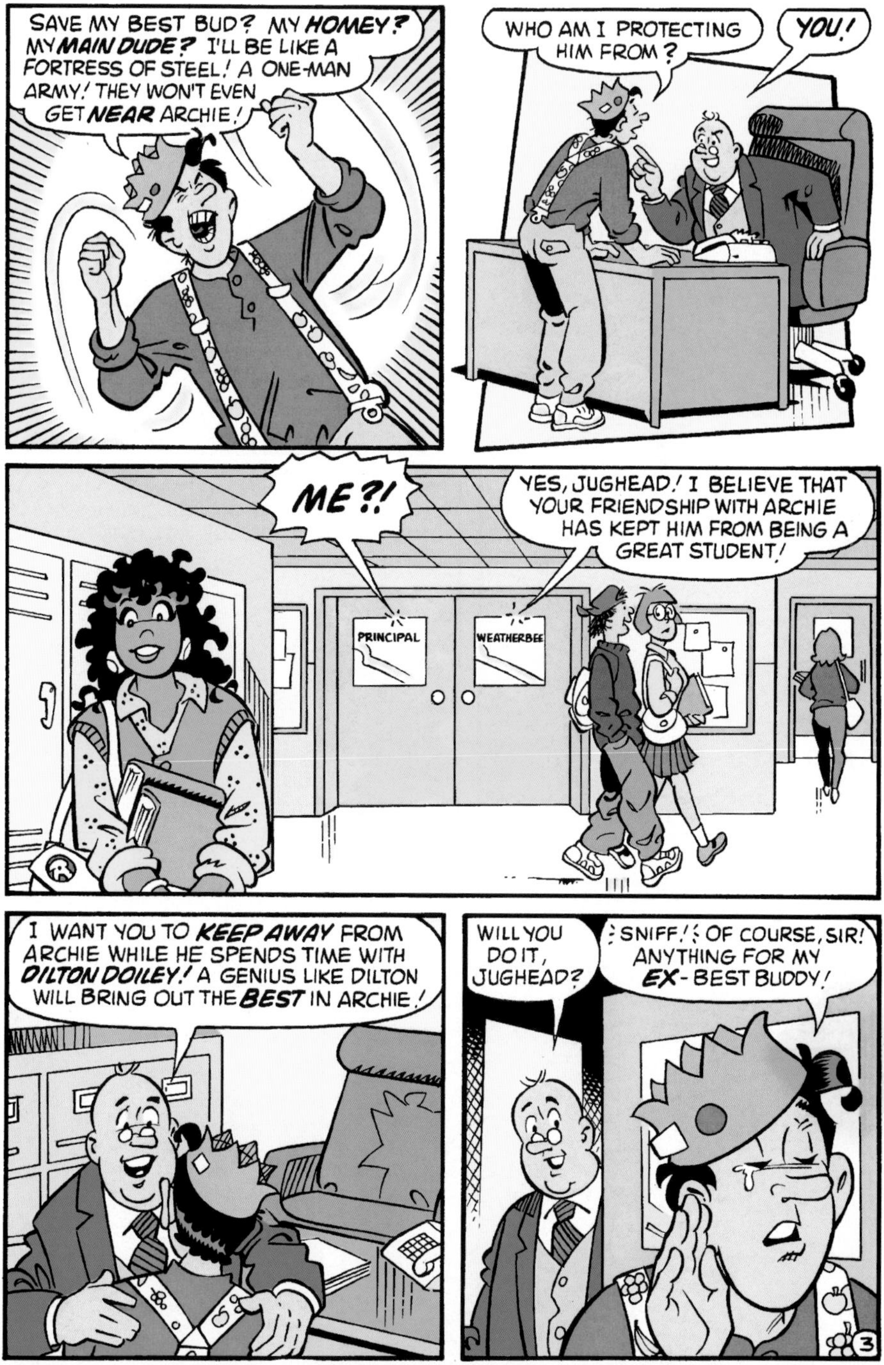
SAVE MY BEST BUD? MY HOMEY? MY MAIN DUDE? I'LL BE LIKE A FORTRESS OF STEEL! A ONE-MAN ARMY! THEY WON'T EVEN GET NEAR ARCHIE!
WHO AM I PROTECTING HIM FROM?
YOU!
ME?!
YES, JUGHEAD! I BELIEVE THAT YOUR FRIENDSHIP WITH ARCHIE HAS KEPT HIM FROM BEING A GREAT STUDENT!
PRINCIPAL
WEATHERBEE
I WANT YOU TO KEEP AWAY FROM ARCHIE WHILE HE SPENDS TIME WITH DILTON DOILEY! A GENIUS LIKE DILTON WILL BRING OUT THE BEST IN ARCHIE!
WILL YOU DO IT, JUGHEAD?
SNIFF! OF COURSE, SIR! ANYTHING FOR MY EX-BEST BUDDY!
3

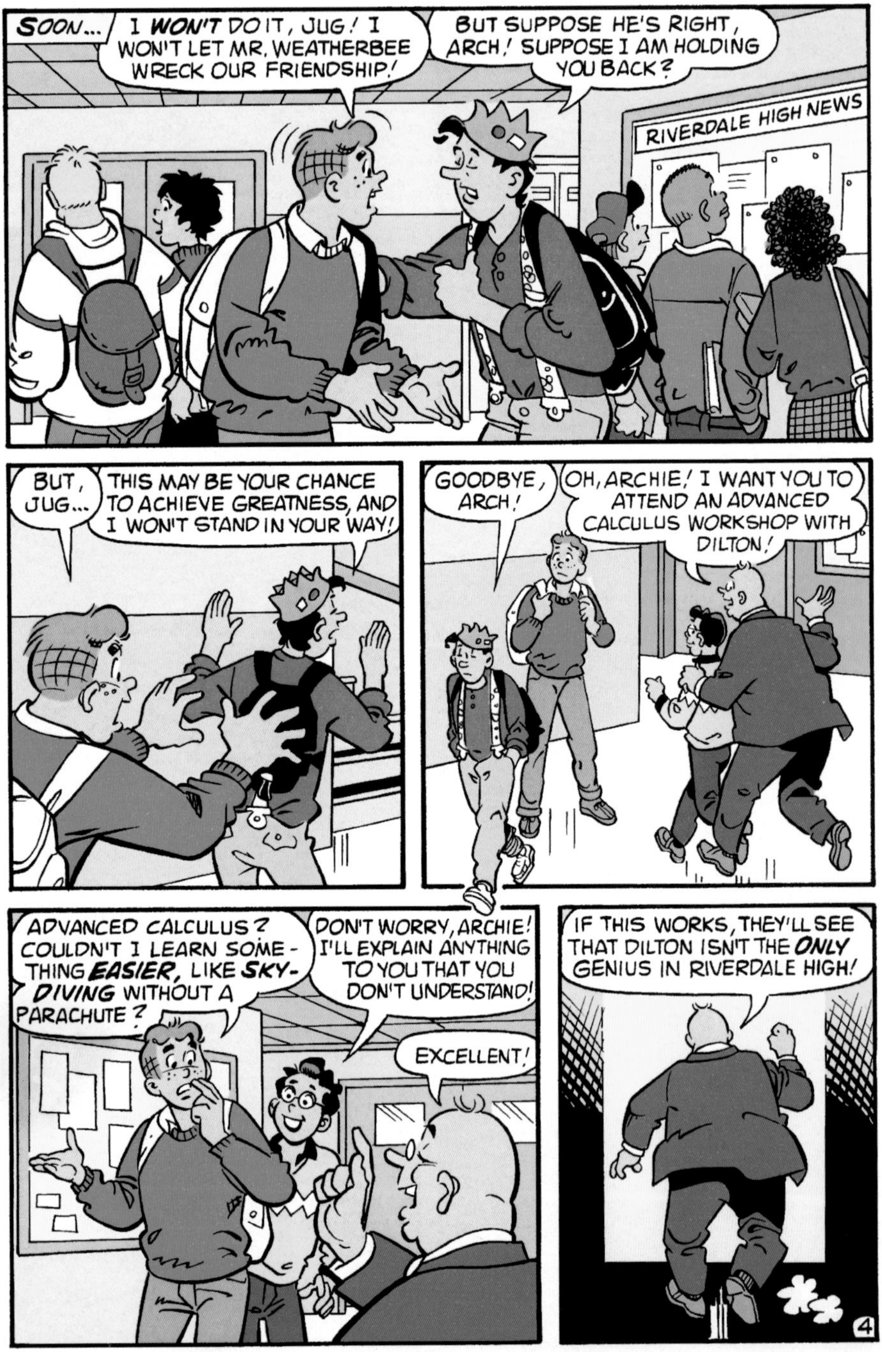
SOON...
I WON'T DO IT, JUG! I WON'T LET MR. WEATHERBEE WRECK OUR FRIENDSHIP!
BUT SUPPOSE HE'S RIGHT, ARCH! SUPPOSE I AM HOLDING YOU BACK?
RIVERDALE HIGH NEWS
BUT, JUG...
THIS MAY BE YOUR CHANCE TO ACHIEVE GREATNESS, AND I WON'T STAND IN YOUR WAY!
GOODBYE, ARCH!
OH, ARCHIE! I WANT YOU TO ATTEND AN ADVANCED CALCULUS WORKSHOP WITH DILTON!
ADVANCED CALCULUS? COULDN'T I LEARN SOMETHING EASIER, LIKE SKY-DIVING WITHOUT A PARACHUTE?
DON'T WORRY, ARCHIE! I'LL EXPLAIN ANYTHING TO YOU THAT YOU DON'T UNDERSTAND!
EXCELLENT!
IF THIS WORKS, THEY'LL SEE THAT DILTON ISN'T THE ONLY GENIUS IN RIVERDALE HIGH!
4

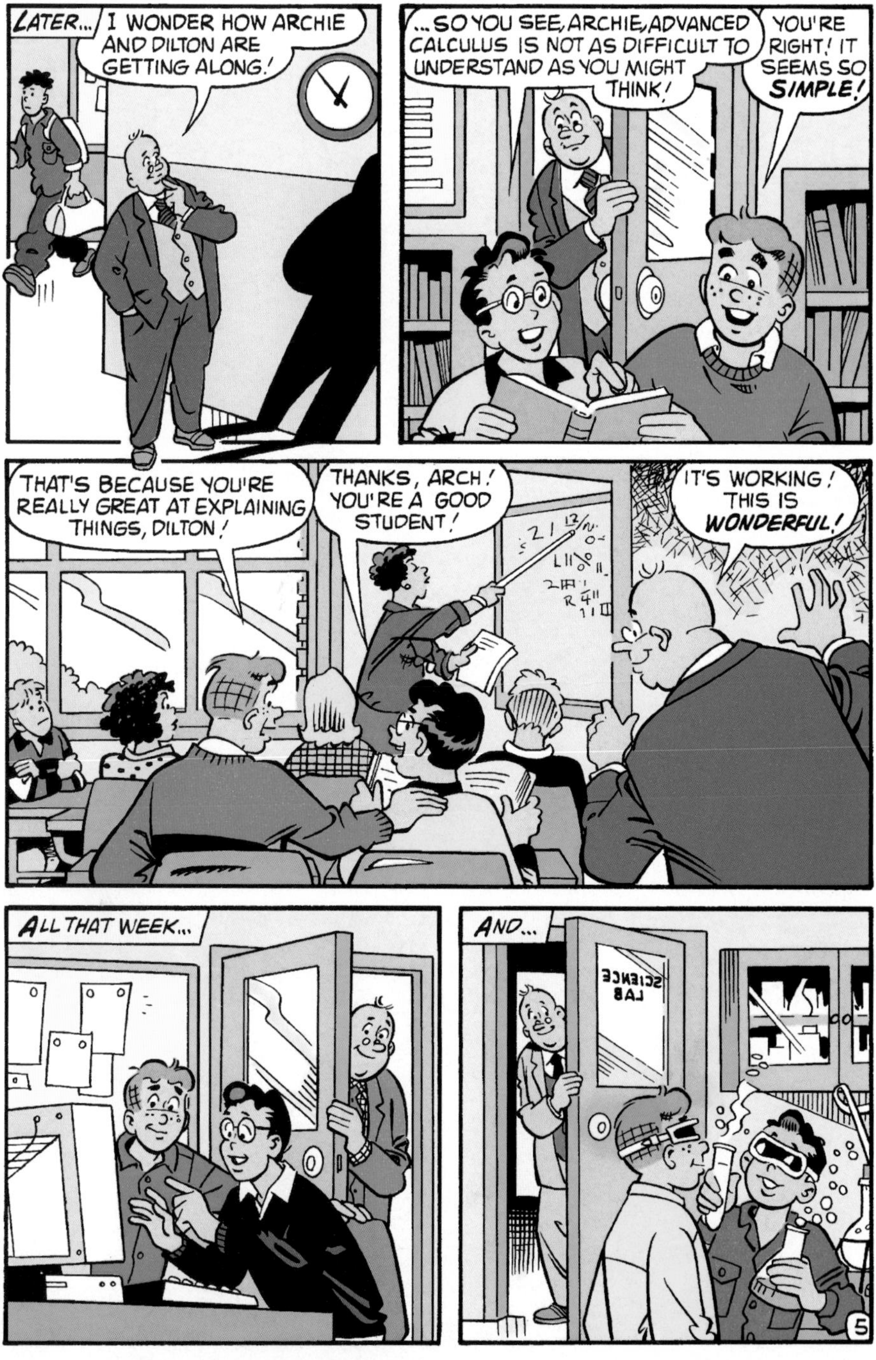
LATER...
I WONDER HOW ARCHIE AND DILTON ARE GETTING ALONG!
...SO YOU SEE, ARCHIE, ADVANCED CALCULUS IS NOT AS DIFFICULT TO UNDERSTAND AS YOU MIGHT THINK!
YOU'RE RIGHT! IT SEEMS SO SIMPLE!
THAT'S BECAUSE YOU'RE REALLY GREAT AT EXPLAINING THINGS, DILTON!
THANKS, ARCH! YOU'RE A GOOD STUDENT!
IT'S WORKING! THIS IS WONDERFUL!
ALL THAT WEEK...
AND...
5

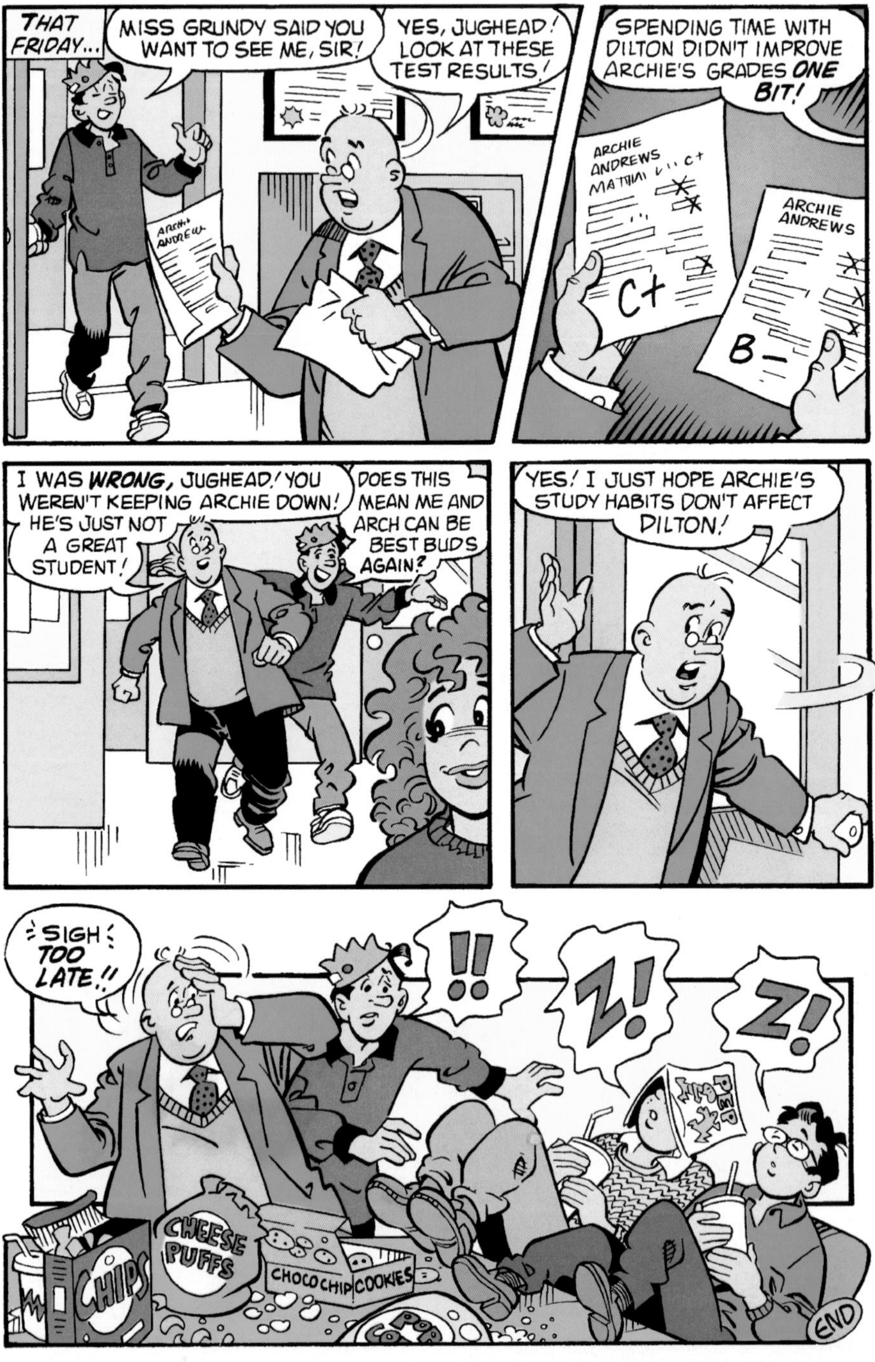
THAT FRIDAY...
MISS GRUNDY SAID YOU WANT TO SEE ME, SIR!
YES, JUGHEAD! LOOK AT THESE TEST RESULTS!
SPENDING TIME WITH DILTON DIDN'T IMPROVE ARCHIE'S GRADES ONE BIT!
ARCHIE ANDREWS
C+
ARCHIE ANDREWS
B–
I WAS WRONG, JUGHEAD! YOU WEREN'T KEEPING ARCHIE DOWN!
HE'S JUST NOT A GREAT STUDENT!
DOES THIS MEAN ME AND ARCH CAN BE BEST BUDS AGAIN?
YES! I JUST HOPE ARCHIE'S STUDY HABITS DON'T AFFECT DILTON!
SIGH TOO LATE!!
!!
Z!
Z!
CHEESE PUFFS
CHIPS
CHOCO CHIP COOKIES
END

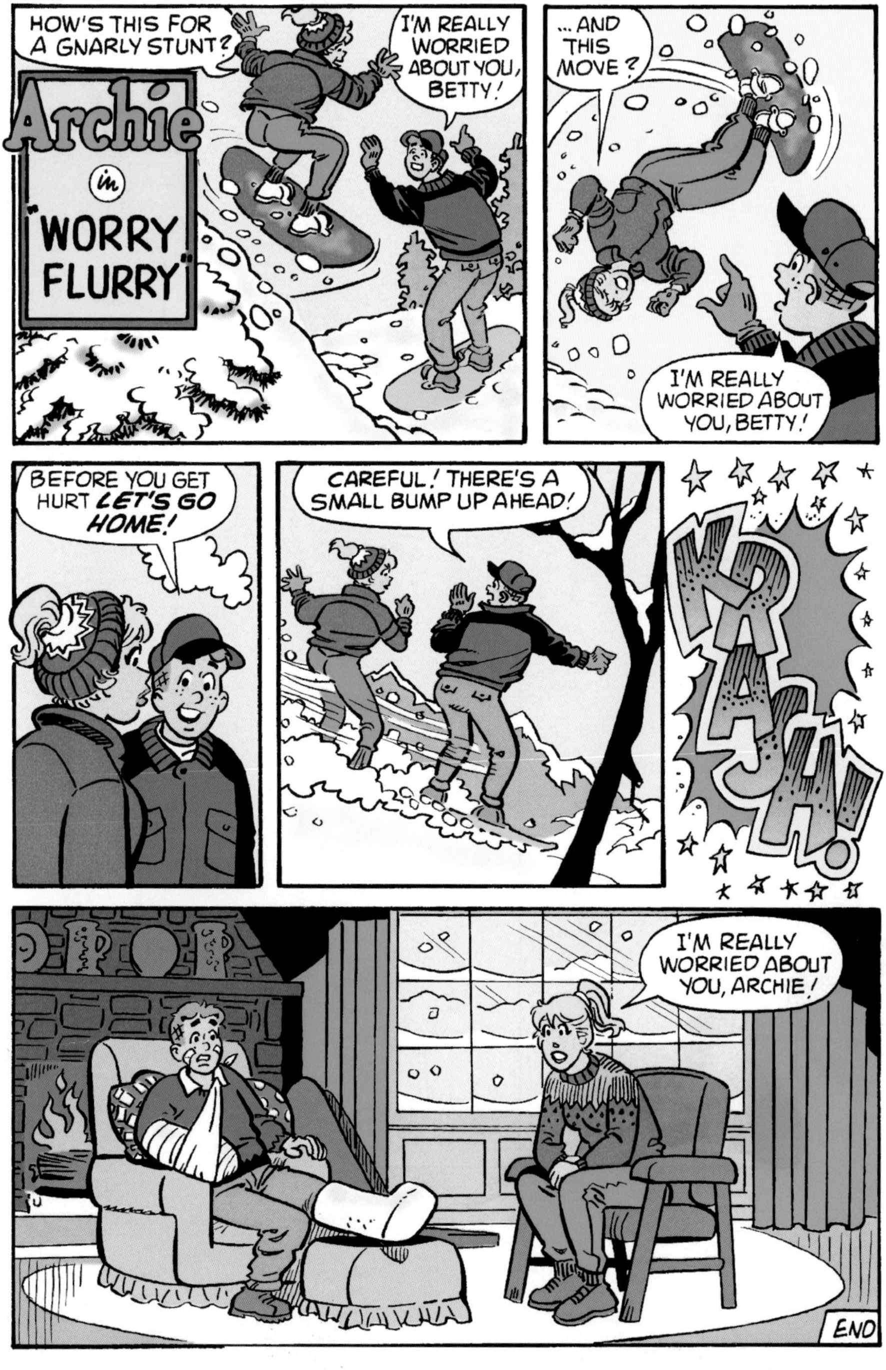
HOW'S THIS FOR A GNARLY STUNT?
Archie
in
"WORRY FLURRY"
I'M REALLY WORRIED ABOUT YOU, BETTY!
...AND THIS MOVE?
I'M REALLY WORRIED ABOUT YOU, BETTY!
BEFORE YOU GET HURT LET'S GO HOME!
CAREFUL! THERE'S A SMALL BUMP UP AHEAD!
KRAJH!
I'M REALLY WORRIED ABOUT YOU, ARCHIE!
END

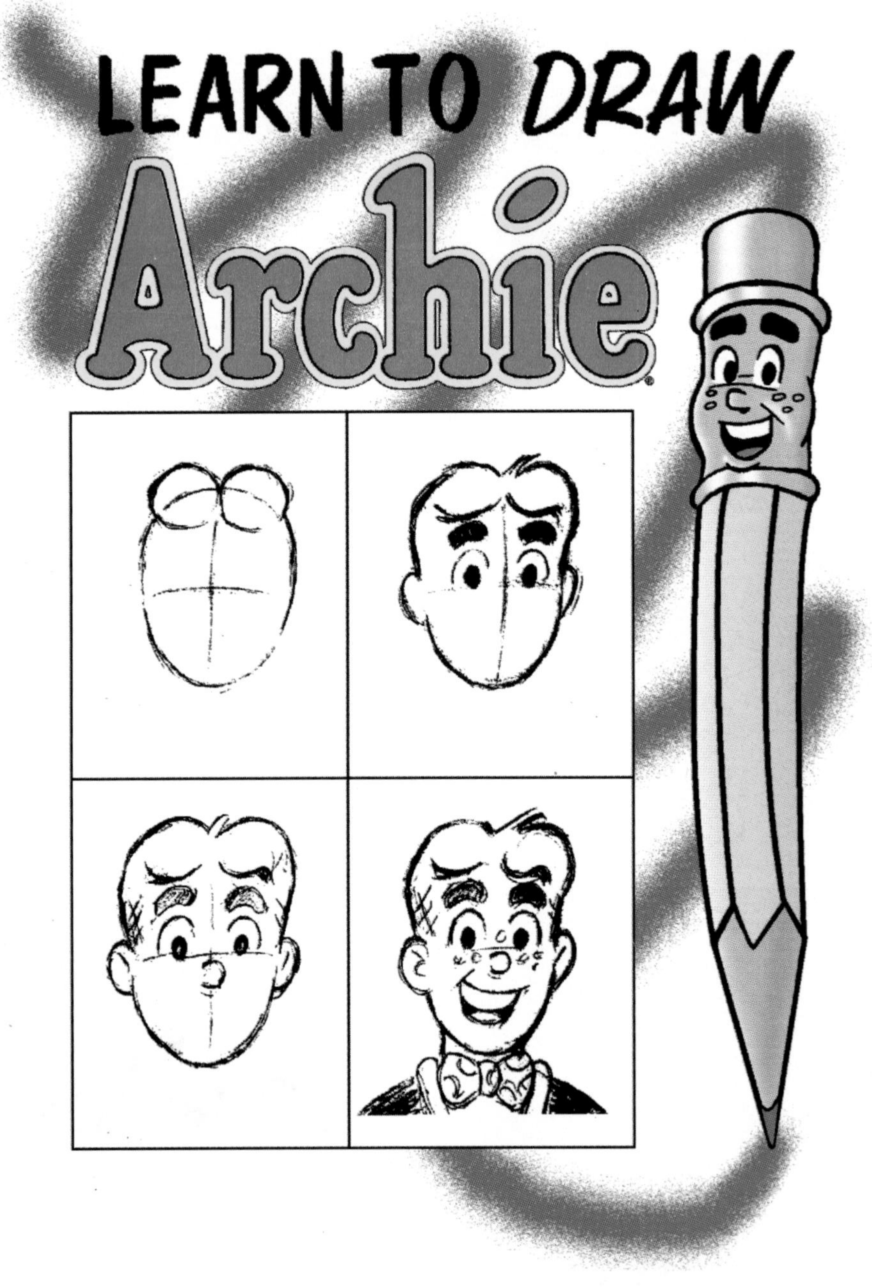
LEARN TO DRAW
Archie

Archie in "Don't Look Now"

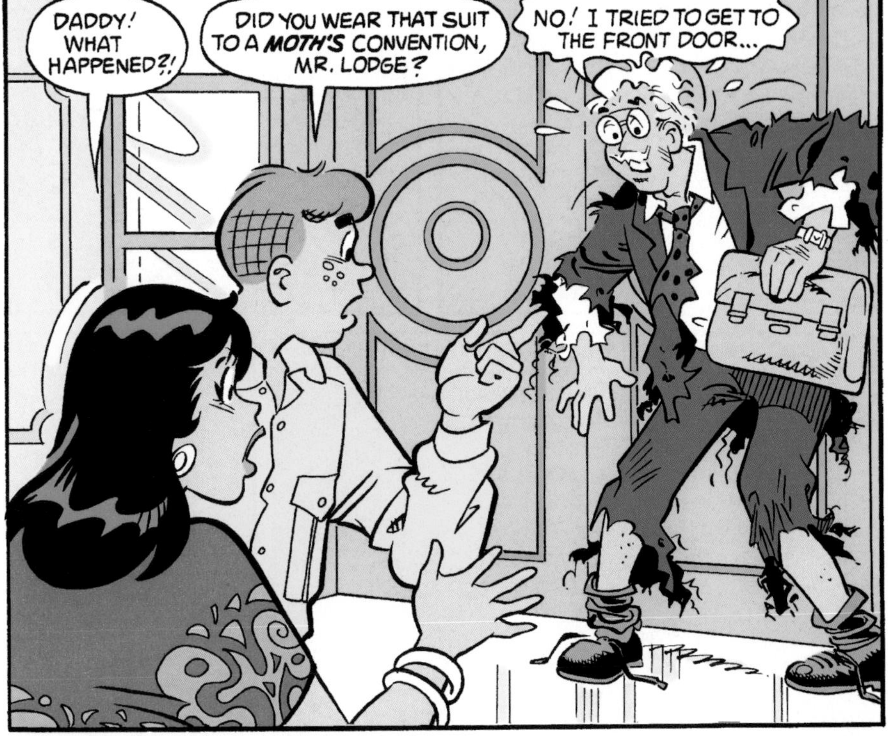
DADDY! WHAT HAPPENED?!
DID YOU WEAR THAT SUIT TO A MOTH'S CONVENTION, MR. LODGE?
NO! I TRIED TO GET TO THE FRONT DOOR...

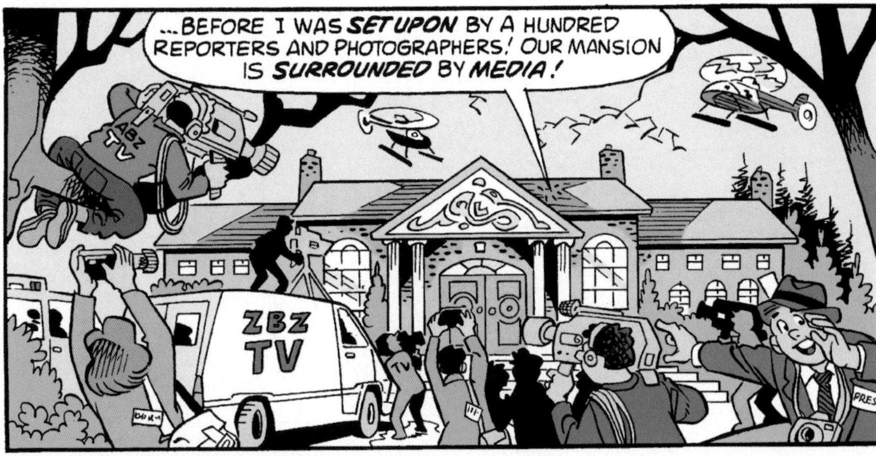
...BEFORE I WAS SET UPON BY A HUNDRED REPORTERS AND PHOTOGRAPHERS! OUR MANSION IS SURROUNDED BY MEDIA!
ABZ TV
ZBZ TV
TV
PRESS

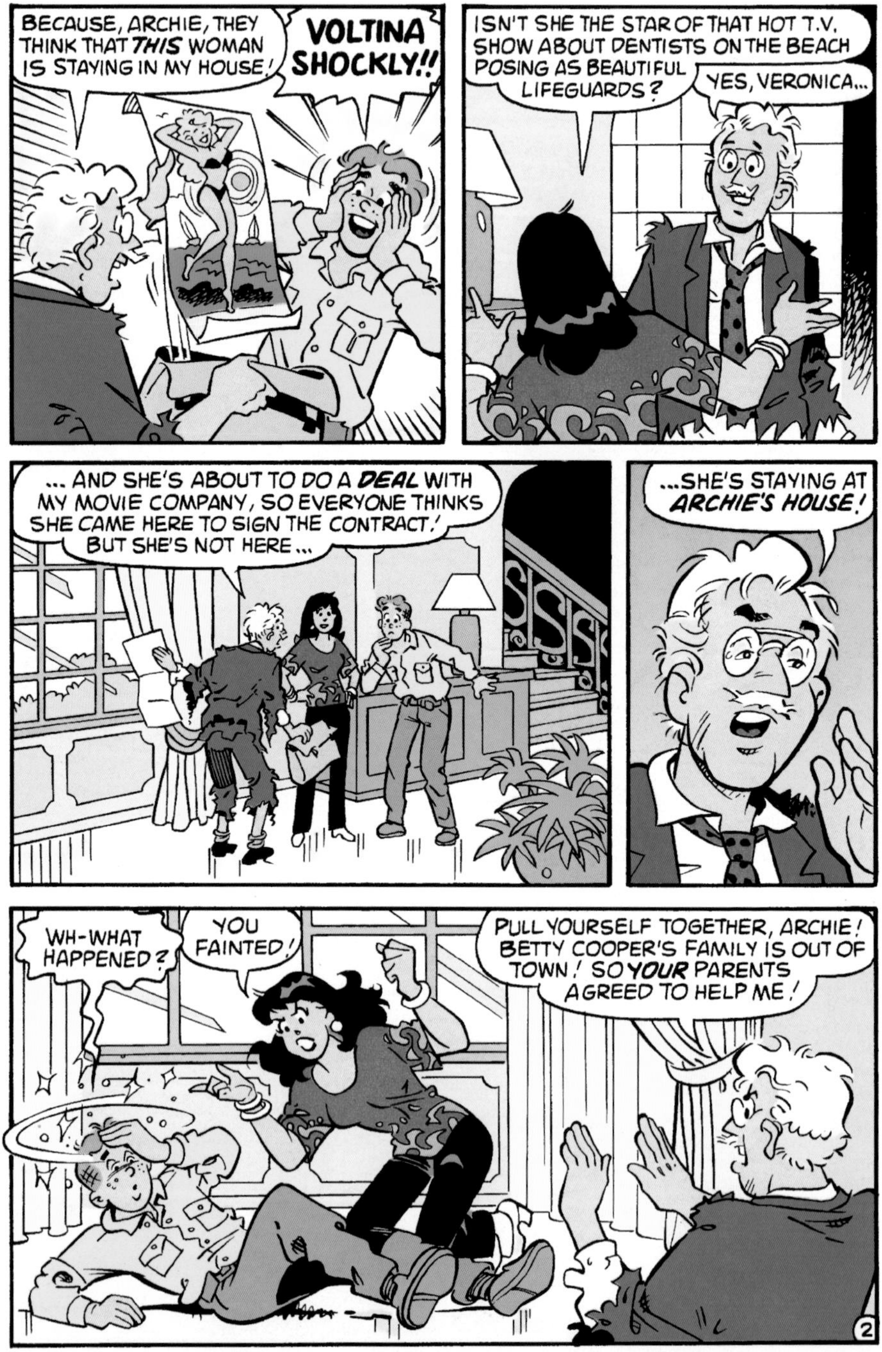
BECAUSE, ARCHIE, THEY THINK THAT THIS WOMAN IS STAYING IN MY HOUSE!
VOLTINA SHOCKLY!!
ISN'T SHE THE STAR OF THAT HOT T.V. SHOW ABOUT DENTISTS ON THE BEACH POSING AS BEAUTIFUL LIFEGUARDS?
YES, VERONICA...
... AND SHE'S ABOUT TO DO A DEAL WITH MY MOVIE COMPANY, SO EVERYONE THINKS SHE CAME HERE TO SIGN THE CONTRACT! BUT SHE'S NOT HERE...
...SHE'S STAYING AT ARCHIE'S HOUSE!
WH-WHAT HAPPENED?
YOU FAINTED!
PULL YOURSELF TOGETHER, ARCHIE! BETTY COOPER'S FAMILY IS OUT OF TOWN! SO YOUR PARENTS AGREED TO HELP ME!
2

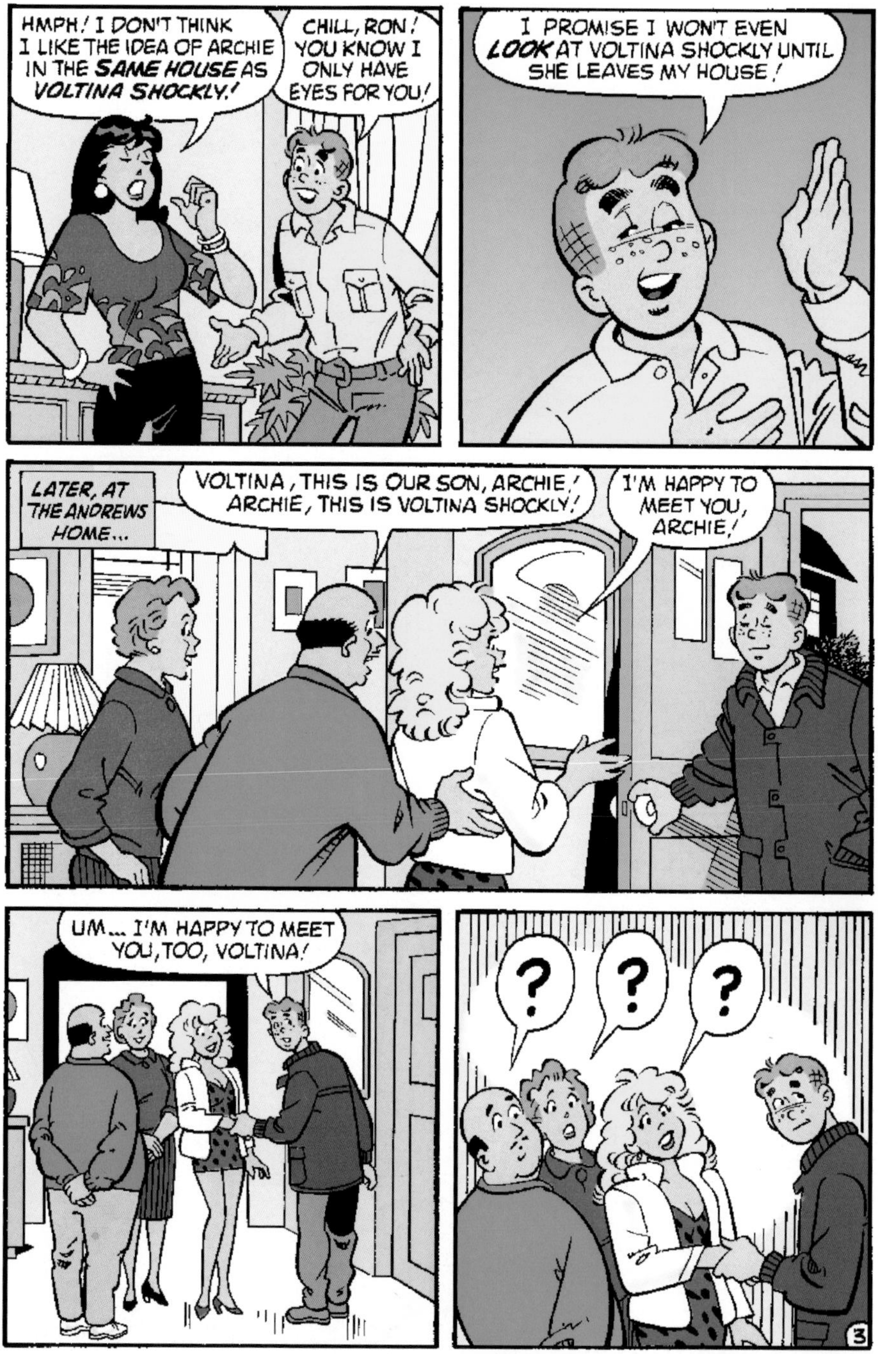
HMPH! I DON'T THINK I LIKE THE IDEA OF ARCHIE IN THE SAME HOUSE AS VOLTINA SHOCKLY!
CHILL, RON! YOU KNOW I ONLY HAVE EYES FOR YOU!
I PROMISE I WON'T EVEN LOOK AT VOLTINA SHOCKLY UNTIL SHE LEAVES MY HOUSE!
LATER, AT THE ANDREWS HOME...
VOLTINA, THIS IS OUR SON, ARCHIE! ARCHIE, THIS IS VOLTINA SHOCKLY!
I'M HAPPY TO MEET YOU, ARCHIE!
UM... I'M HAPPY TO MEET YOU, TOO, VOLTINA!
?
?
?
3

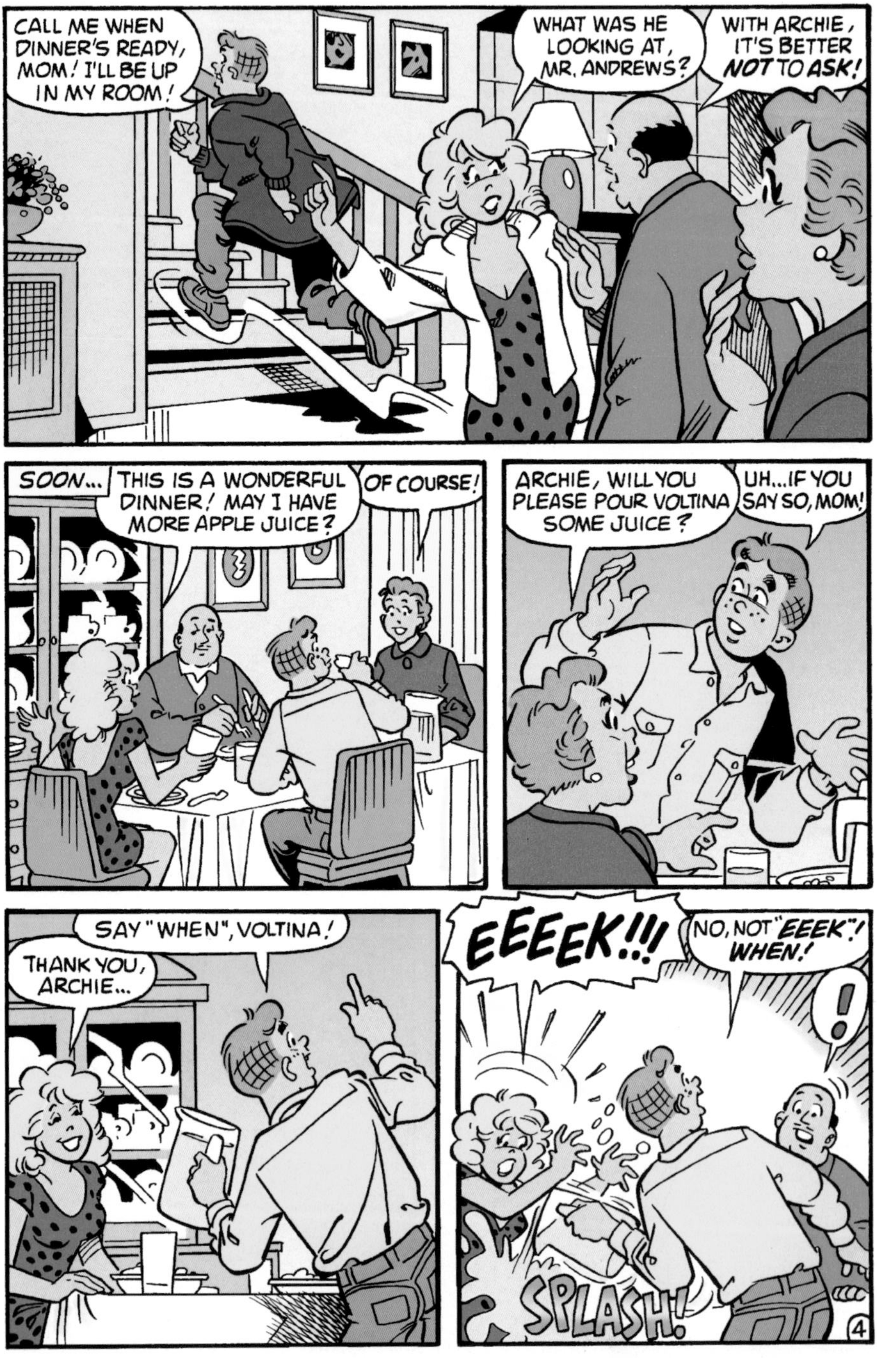
CALL ME WHEN DINNER'S READY, MOM! I'LL BE UP IN MY ROOM!
WHAT WAS HE LOOKING AT, MR. ANDREWS?
WITH ARCHIE, IT'S BETTER NOT TO ASK!
SOON...
THIS IS A WONDERFUL DINNER! MAY I HAVE MORE APPLE JUICE?
OF COURSE!
ARCHIE, WILL YOU PLEASE POUR VOLTINA SOME JUICE?
UH...IF YOU SAY SO, MOM!
SAY "WHEN", VOLTINA!
THANK YOU, ARCHIE...
EEEEK!!!
NO, NOT "EEEK"! WHEN!
!
SPLASH!
4

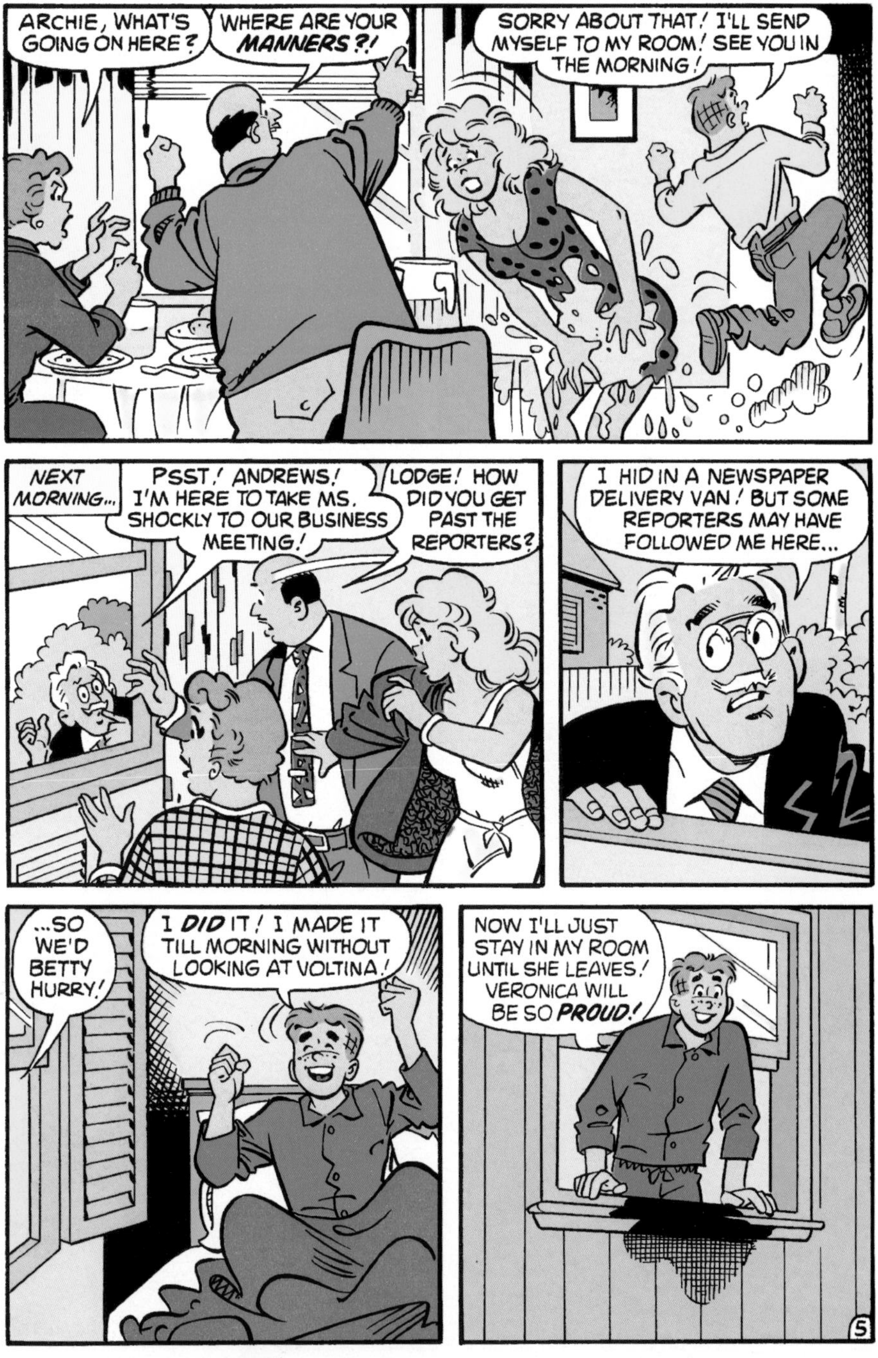
ARCHIE, WHAT'S GOING ON HERE?
WHERE ARE YOUR MANNERS?!
SORRY ABOUT THAT! I'LL SEND MYSELF TO MY ROOM! SEE YOU IN THE MORNING!
NEXT MORNING...
PSST! ANDREWS! I'M HERE TO TAKE MS. SHOCKLY TO OUR BUSINESS MEETING!
LODGE! HOW DID YOU GET PAST THE REPORTERS?
I HID IN A NEWSPAPER DELIVERY VAN! BUT SOME REPORTERS MAY HAVE FOLLOWED ME HERE...
...SO WE'D BETTY HURRY!
I DID IT! I MADE IT TILL MORNING WITHOUT LOOKING AT VOLTINA!
NOW I'LL JUST STAY IN MY ROOM UNTIL SHE LEAVES! VERONICA WILL BE SO PROUD!
5

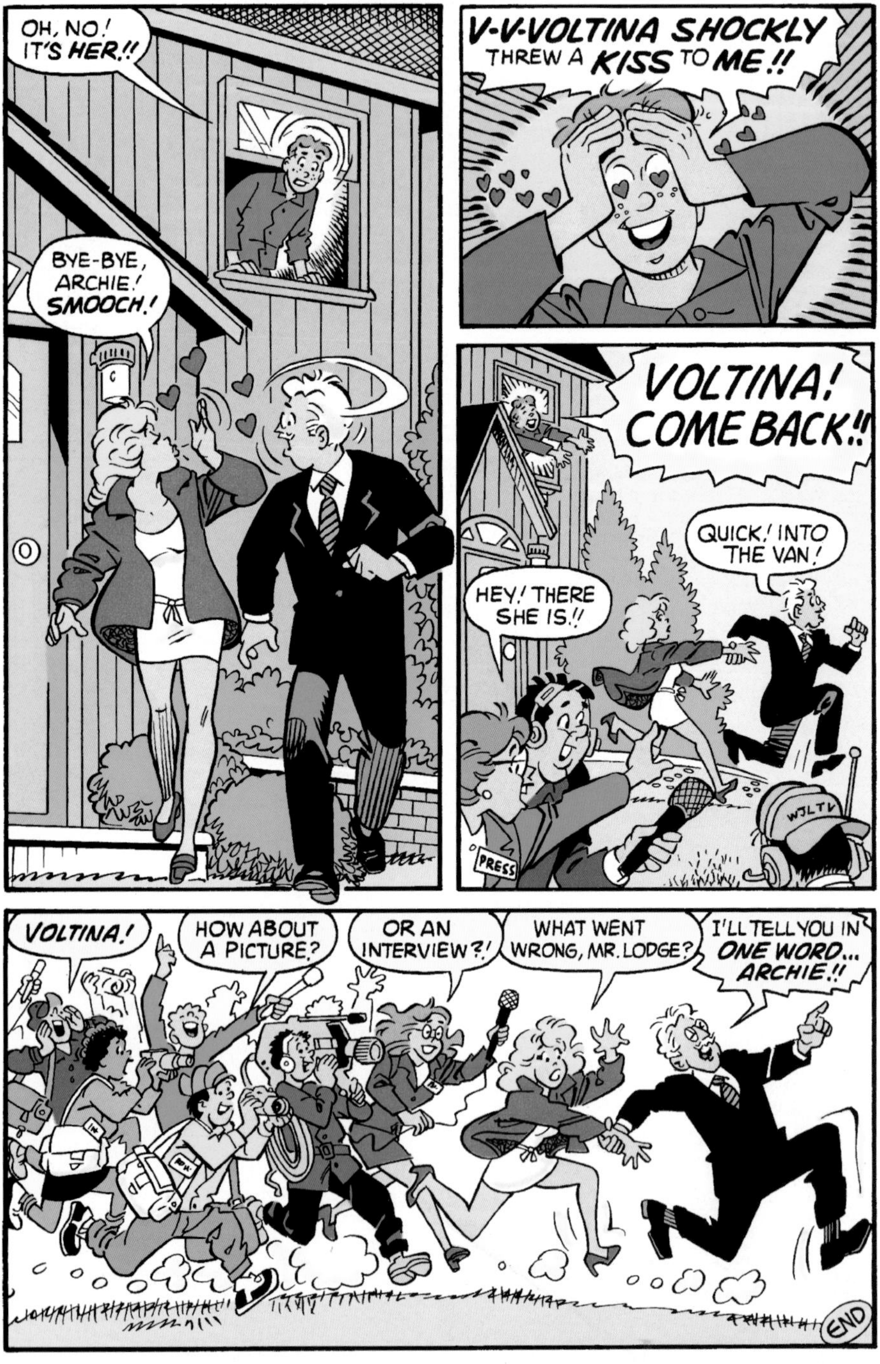
OH, NO! IT'S HER!!
BYE-BYE, ARCHIE! SMOOCH!
V-V-VOLTINA SHOCKLY THREW A KISS TO ME!!
VOLTINA! COME BACK!!
QUICK! INTO THE VAN!
HEY! THERE SHE IS!!
PRESS
WJLTV
VOLTINA!
HOW ABOUT A PICTURE?
OR AN INTERVIEW?!
WHAT WENT WRONG, MR. LODGE?
I'LL TELL YOU IN ONE WORD... ARCHIE!!
END

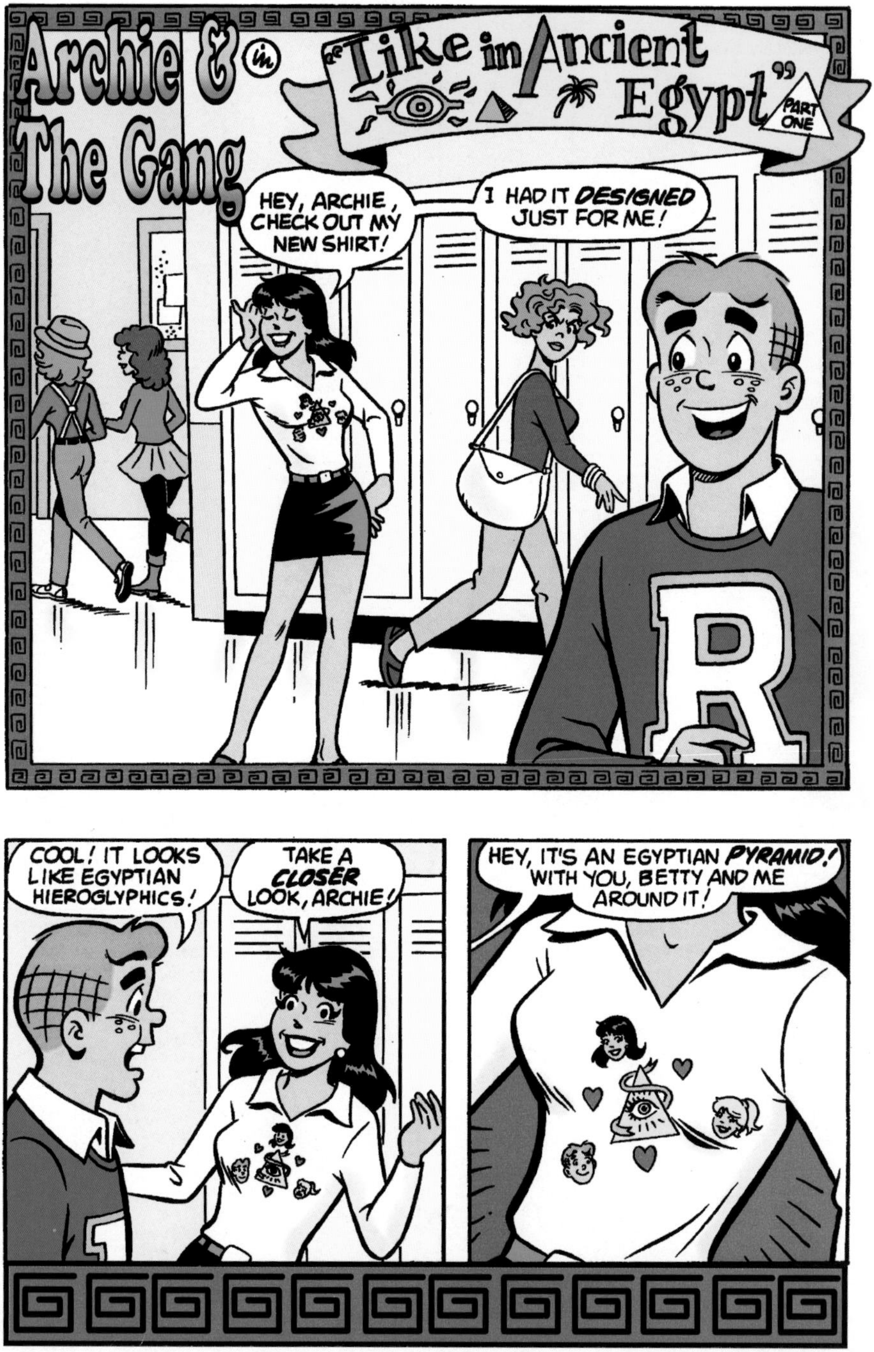
Archie & The Gang
in
"Like in Ancient Egypt" PART ONE
HEY, ARCHIE, CHECK OUT MY NEW SHIRT!
I HAD IT DESIGNED JUST FOR ME!
COOL! IT LOOKS LIKE EGYPTIAN HIEROGLYPHICS!
TAKE A CLOSER LOOK, ARCHIE!
HEY, IT'S AN EGYPTIAN PYRAMID! WITH YOU, BETTY AND ME AROUND IT!

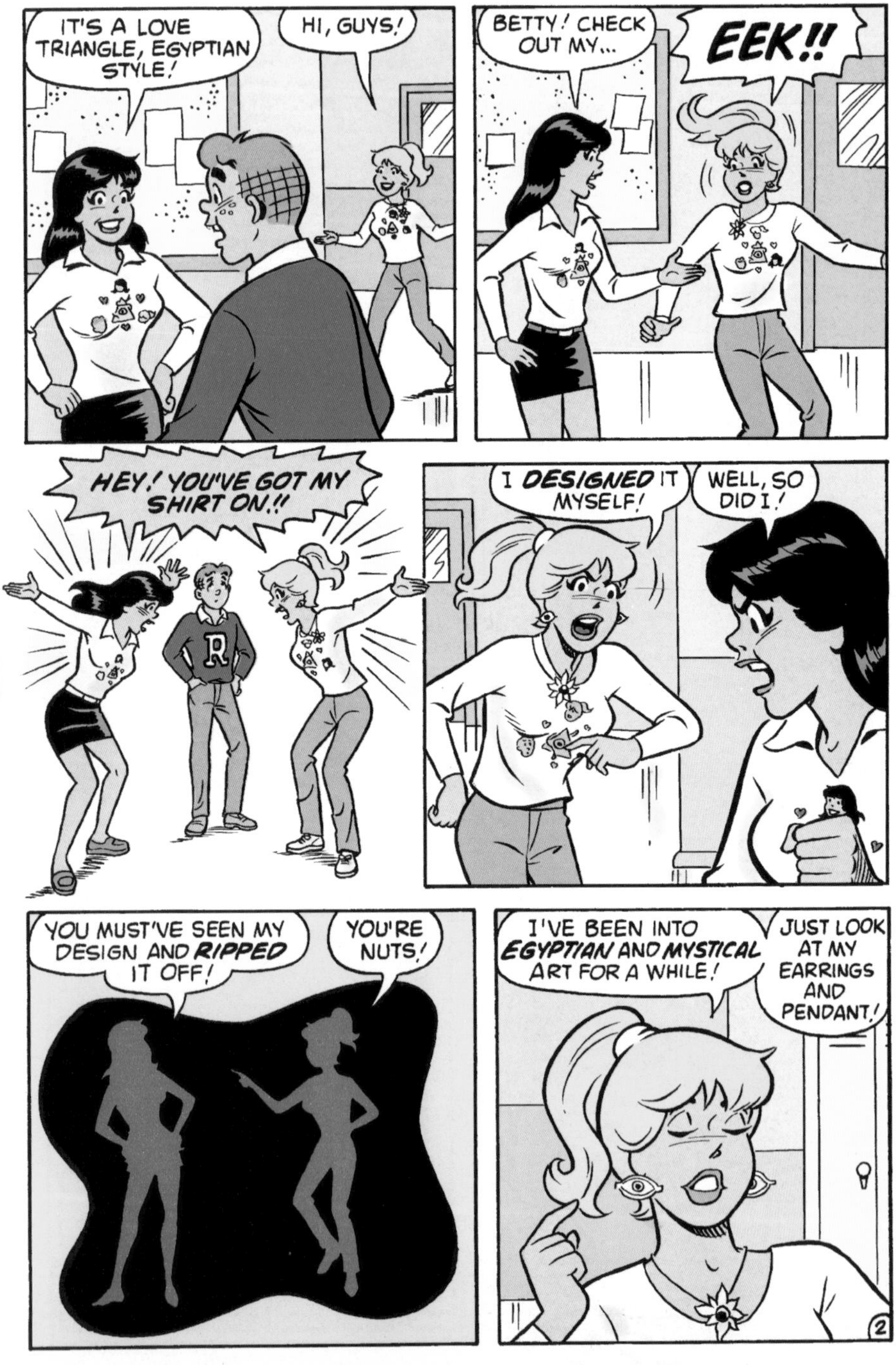
IT'S A LOVE TRIANGLE, EGYPTIAN STYLE!
HI, GUYS!
BETTY! CHECK OUT MY...
EEK!!
HEY! YOU'VE GOT MY SHIRT ON!!
I DESIGNED IT MYSELF!
WELL, SO DID I!
YOU MUST'VE SEEN MY DESIGN AND RIPPED IT OFF!
YOU'RE NUTS!
I'VE BEEN INTO EGYPTIAN AND MYSTICAL ART FOR A WHILE!
JUST LOOK AT MY EARRINGS AND PENDANT!
2

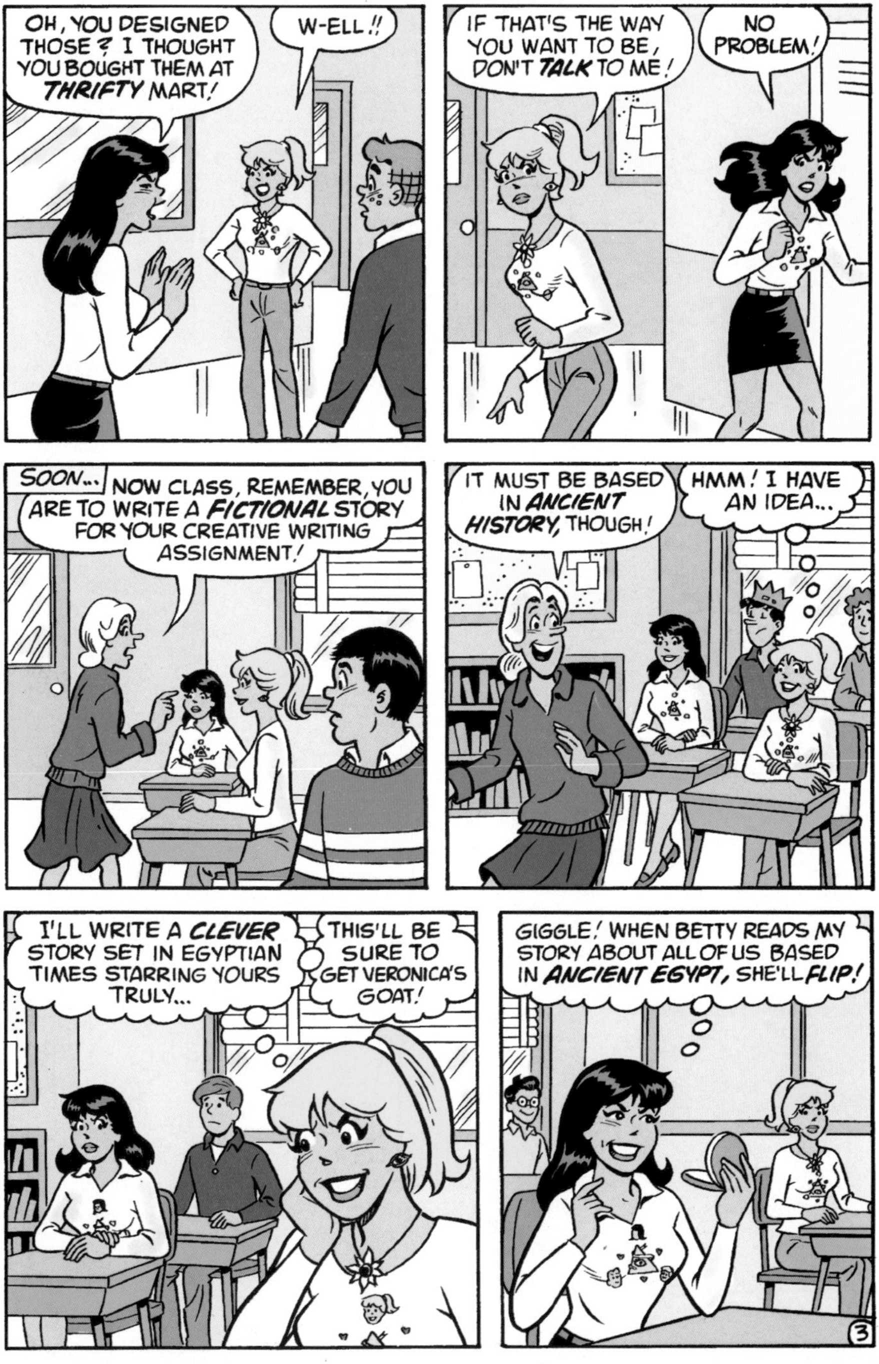
OH, YOU DESIGNED THOSE? I THOUGHT YOU BOUGHT THEM AT THRIFTY MART!
W-ELL!!
IF THAT'S THE WAY YOU WANT TO BE, DON'T TALK TO ME!
NO PROBLEM!
SOON...
NOW CLASS, REMEMBER, YOU ARE TO WRITE A FICTIONAL STORY FOR YOUR CREATIVE WRITING ASSIGNMENT!
IT MUST BE BASED IN ANCIENT HISTORY, THOUGH!
HMM! I HAVE AN IDEA...
I'LL WRITE A CLEVER STORY SET IN EGYPTIAN TIMES STARRING YOURS TRULY...
THIS'LL BE SURE TO GET VERONICA'S GOAT!
GIGGLE! WHEN BETTY READS MY STORY ABOUT ALL OF US BASED IN ANCIENT EGYPT, SHE'LL FLIP!
3

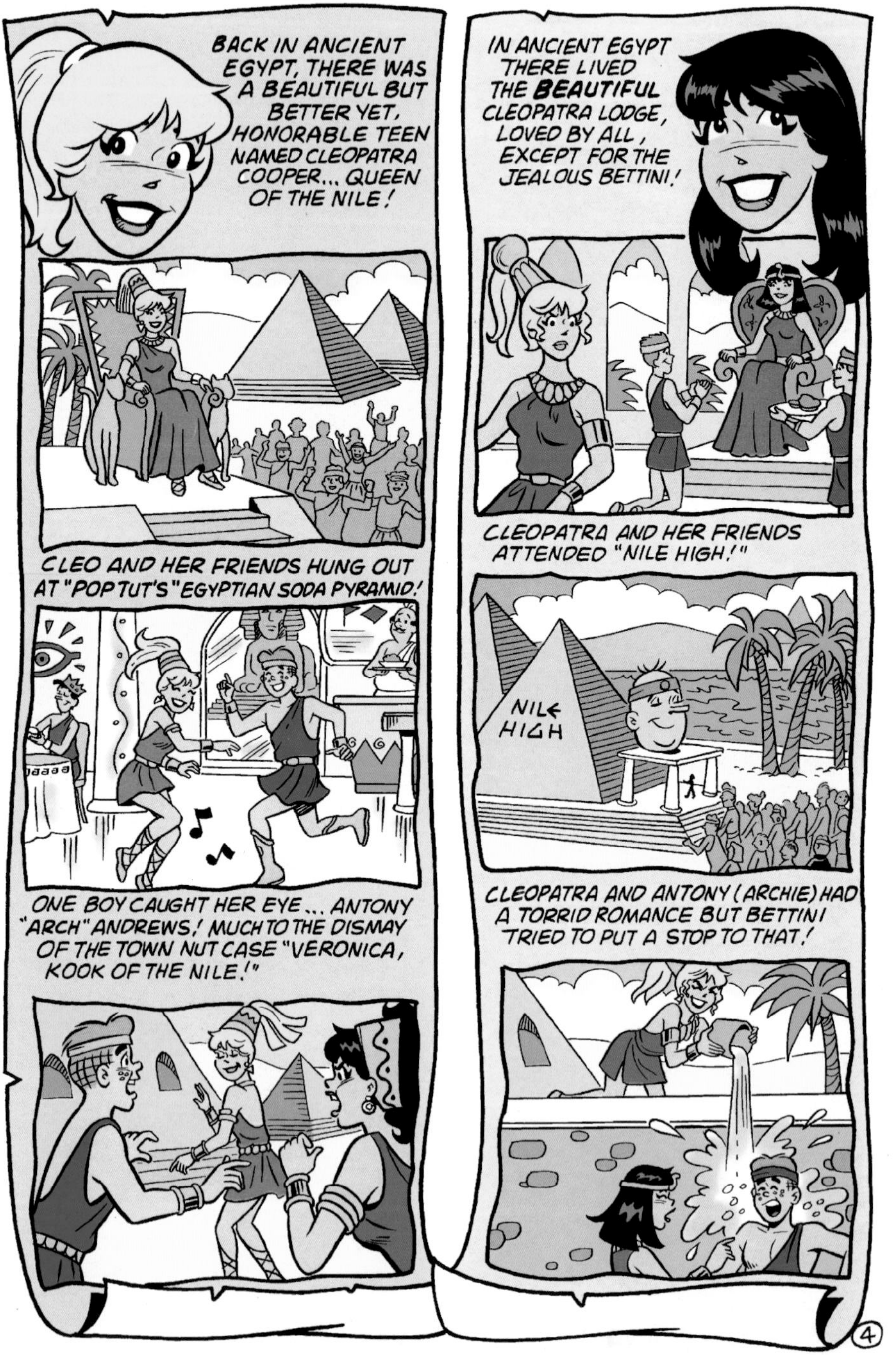
BACK IN ANCIENT EGYPT, THERE WAS A BEAUTIFUL BUT BETTER YET, HONORABLE TEEN NAMED CLEOPATRA COOPER... QUEEN OF THE NILE!
CLEO AND HER FRIENDS HUNG OUT AT "POP TUT'S" EGYPTIAN SODA PYRAMID!
ONE BOY CAUGHT HER EYE... ANTONY "ARCH" ANDREWS! MUCH TO THE DISMAY OF THE TOWN NUT CASE "VERONICA, KOOK OF THE NILE!"
IN ANCIENT EGYPT THERE LIVED THE BEAUTIFUL CLEOPATRA LODGE, LOVED BY ALL, EXCEPT FOR THE JEALOUS BETTINI!
CLEOPATRA AND HER FRIENDS ATTENDED "NILE HIGH!"
NILE HIGH
CLEOPATRA AND ANTONY (ARCHIE) HAD A TORRID ROMANCE BUT BETTINI TRIED TO PUT A STOP TO THAT!
4

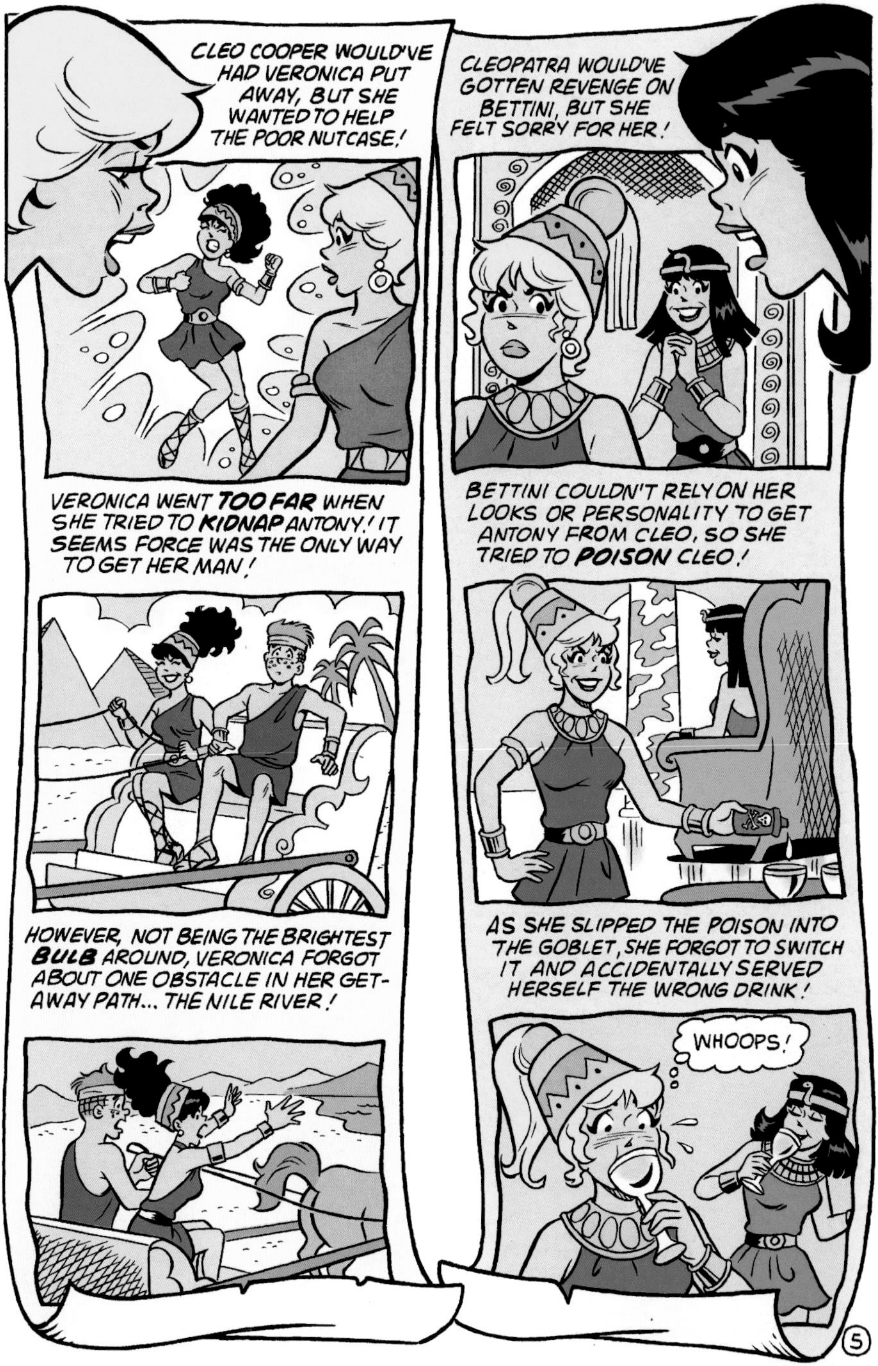
CLEO COOPER WOULD'VE HAD VERONICA PUT AWAY, BUT SHE WANTED TO HELP THE POOR NUTCASE!
VERONICA WENT TOO FAR WHEN SHE TRIED TO KIDNAP ANTONY! IT SEEMS FORCE WAS THE ONLY WAY TO GET HER MAN!
HOWEVER, NOT BEING THE BRIGHTEST BULB AROUND, VERONICA FORGOT ABOUT ONE OBSTACLE IN HER GET-AWAY PATH... THE NILE RIVER!
CLEOPATRA WOULD'VE GOTTEN REVENGE ON BETTINI, BUT SHE FELT SORRY FOR HER!
BETTINI COULDN'T RELY ON HER LOOKS OR PERSONALITY TO GET ANTONY FROM CLEO, SO SHE TRIED TO POISON CLEO!
AS SHE SLIPPED THE POISON INTO THE GOBLET, SHE FORGOT TO SWITCH IT AND ACCIDENTALLY SERVED HERSELF THE WRONG DRINK!
WHOOPS!
5

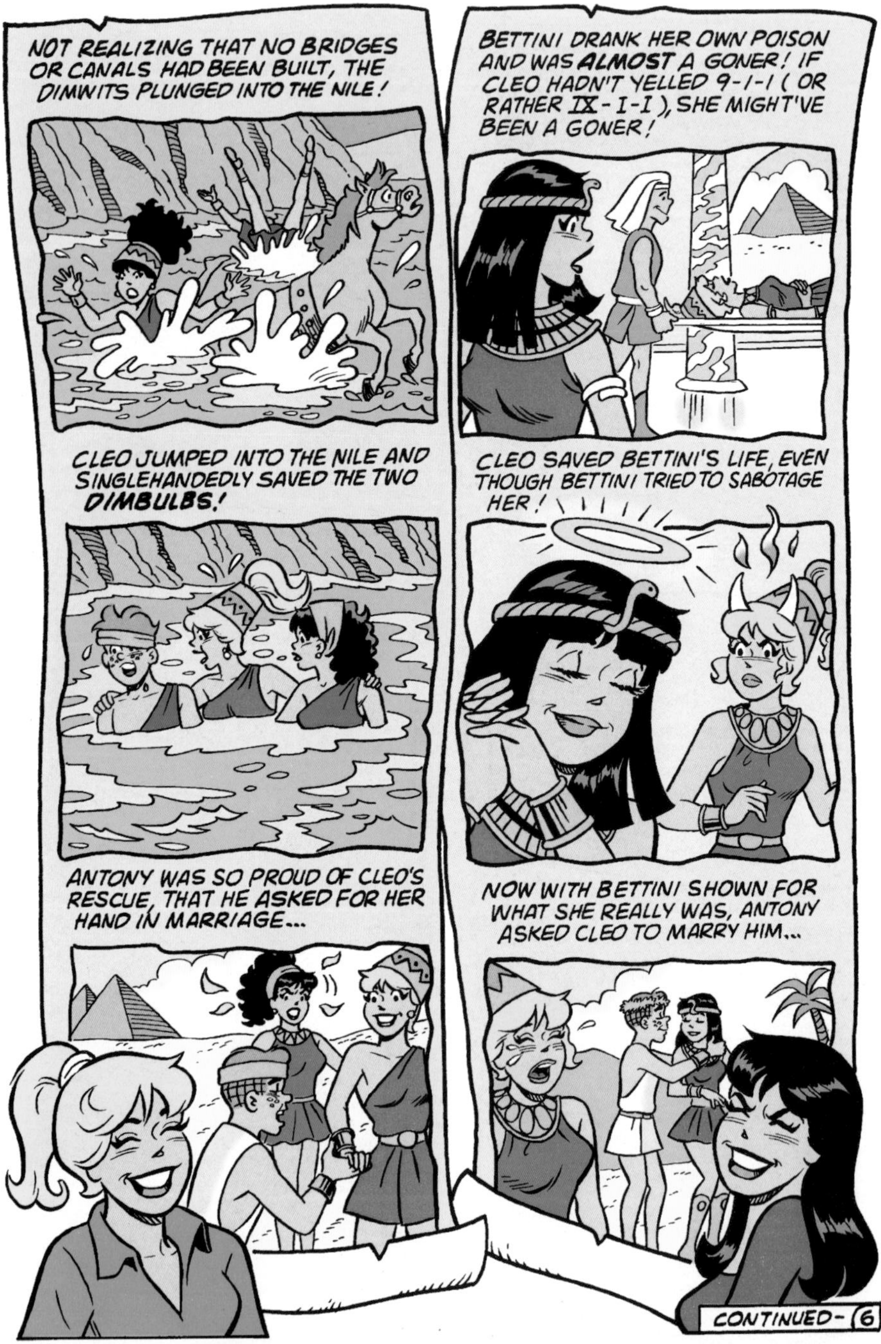
NOT REALIZING THAT NO BRIDGES OR CANALS HAD BEEN BUILT, THE DIMWITS PLUNGED INTO THE NILE!
CLEO JUMPED INTO THE NILE AND SINGLEHANDEDLY SAVED THE TWO DIMBULBS!
ANTONY WAS SO PROUD OF CLEO'S RESCUE, THAT HE ASKED FOR HER HAND IN MARRIAGE...
BETTINI DRANK HER OWN POISON AND WAS ALMOST A GONER! IF CLEO HADN'T YELLED 9-1-1 (OR RATHER IX - I-I), SHE MIGHT'VE BEEN A GONER!
CLEO SAVED BETTINI'S LIFE, EVEN THOUGH BETTINI TRIED TO SABOTAGE HER!
NOW WITH BETTINI SHOWN FOR WHAT SHE REALLY WAS, ANTONY ASKED CLEO TO MARRY HIM...
CONTINUED- 6

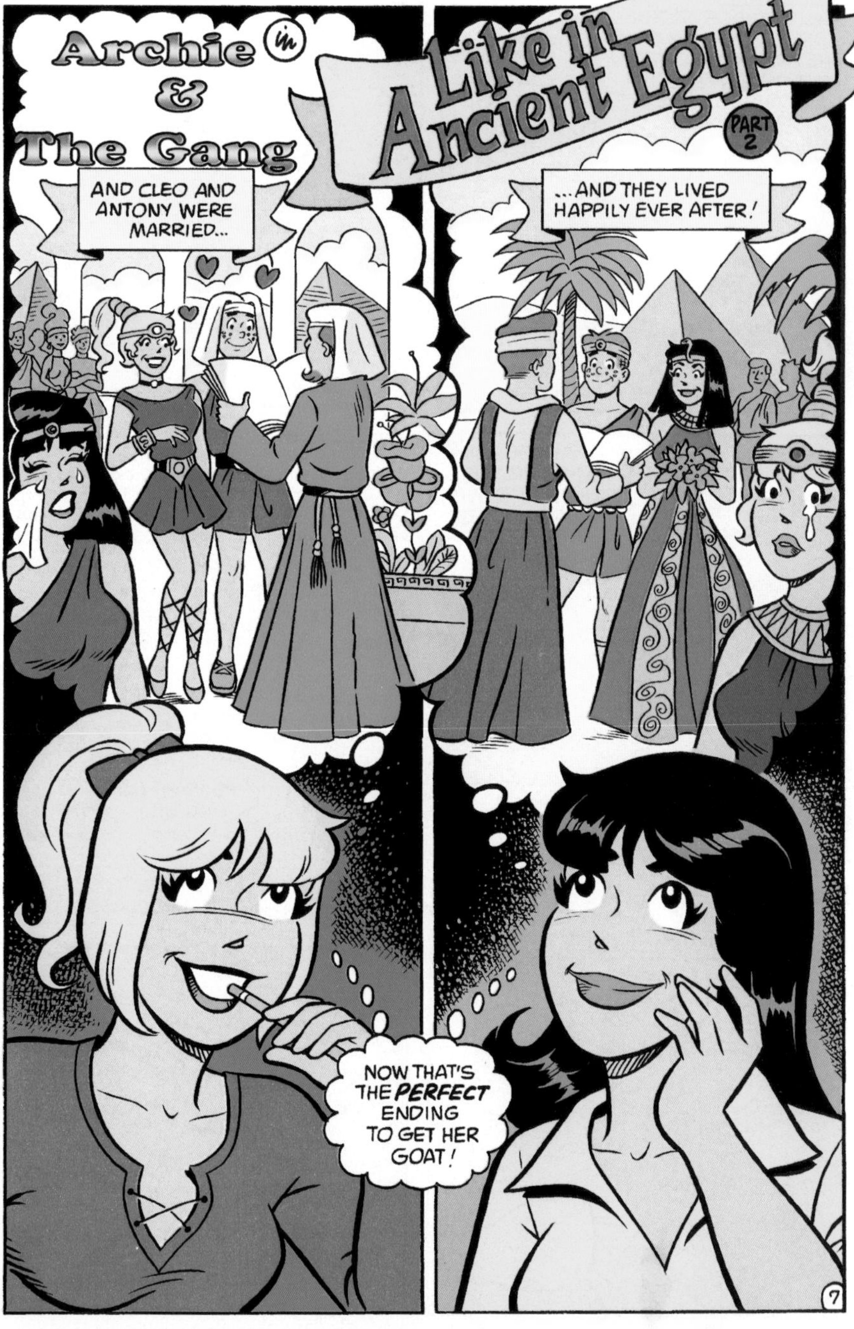
Archie in & The Gang
Like in Ancient Egypt
PART 2
AND CLEO AND ANTONY WERE MARRIED...
...AND THEY LIVED HAPPILY EVER AFTER!
NOW THAT'S THE *PERFECT* ENDING TO GET HER GOAT!
7

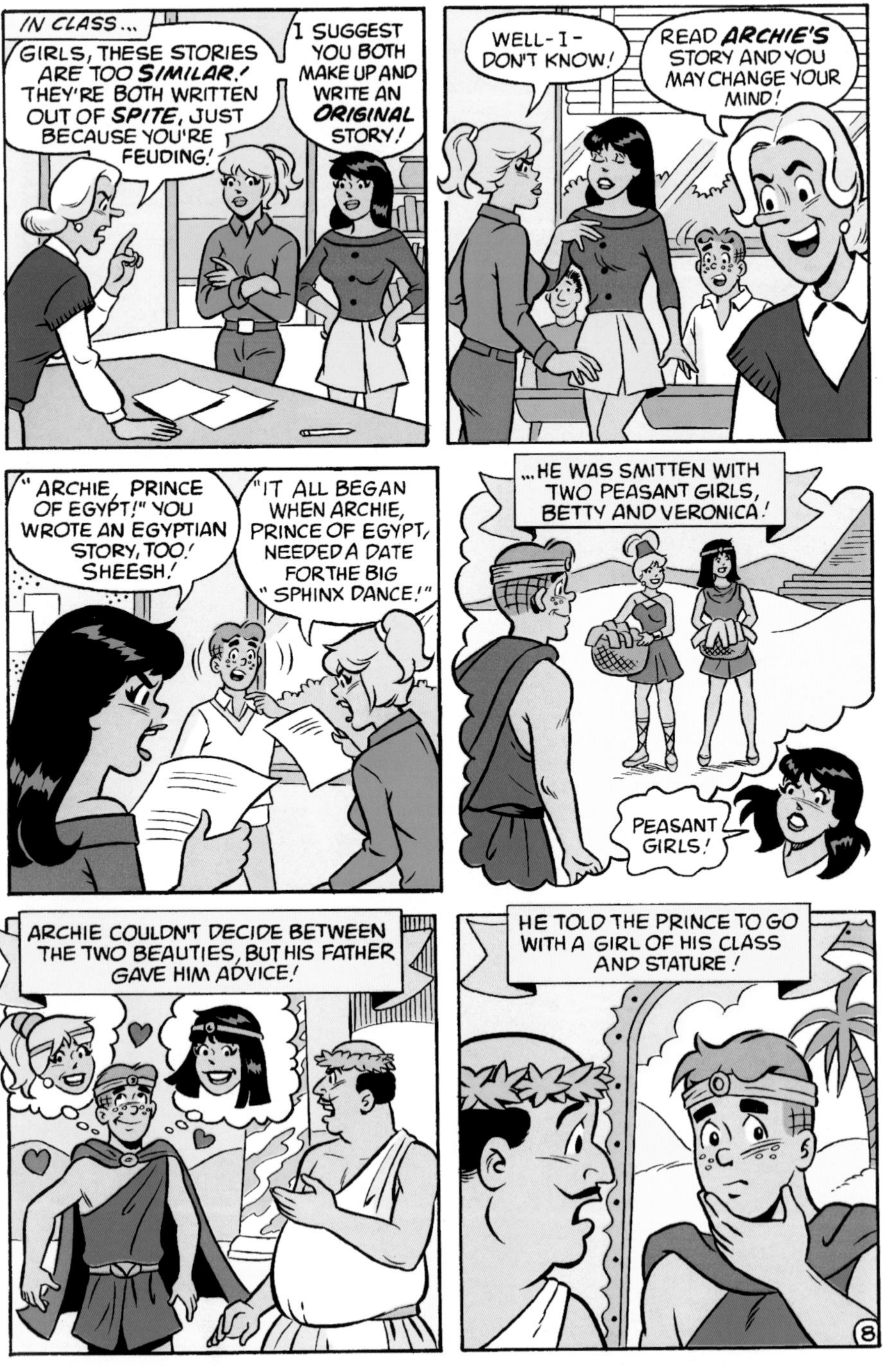
IN CLASS...
GIRLS, THESE STORIES ARE TOO SIMILAR! THEY'RE BOTH WRITTEN OUT OF SPITE, JUST BECAUSE YOU'RE FEUDING!
I SUGGEST YOU BOTH MAKE UP AND WRITE AN ORIGINAL STORY!
WELL-I-DON'T KNOW!
READ ARCHIE'S STORY AND YOU MAY CHANGE YOUR MIND!
"ARCHIE, PRINCE OF EGYPT!" YOU WROTE AN EGYPTIAN STORY, TOO! SHEESH!
"IT ALL BEGAN WHEN ARCHIE, PRINCE OF EGYPT, NEEDED A DATE FOR THE BIG "SPHINX DANCE!"
...HE WAS SMITTEN WITH TWO PEASANT GIRLS, BETTY AND VERONICA!
PEASANT GIRLS!
ARCHIE COULDN'T DECIDE BETWEEN THE TWO BEAUTIES, BUT HIS FATHER GAVE HIM ADVICE!
HE TOLD THE PRINCE TO GO WITH A GIRL OF HIS CLASS AND STATURE!
8

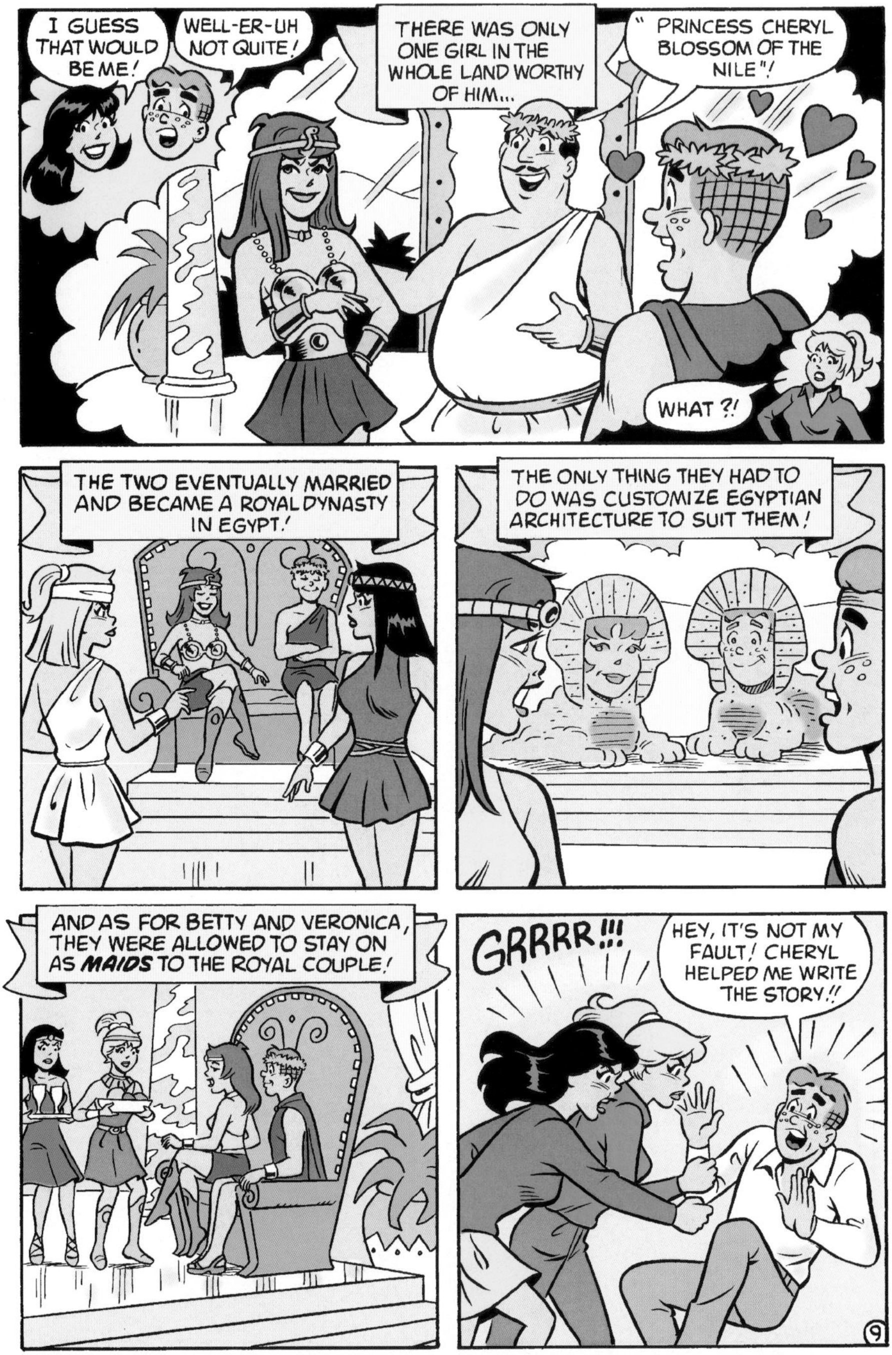
I GUESS THAT WOULD BE ME!
WELL-ER-UH NOT QUITE!
THERE WAS ONLY ONE GIRL IN THE WHOLE LAND WORTHY OF HIM...
"PRINCESS CHERYL BLOSSOM OF THE NILE"!
WHAT?!
THE TWO EVENTUALLY MARRIED AND BECAME A ROYAL DYNASTY IN EGYPT!
THE ONLY THING THEY HAD TO DO WAS CUSTOMIZE EGYPTIAN ARCHITECTURE TO SUIT THEM!
AND AS FOR BETTY AND VERONICA, THEY WERE ALLOWED TO STAY ON AS MAIDS TO THE ROYAL COUPLE!
GRRRR!!!
HEY, IT'S NOT MY FAULT! CHERYL HELPED ME WRITE THE STORY!!
9

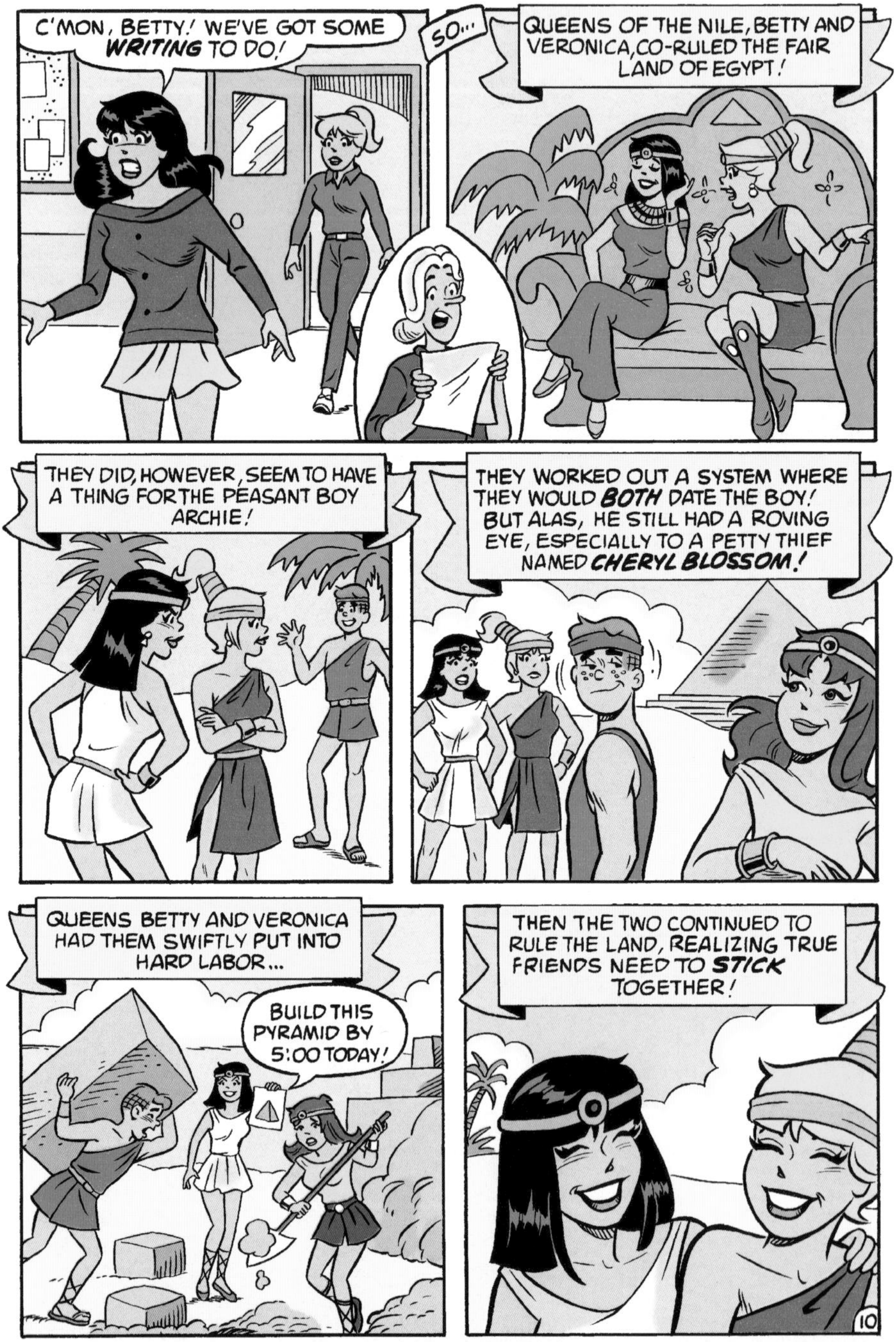
C'MON, BETTY! WE'VE GOT SOME WRITING TO DO!
SO...
QUEENS OF THE NILE, BETTY AND VERONICA, CO-RULED THE FAIR LAND OF EGYPT!
THEY DID, HOWEVER, SEEM TO HAVE A THING FOR THE PEASANT BOY ARCHIE!
THEY WORKED OUT A SYSTEM WHERE THEY WOULD BOTH DATE THE BOY! BUT ALAS, HE STILL HAD A ROVING EYE, ESPECIALLY TO A PETTY THIEF NAMED CHERYL BLOSSOM!
QUEENS BETTY AND VERONICA HAD THEM SWIFTLY PUT INTO HARD LABOR...
BUILD THIS PYRAMID BY 5:00 TODAY!
THEN THE TWO CONTINUED TO RULE THE LAND, REALIZING TRUE FRIENDS NEED TO STICK TOGETHER!
10

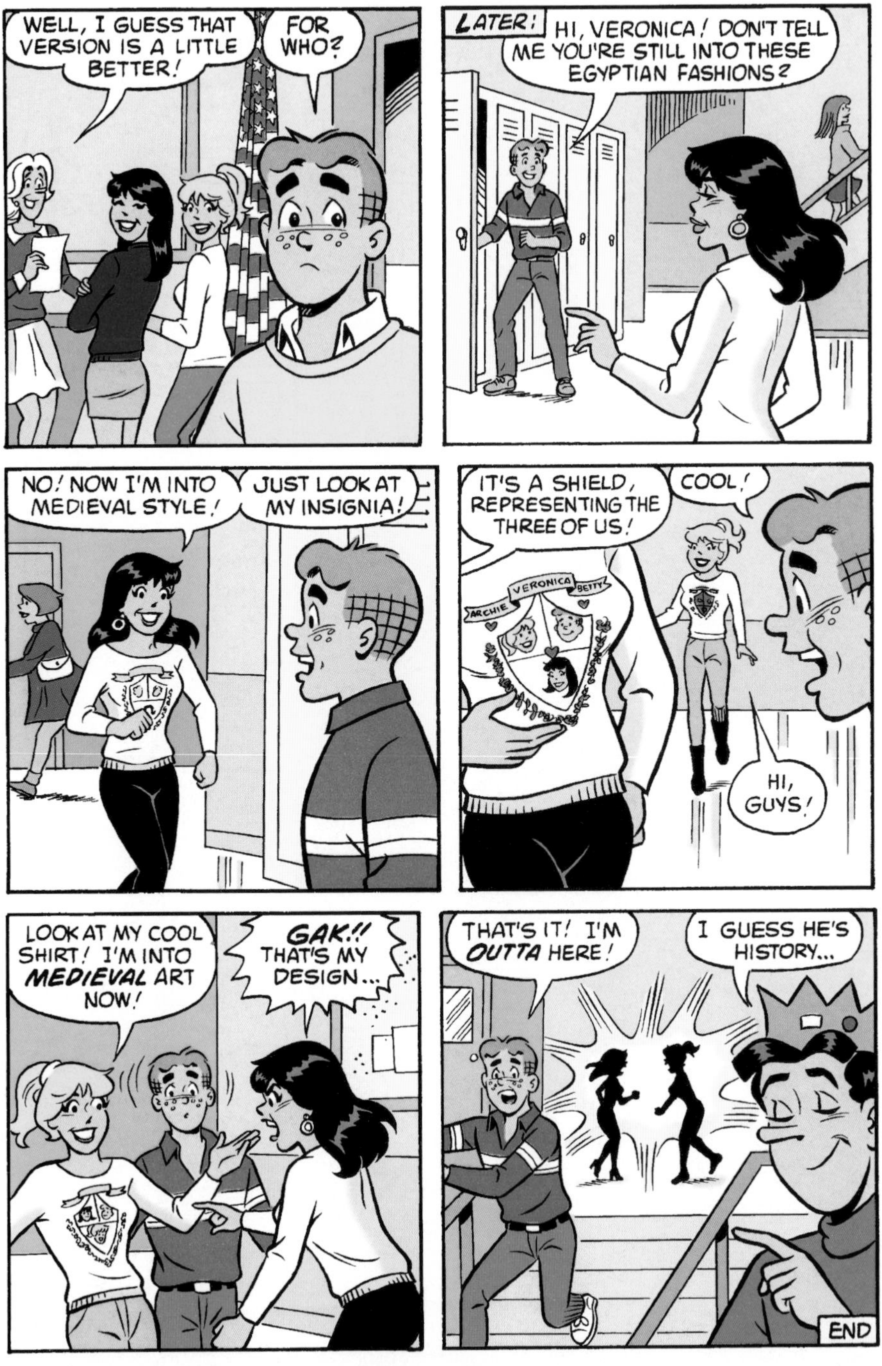
WELL, I GUESS THAT VERSION IS A LITTLE BETTER!
FOR WHO?
LATER:
HI, VERONICA! DON'T TELL ME YOU'RE STILL INTO THESE EGYPTIAN FASHIONS?
NO! NOW I'M INTO MEDIEVAL STYLE!
JUST LOOK AT MY INSIGNIA!
IT'S A SHIELD, REPRESENTING THE THREE OF US!
VERONICA
ARCHIE
BETTY
COOL!
HI, GUYS!
LOOK AT MY COOL SHIRT! I'M INTO MEDIEVAL ART NOW!
GAK!! THAT'S MY DESIGN...
THAT'S IT! I'M OUTTA HERE!
I GUESS HE'S HISTORY...
END

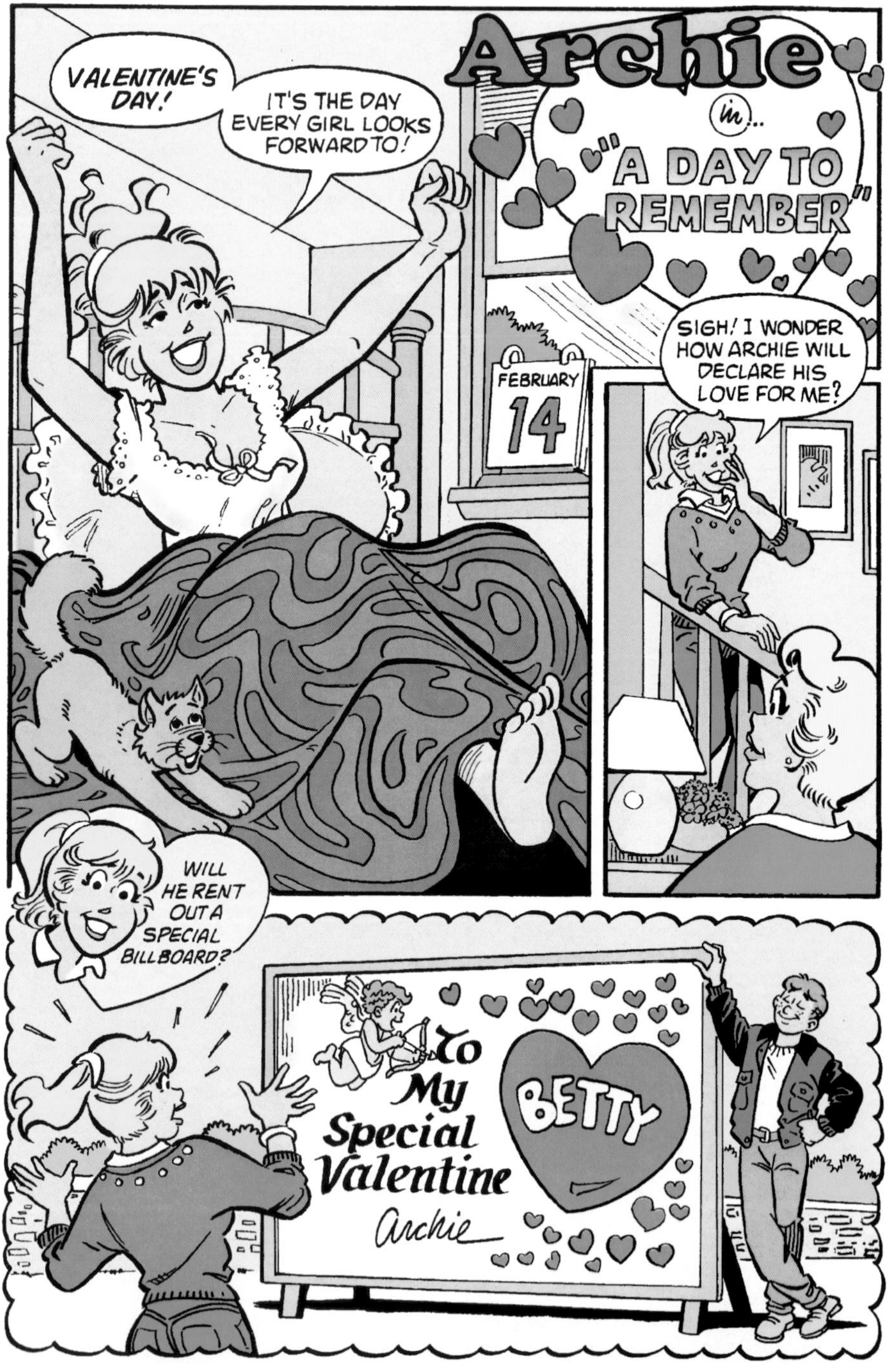
Archie
in...
"A DAY TO REMEMBER"
VALENTINE'S DAY!
IT'S THE DAY EVERY GIRL LOOKS FORWARD TO!
FEBRUARY 14
SIGH! I WONDER HOW ARCHIE WILL DECLARE HIS LOVE FOR ME?
WILL HE RENT OUT A SPECIAL BILLBOARD?
To My Special Valentine
BETTY
Archie

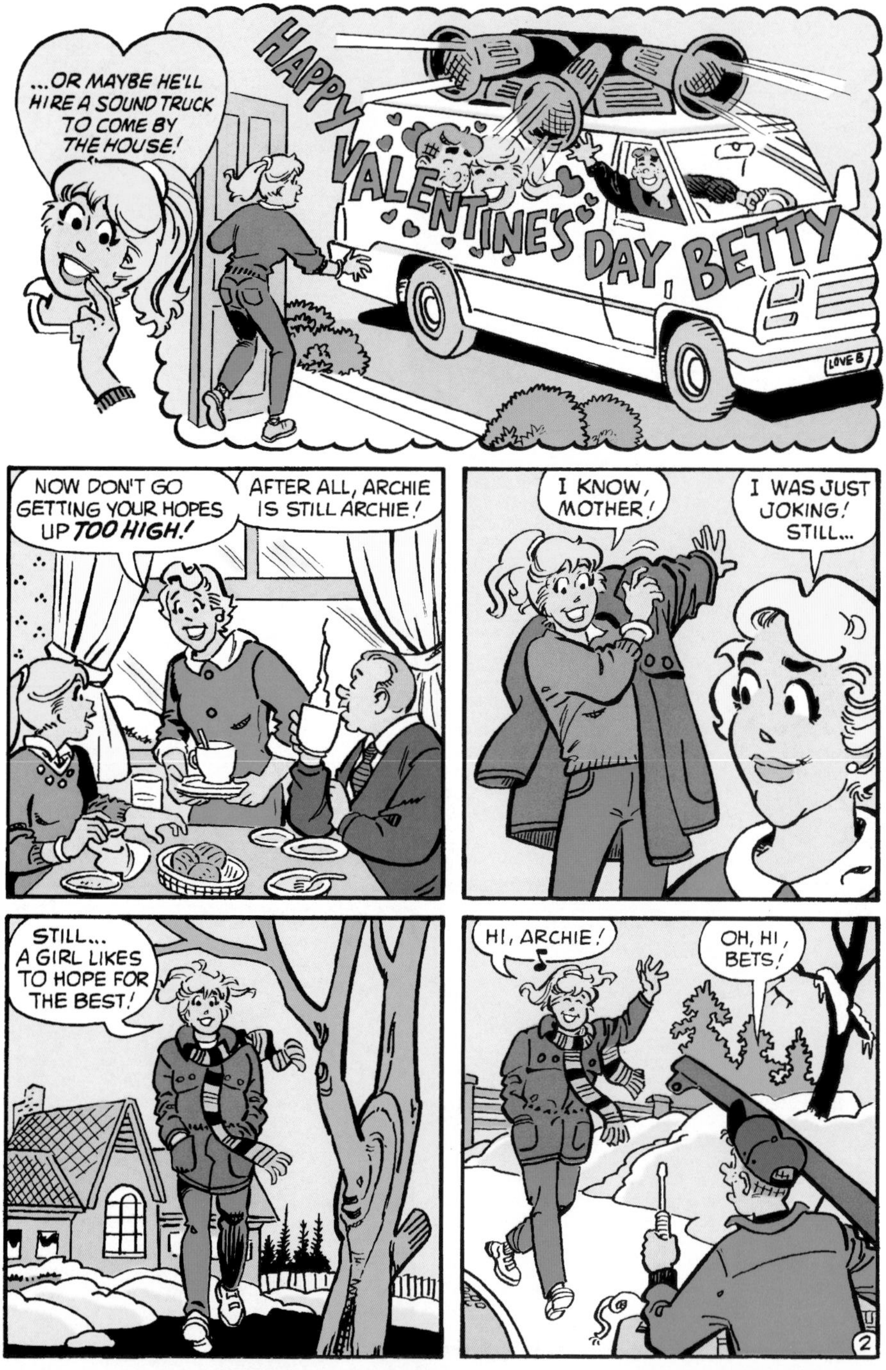
...OR MAYBE HE'LL HIRE A SOUND TRUCK TO COME BY THE HOUSE!
HAPPY VALENTINE'S DAY, BETTY
LOVE B
NOW DON'T GO GETTING YOUR HOPES UP TOO HIGH!
AFTER ALL, ARCHIE IS STILL ARCHIE!
I KNOW, MOTHER!
I WAS JUST JOKING! STILL...
STILL... A GIRL LIKES TO HOPE FOR THE BEST!
HI, ARCHIE!
OH, HI, BETS!
2

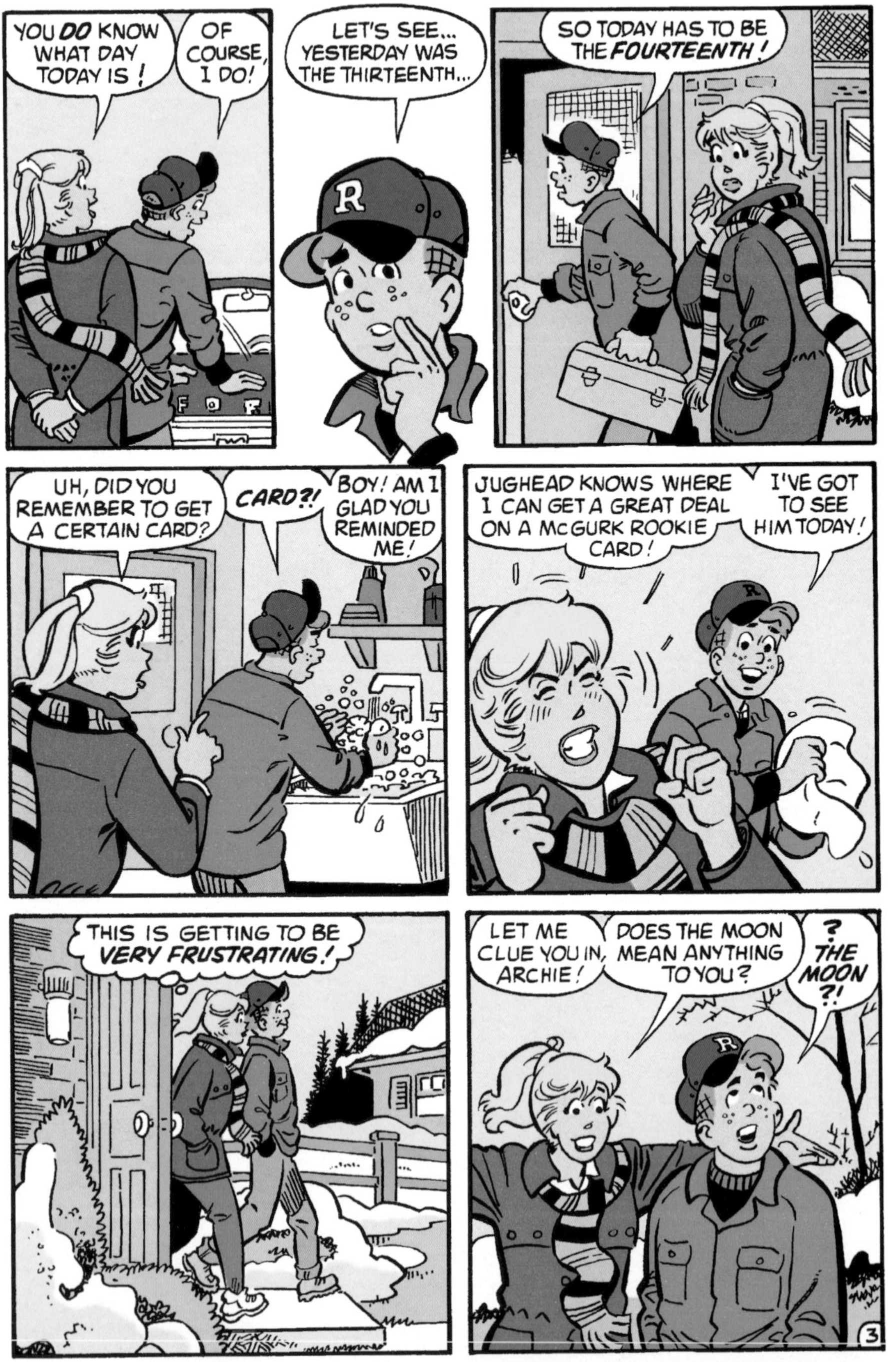
YOU DO KNOW WHAT DAY TODAY IS!
OF COURSE, I DO!
LET'S SEE... YESTERDAY WAS THE THIRTEENTH...
SO TODAY HAS TO BE THE FOURTEENTH!
UH, DID YOU REMEMBER TO GET A CERTAIN CARD?
CARD?!
BOY! AM I GLAD YOU REMINDED ME!
JUGHEAD KNOWS WHERE I CAN GET A GREAT DEAL ON A McGURK ROOKIE CARD!
I'VE GOT TO SEE HIM TODAY!
THIS IS GETTING TO BE VERY FRUSTRATING!
LET ME CLUE YOU IN, ARCHIE!
DOES THE MOON MEAN ANYTHING TO YOU?
? THE MOON ?!
3

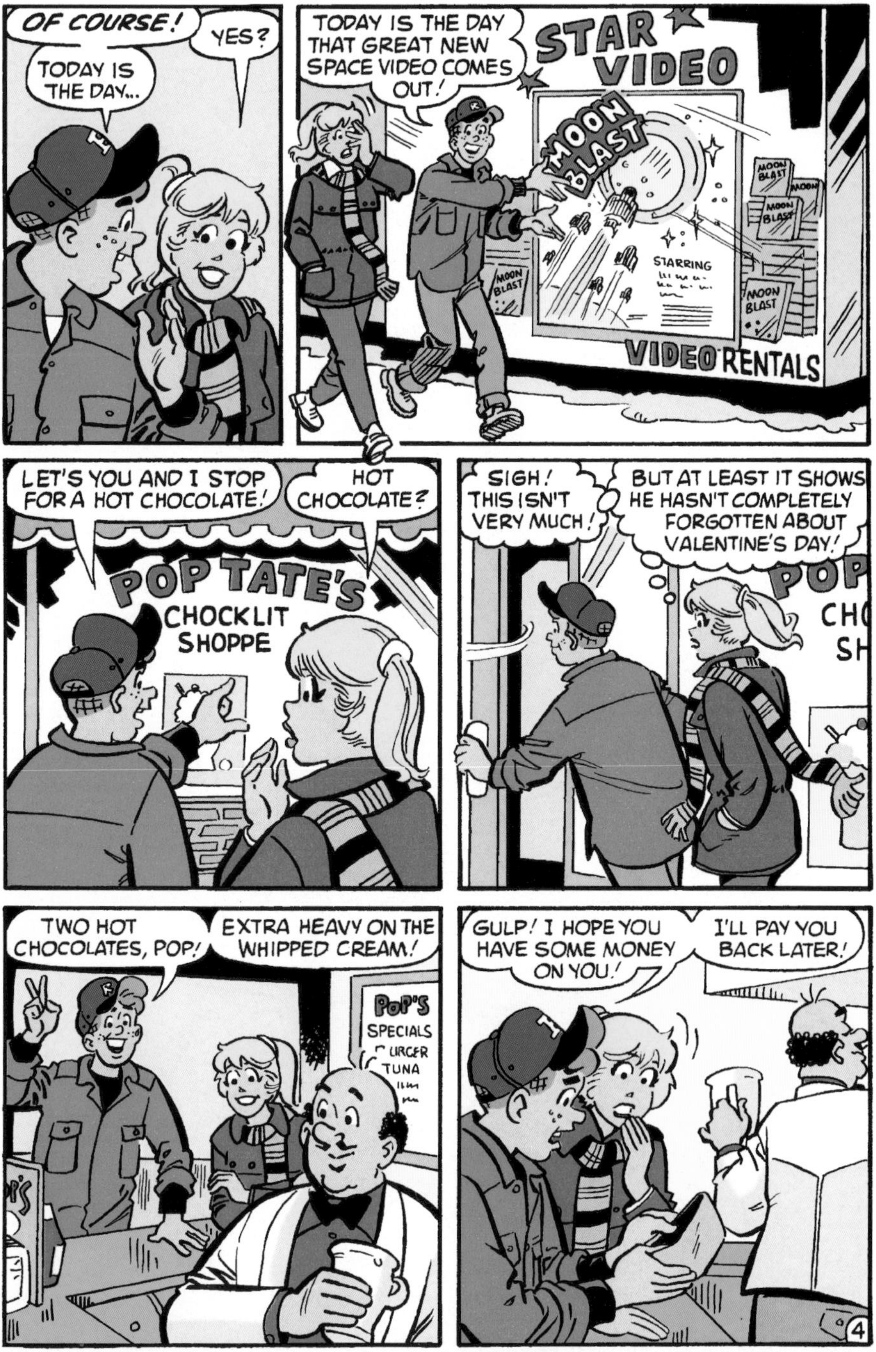
OF COURSE!
YES?
TODAY IS THE DAY...
TODAY IS THE DAY THAT GREAT NEW SPACE VIDEO COMES OUT!
STAR VIDEO
MOON BLAST
STARRING
VIDEO RENTALS
LET'S YOU AND I STOP FOR A HOT CHOCOLATE!
HOT CHOCOLATE?
POP TATE'S
CHOCKLIT SHOPPE
SIGH! THIS ISN'T VERY MUCH!
BUT AT LEAST IT SHOWS HE HASN'T COMPLETELY FORGOTTEN ABOUT VALENTINE'S DAY!
TWO HOT CHOCOLATES, POP!
EXTRA HEAVY ON THE WHIPPED CREAM!
POP'S
SPECIALS
TUNA
GULP! I HOPE YOU HAVE SOME MONEY ON YOU!
I'LL PAY YOU BACK LATER!
4

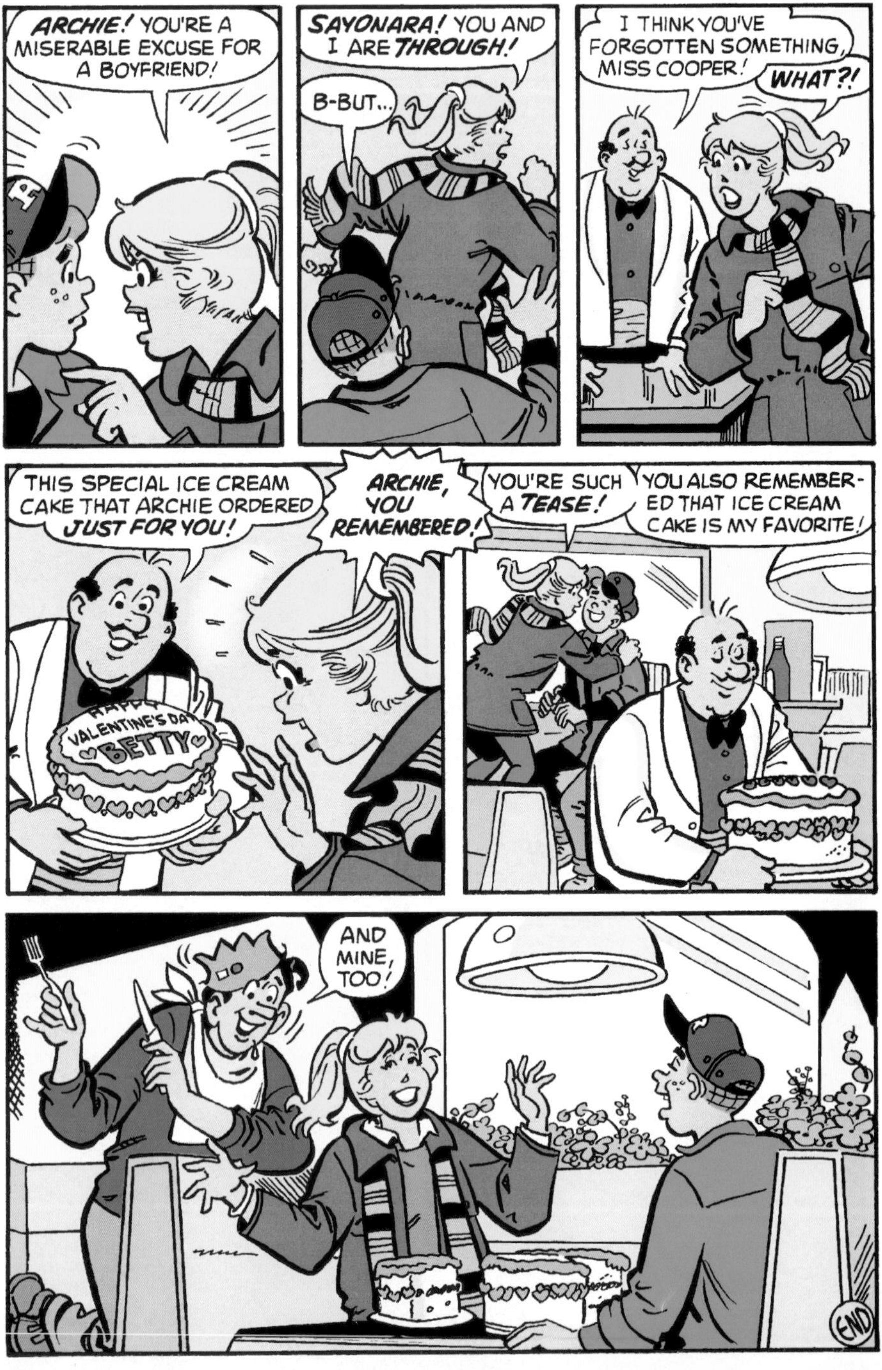
ARCHIE! YOU'RE A MISERABLE EXCUSE FOR A BOYFRIEND!
SAYONARA! YOU AND I ARE THROUGH!
B-BUT...
I THINK YOU'VE FORGOTTEN SOMETHING, MISS COOPER!
WHAT?!
THIS SPECIAL ICE CREAM CAKE THAT ARCHIE ORDERED JUST FOR YOU!
ARCHIE, YOU REMEMBERED!
HAPPY VALENTINE'S DAY BETTY
YOU'RE SUCH A TEASE!
YOU ALSO REMEMBERED THAT ICE CREAM CAKE IS MY FAVORITE!
AND MINE, TOO!
END